W9-CMF-821

THE
—
JOB PIRATE

Bleeding Heart Publications is a South East Asia-based publishing house that specializes in English language short fiction booklets and full-length creative non-fiction. Our publications sell primarily in the United States and are available online and in stores.

Copyright ©2013 BH Publications Pte Ltd.

All rights reserved.

No part of this book may be reproduced, stored in a retrieval system, or transmitted by any means, electronic, mechanical, photocopying, record-ing, or otherwise, without written permission from the copyright holder.

Distributed by Greenleaf Book Group

For ordering information or special discounts for bulk purchases, please contact Greenleaf Book Group at PO Box 91869, Austin, TX 78709, 512.891.6100.

Design and composition by Greenleaf Book Group
Cover design by Greenleaf Book Group and Debbie Berne

Cataloging-in-Publication data is available.

ISBN 978-0-9905732-0-3

Part of the Tree Neutral® program, which offsets the number of trees consumed in the production and printing of this book by taking proactive steps, such as planting trees in direct proportion to the number of trees used: www.treeneutral.com

TreeNeutral®

Printed in the United States of America on acid-free paper

15 16 17 18 19 20   10 9 8 7 6 5 4 3 2 1

First Edition

THE

JOB PIRATE

AN ENTERTAINING TALE
OF MY JOB-HOPPING JOURNEY
IN AMERICA

BRANDON CHRISTOPHER

Bleeding Heart
PUBLICATIONS

Previous Works by Brandon Christopher

Emily's Little Pilot of Loquacious Weather
2013 Transfusions
BH Publications

Nightville
2011
L & L Dreamspell

Dirty Little Altar Boy
2007
Ghost Pants Press
(To be re-released by BH Publications 2015)

CONTENTS

Acknowledgments *vii*

Intro: The Mire of My Livelihood *1*

1   The Hunter Becomes the Hunted *7*

2   The Mortuary Driver *19*

3   The Citadel of Toaster Ovens *27*

4   Meat Burrito and a Side of Beans *37*

5   McPlumbers *59*

6   Little Generals *75*

7   The Grilled Cheese Epiphany *81*

8   Moving in Place *85*

9   The Broken Toys of Hollywood *95*

10   The Electrifying Case of the Broken
     Windshield *103*

11   The Grand Disillusion *121*

12   Operation Hot Fudge *135*

13   The Thespian Loses His Coat *147*

14   The Rise and Tragic Fall *153*

15   The Blessed Do-Over *187*

16   That Motherfucker Carlos *201*

17   Most of a Day at Whispering Meadows *209*

18   The Porn Is Mightier than the Sword *223*

19   Wax Is Thicker than Pride *253*

20   A Staring Contest with 40 *271*

Afterword *275*

About the Author *285*

ACKNOWLEDGMENTS

The Job Pirate isn't just a collection of true stories about all my poor career choices; it's also a chronicle of the last two decades of my life—the good times, the bad times, the hungry times, but always the real times. So there are a lot of people that are owed a big thank you . . . and perhaps even an explanation. First and foremost, I would like to thank my folks, Fred and Peggi, for always being understanding of their middle kid with a keen gift for finding trouble. I owe an enormous deal of gratitude to Cali, Kyle, and Gordon at Bleeding Heart Publications for believing in me and giving me the softcover soapbox on which to stand and rant about all my crazy jobs. I'd also like to thank Colin, Sean, Scott, Lisa, Bryan, and Laura for always being there for me, sometimes being the fodder for my stories, and for keeping me on the path. I should probably thank all the coworkers I've written about, with a special shout-out to Sherry, Natalie, Joel, Carlos, and Tony (you'll see why). Three or four of the eighty-one bosses I've had probably deserve a "thanks," or at least a proper "I quit," but I must have had a good reason for leaving in the first place, so we'll just call that one a draw. And since we're coming clean, I probably owe David Byrne about $90 in royalties for the amount of times I listened to "Road to Nowhere" while driving home after getting fired.

THE MIRE OF
MY LIVELIHOOD

To see me in your office is surely cause for speculation. I look like you, I work like you, but I am not like you, and some part of you knows this. Some elemental part of you, deep down inside, knows that I am an imposter in your workplace. But your—actually, *our*—employer doesn't know this yet; he doesn't realize the person he just gave a unique login and password to is a professional at what he does for a living. But this particular profession isn't what he does for a living—at least it wasn't three days before the interview.

That new employee that you see hanging his vintage blazer onto the backrest of his swivel chair is me. My cubicle is right next to yours. I don't say much, I dine alone, I drink a lot of coffee, and I know my legal right to two cigarette breaks in an eight-hour workday. And yes, you were right, I'm not really the Marketing Strategist I told the boss I was. But I'm sitting here in this cubicle, and the resume that got me this job is in my attaché case right beside me. It clearly states that I have more than enough experience to run this company's *entire* advertising department. So, fuck you, lady in the cubicle next to mine. And fuck your perceptive eyes that caught me checking my Scottrade account this morning. I'll be here between three weeks and a year, so you better get used to the idea of it.

There are careers, there are professions, there are jobs, there are contract jobs, and there are gigs. Both connecting and separating these occupational categories, like a river drifting alongside five ports, is what I like to call the gray area of employment—the mire of my livelihood. Two decades worth of brief occupations, short-lived careers, and both rightful and wrongful terminations, all sewn together like the patched quilt that shields the child from the monsters of adult life. I am a job pirate—a professional pretender for a decent paycheck and health insurance.

I've never subscribed to that old-fashioned American Dream of having just *one* career for 35 years, followed by a cane-bound trance of heart medications, hip problems, and *Law & Order*. Nothing scares me more, to be honest, even as I near dangerously close to middle age myself. Instead, I prefer to taste life. I prefer to taste *many* lives, actually. Eighty-one different lives, at last count. Some lasted a few days, some a few years. Some were so bad that I quit, while others were so good that I was fired. The "greatest recession since the Great Depression" played a part in a good portion of my most recent departures, but the vast majority were just due to my general lack of satisfaction and contentment.

And yet, there's a lot more to it than simply being stubborn, or hard to please, or needing a dental plan. When you start a new job, you invade a little bubble of life that existed long before you ever got there, and will continue to exist long after you have gone—a separate reality running parallel to your own, like string theory in physics. You step through those glass front doors into an entirely new dimension—one that you would have never known supported life had it not been for your hiring. You make new friends, you date new coworkers, you fall into new loves, and you create new enemies. You slowly develop contained little relationships with these new people around you. Relationships with dozens, if not hundreds, of people over the years, whom you never would have met in your entire life had you not taken that job as a floral arranger for seven months, or the door-to-door tie salesman for one day, or the erotic writer of a porn magazine for close to a year.

But this fickle, wayfaring life is not as easy and care-free as it may sound. Claiming eighty-one different job titles means that I have "bent the truth a little" on eighty-one *different* job applications. So, researching a new occupational role beforehand is mandatory. Character exploration is vital to authentic employee development. But a simple Internet search of topics like "job duties of plumber assistant" or "what is an accountant, really?" before your first day will reap rich rewards. And adapting to a new role at all times is the key to success. Learn to not only dress the part but actually live the part of each new job you take. When you're a chauffeur, go out and buy those ridiculous mirrored, police-style sunglasses, and wear them a lot. If you pull a corporate office stint, learn to love wearing Dockers and calmly striped shirts and adapt to expressing your creative side by only decorating your gray cubicle wall with black-and-white printouts of scenes from David Lynch movies. Learn to eat by yourself, and read the newspaper by yourself, especially during that first month at any job. If the job goes over a month you'll make a few friends, maybe go out for a beer after work with the "cool" crowd (who are basically only interested in seeing if you're gay, married, or weird). If the job goes over three months, there are phone numbers exchanged, a few holiday party invites begotten, some of the aforementioned crushes have started to develop, and some flirtations have been established. You'll eventually become part of "the gang," most likely with the two or three other people who stand and smoke cigarettes where the concrete meets the grass. And when layoffs and Januaries come around, you'll be in the bottom tier of employees and one of the first three to be called into the manager's office for the "Sit down, we need to talk" talk.

Like anything in life, there are some highs and lows involved in being a job pirate. And you'll have to ride them both out in order to sustain yourself. Sometimes you're flat broke and drinking Folgers without sugar, and other times you're making $1,400 per week and tipping on every Starbucks latte you order. Sometimes you're surviving on $775 per month, trying to validate your lifestyle choice to yourself over the fourth grilled-cheese-sandwich-and-tap-water dinner in a row, and other times you're buying a pre-owned Lexus after four months at a job that was scored as a result of the Dubious Resume #7. Just don't be alarmed when you're selling that fucking Lexus back to CarMax a few months later—at a $2,600 loss—because you got fired and decided to move to Seattle. Because you're a job pirate, and that's the life. You trade in those career perks for a life of sovereignty, free will, and independence. If you don't like your job, you quit. You'll find another. If a boss yells at you, you yell right back at him. Or better yet, you take a dump on the windshield of his new Mercedes-Benz.

But one of the best benefits of jumping from one profession to another is learning all sorts of new skills and abilities that you never would have acquired had you stayed with just *one* career. But now you wield these new talents, just in case some future predicament requires you to properly buckle a corpse onto a gurney, twist an arm without breaking it, or come up with seventeen different euphemisms for the word "testicles." Your life becomes rich with extraordinary new abilities and delightful conversation starters. You are the protagonist in your own living novel, with each new job serving as a chapter or plot twist.

When you're a corporate ghost lurking temporarily inside the cubicle kingdoms of America—milling about all those melancholic coworkers with their fixed lives, fat families, and 401(k)s—you'll probably find yourself smiling a little too often during conversations. You'll smile partly to mask the envy, and partly to celebrate the relief. You know you won't ever have the same type of life security that Dottie in Human Resources will have, but you will have something just as valuable: your autonomy. Sure, most months become little wars of attrition—deciding which bills to pay and deducing how many possible dinners a pack of four chicken breasts will actually make—but all those little fights keep your mind off all the big fights out there. The struggle helps you stay focused on the immediate: that precious yolk of time between yesterday and tomorrow.

Some might think it silly to burn through so many jobs during an economic period where so many have found it impossible to find work. I don't consider it silly at all; I consider it good experience for the disappearing job market ahead. It's not my fault that most major American corporations moved their production facilities to China or India because labor is cheaper there; it's not my fault American car companies went belly-up because of their fat union pensions and piss-poor products; and I had nothing to do with L.A.'s slow death at the hands of outrageous film budgets reduced by millions overnight because production is cheaper in Canada. I was dealt the same cards as everybody else, and I'm surviving just fine. I will admit that for every job I deceivingly take, someone rightfully qualified may stay unemployed as a result. But the flipside is, for every job that

I get fired from (or quit), a fresh new job opens up for some-one else. It's the cosmic balance of things. An employee like me makes employers cherish employees like Dottie.

A week, a month, a year, it doesn't really matter how long you were there, or how it ended. Because there's a whole world in between that first and last day, just begging you to dig your teeth into it. The key is to celebrate the finite. Like realizing you're in a dream, once you accept the fact that you're only there temporarily—that you won't be calling *those* people "coworkers" in three years, let alone three months—a calm clarity takes over; a soothing, bulletproof understanding that your short-term destiny is all up to you.

It's a tricky world out there these days, and you've got to be just as tricky to survive it. The workers of today must be willing to venture into unknown territories and adapt to new lifestyles or forever be left in the wake of retail serfdom. Employers care about their business surviving, not *your* sur-vival. The sooner you realize this the better off you are. It's a changed world. Pensions are nearly obsolete, 401(k)s are like family dogs without leashes that may or may not come home with you, and the gentleman's handshake is now followed by a squirt of Purell sanitizer. Acclimate, or it's adios time.

THE HUNTER BECOMES THE HUNTED

JOB #15

"Please, have a seat anywhere," the 20-something supervisor motioned across the large windowless room, which was sectioned into two rectangles by Formica folding tables and chairs.

I was the third in line to get in, right behind a heavyset woman with a cane and a girl right out of college. You could tell she was right out of college because she was the only one who was still holding out a resume. The rest of us knew something was a little off with this interview, but we stayed around to see if maybe we were wrong. I eyed the supervisor as I walked by him, taking note of his oversized shirt that billowed out when he raised his arms—must have been on sale. His tie was atrocious and hung too low below the belt. His hair was as manicured as the thin strip of black fuzz that traced his missing jaw line. Ten feet through the door and I already didn't like where this operation was headed, but I took a seat at one of the back tables nonetheless. The room filled up quickly; I hadn't realized there were that many people in line behind me. I glanced around at all my fellow salespeople and assessed their clothing, their shoes, their attentiveness to the surroundings and the situation. We were from all walks of life and couldn't have been more different, yet there we were together all dressed in our very best pieced-together outfits that one wears when trying to get a job. We just weren't expecting there to be twenty of us.

The supervisor walked to the front of the room and raised his arms; the shirt ballooned out again. "Hello there, everyone. My name's Gary, and I hope you're all as excited as I am to be here today. But first I have some good news and some bad news that I need to share with you," he said with a wink and a sly grin to the woman sitting at the table nearest him. "The good news is, you all got the job! The bad news is . . . there is no bad news! You're all going to make lots of money!"

A few people laughed, some out of courtesy and some out of honest excitement. But I knew what he really meant. I knew that if this company was going to hire all twenty of us for sales positions then there would be no salary, only commission on what we sold. One glance around the room made that clear. Sitting next to me were two old Vietnamese ladies who spoke no English. One was doing Sudoku while the other rested her chin on her cane like Yoda.

Up front, Gary fiddled with a projector as a giant stock-photo of a glass of water went in and out of focus on the white wall behind him. He finally got it clear enough so we could see the crisp droplets trickling down the glass, and he turned back to us.

"I want to thank you all for coming down here today, and for being part of a company I know you'll love as much as I do. I know the ad that brought you here was kind of vague, and you're all probably sitting there wondering what this job is, right? Will I be stuck in some crummy store all day, right? Answering phones, right? Wrong! I wasn't lying when I said that you could make up to $10,000 a month *and* be outdoors all day *and* be your own boss . . . set your own hours, work when you want to, be with your family. Interested?"

He cupped his hand behind his ear and arched forward as if waiting to hear all of us cheering for "More, more, more!" But the only answer he got was from the old Vietnamese lady next to me, who raised her hand and replied very matter-of-factly, "Yes, I am interested." I guess she *did* speak English. Then a couple of other people nodded their heads. Then so did I, but only because I was sitting right beside the lady who spoke first. It definitely wasn't the punchy reply he was expecting, but the supervisor handled it gracefully. He jumped back into his pitch before any more momentum could be lost.

"Great! Now, I bet you're all asking yourselves how you can achieve all this, right? Lots of money, setting your own hours, working outdoors . . . That sounds too good to be true, right? Wrong!" He violently pressed his thumb down onto the remote control, and the glass of water behind him turned into a faucet pouring water into a sink, then a pie chart full of percentages and numbers. "Almost 90 percent of Los Angeles residents drink tap water without any filtration. If you look here . . . see all the bacteria and cancer-causing agents found in just one glass of tap water? Same with a shower. Just because you don't drink it doesn't mean it's not entering your pores, your skin, your . . . But look at how these numbers change when using an AquaTastic water purifier! Just look at that. AquaTastic actually prevents almost 99 percent of contaminants from getting through, making you sick, killing you. We've done the numbers, folks, and AquaTastic filtration systems will sell themselves. Seriously."

The supervisor proceeded to lionize his filtration system for another 20 minutes before getting to the part about how much money he had made in the past year alone. He explained the patented charcoal filter system "designed in Finland and so cutting edge that most of America didn't even know about it yet." Then when someone at the front table raised their hand and asked how come the display model said "Made in Pakistan" on the bottom, he explained that Pakistan was the world leader in cutting-edge plastics, like the plastic used to make the AquaTastic water filtration system. Then he said, "Good question!" with a finger gun at the guy.

"Any other questions?" the supervisor asked us, and several hands shot up.

"So, we're selling these filter systems? That's the job?" a middle-aged guy asked.

"No . . . they sell themselves!" the supervisor exclaimed with a grin. "We have two patented models, which you'll be selling: the AquaTastic faucet filter for purified drinking water—which pays for itself within a year from all the bottled water customers won't have to buy any longer. And there's also the AquaTastic shower filter, which screws right onto most showerheads and filters all the bad stuff out. Both amazing!"

"Where's the store? Where do we work from?"

"Great question! That's the beautiful part: no store! *You* are the store! Customers are everywhere. Your neighbors, your friends, your schools . . . drive to any neighborhood you like and you'll have all the sales you can imagine!

Remember, these things will sell themselves. People will thank you. You're saving their lives."

"So we walk around and sell these? From my sales experience, people don't like it when you show up at their door trying to sell stuff. They think it's a rip-off."

"Apparently, you weren't selling AquaTastic!" the supervisor replied with a loud laugh and pointed to someone else.

"Do we get a paycheck or anything? Or is this just like a commission thing?"

"Great question! Neither! Seriously, you get it all! You get all the money. Everything you make goes right into your own pocket. When you sell one of our filters at $89.99, you put that $89.99 right into your own pocket."

The same woman blurted out, "How?" before the supervisor could point to someone else. His smile was waning but still toothy enough to launch into the mathematics of the deal. "This is where we really work with you, folks. We want you to succeed here. We want people to be healthy and drinking pure water all across this country. That's why we sell our AquaTastic filtration systems to you at half the price of retail! Yes, really! What we do is give these to you for just $44.99 and you turn around and sell them for double that. And they'll still sell themselves. It's an amazing deal!"

Half of the crowd immediately shifted in their seats at the thought of having to buy *anything* for the sake of getting a job; the supervisor saw this and tried to salvage his pitch from all of us who had just seen behind Oz's curtain. "I can tell that you're all a little worried about that part, but you've got to spend money to make money, right? Wrong! I'm so sure you'll make a fortune selling these systems that you won't have to pay us back until you've made some sales. AquaTastic has its very own lending system with a very desirable APR. It's like a loan between friends, and we won't charge you a cent for 45 days. After you've met with someone from our AquaTastic credit team, you can pick up as many filtration systems as you want and get started getting rich. Think about it, if you sell ten of these a day, you just made yourself a lot of money . . . like a week's salary for some of you. For one day of work!"

The room grew quiet as people did the math. The supervisor knew he was losing most of us the longer we thought about it. But he had an ace up his sleeve just for this very moment—what would be called "the turn" in a magic trick. He waved to the back of the room, and two attractive women in pantsuits wheeled a dolly with several large boxes to the front. Gary opened one of the cardboard boxes and pulled out a crisply packaged AquaTastic faucet filter, then opened another box and pulled out the shower filter. He displayed both white devices on the table beside the projector so we could see how pretty they were.

"Listen, I know what you're thinking, folks. Some of you are thinking 'this is too good to be true,' and others are thinking 'this must be a scam.' Both are wrong. This really is that good. And I'm so sure of it, and I'm so sure of all of you, that I want you each to take home a set of these and try them out overnight. Then you can come back here tomorrow and tell me how good they are. That's how confident I am in this product. And I want you to be that confident, too, so you can sell a million of them. You just need to try them out to know how good they really are. I'm telling ya, they sell themselves."

It was a clever approach and had most if not all of the room nodding their heads—not so much for the actual job but for getting to take something home for free. It was meant to build up a level of trust between the supervisor and us, and it seemed to be working. But nothing ever comes for free; people just don't want to accept that.

"Anybody's who's interested, please come on up and take your two complimentary filtration systems—a $200 value. That's the level of faith I have in this product . . . and in you. Try it out tonight; take the first pure shower you've probably ever had in your life. And I know you'll all come back tomorrow raving about it and ready to get to work. All I ask is that you sign my list up here so I know you each got two."

The entire room rushed to the open path between the tables and formed a line. I could not believe how fast those two old Vietnamese ladies were—from the back table to the front of the room in record speed; we bookended the line by the time I got there. It was a slow-moving parade for giving away free stuff, and when I reached the front where Gary and his assistants were, I realized why. There were two clipboards filled with scribbled home addresses, signatures, and phone numbers on the table before me. One of the ladies offered me a pen and asked to see my ID and social security card, which I vaguely recalled being asked to bring the day before.

"But I'm not sure if I want this job yet . . . I want to be sure of the product first," I replied, giving her my best poker face.

Gary shook my hand and asked my name. I gave him the first moniker that popped into my mind. "Conrad, I know exactly how you feel. I was the same way. I wouldn't sell an inferior product no matter how much you paid me. This is just for precaution, in case some of these people don't come back. Or don't bring back the filter systems. It's just a little formality. I wish I could trust everybody like I trust you."

I glanced back at all of the salespeople admiring their shiny, new packages and sneered so that the supervisor could see me. I nodded. "Smart move. You can never be too sure with people these days, especially with a product as pioneering as this. I'm really proud to be a part of your organization . . . an organization that might improve a lot of lives. I will do this!"

He shook my hand again, and I smiled one of the loudest, friendliest smiles I could bullshit and still get away with; I even revealed my missing tooth. I had decided about a minute into this interview that I wouldn't be entering the lucrative world of selling AquaTastic water filters to friends and loved ones, but I did really want to have "the first pure shower I've probably ever had in my life." Ever since he had said it that was all I could think about. How amazing would it be to bathe in fresh, pure water? Like melted glacier water, I imagined. Crystal purity showering down upon me, forgiving me of my sins and washing me free of my impurities. Like the warm tears of gods bathing the unclean right off me.

I figured I should at least try it for the night; maybe bring it back tomorrow, maybe not. I assumed most of the crowd felt the same way. So I grabbed the pen and exclaimed, "This sounds great! I want a piece of this!"

"It will be the best investment of your life," was what Gary said to me before turning away to answer a question from the young woman with the resume. And that's when I really realized we all were getting duped—and not just by a shitty product. When he said "investment," it awakened the frugal part of me. Although this very same frugal part of me had lost $700 in the stock market the year prior, it still knew its business and that part of me knew something wasn't right with this scenario. I scanned the page on the clipboard and noticed the tell-tale signs: mother's maiden name, social security number, home address, yet nothing about citizenship or past employment. This clipboard wasn't a sign-up list; it was a credit application, and the nineteen people before me had all just signed up without even realizing it. And they had all just purchased two of their very own AquaTastic water filtrations systems at $44.99 a pop. The guy was right about one thing: These fuckers really did sell themselves.

Even knowing this, I still really wanted that shower purifier. I wanted to feel that first pure shower of my life. There was no way I was going to actually buy the filter system, but there must have been some way I could leave there with one. Then the devious part of me kicked in with a plan, replacing the frugal part's cause for concern. While the supervisor and assistant were answering questions from the crowd surrounding the table, I wrote down that my full name was Conrad Reinhardt Racer and gave an address near my old apartment. As for my mother's maiden name, well, she came from a long line of Eskovitos from the hills of Poland. I returned the pen and eagerly grabbed my two new water purification systems and prepared to disappear into the crowd when the female assistant politely grasped my wrist and said, "Oh, wait, wait . . . Mr. Racer, you forgot your social security number here," and she pointed the pen to the big blank line which I'd completely neglected to fill out. "And I'm supposed to check your social security card too."

I had jumped the gun in my excitement. I was caught in my grand lie and only had a split-second to figure a way out. I was too close to the prize to say that I had forgotten my paperwork in the car, only to rush out and escape empty-handed. I was too close; I had come too far. I could already feel the pure, warm sunshine water showering down upon me, and I wasn't going to leave without getting a taste of it. I would have to go for the gamble . . . I would have to go all or nothing on this one.

"I'm afraid I lost my social security card years ago, but I can get you the number. I believe I told the lady on the phone this before deciding to come here," I said with a trusting smile.

"Sir, Mr. Racer, I'm going to need something, some kind of legal document with that number on it," she replied.

I pulled out my wallet and fumbled through it as if looking for something that would work, but I knew I didn't have anything in there. But I did find a Bank of America business card with my new phone number handwritten on the back of it—a number so new, in fact, that I hadn't yet remembered it and was forced to keep reminders of it scribbled on papers in my wallet. I pulled it out and showed her both sides of the card. "This is what the bank gave me when I said I needed some kind of proof of my social security number today. They said this would do it . . . it has the name of the bank on there. I don't know how much more legal you can get than Bank of America."

"Oh, okay . . ." she took my card, examined it, then wrote 8-1-8-5-0-8-5-0-5-4 in the blank area on the application and handed it back to me. "Wow, 8-1-8, those are the same numbers as my area code. Must make it easy to remember that way."

"I still forget it . . . need to keep it written down, as you can see." I couldn't believe she hadn't noticed the tenth number in mine when all the other's only had nine. But she was young and cute and wasn't hired for details like that.

I took my two new water purifiers and gradually drifted to the back of the room. The old Vietnamese lady and I met eyes, and we flashed our new toys at one another with big smiles. Then Gary happily shouted for us all to go home and enjoy our purified showers and drinking water for the night, and to return the next day at 9:00 a.m. ready for a big day of making money. He also made it clear that we were to return the purifiers with all of the packaging intact.

I don't know how many of us went back that next day to begin work selling those overpriced water purifiers, but I can assume not many. And I'm sure the ones who never went back must have thought they had the best bit of luck imaginable until that credit card statement came in the mail a few weeks later saying they had been billed. Maybe that might finally show them that nothing in this life is free. Unless you're wily like me, of course.

I got the first angry message on my answering machine about four days later. It seemed that Gary had finally broken the code of Conrad Reinhardt Racer's social security number actually being his phone number. I didn't pick up until his third phone call of the day, and that's when I told him how absolutely right he was: That first shower with the AquaTastic filtration system was simply amazing, and it really did feel like the first pure shower that I had ever taken in my life. I then went into great detail about how wonderful I had felt since drinking the purified tap water for the past four days, and how many lives his devices would affect. I told him the $89.99 retail price for these babies was well worth it, and they would most definitely sell themselves— they sold me. Then I explained how the hunter had become the hunted.

THE MORTUARY DRIVER

JOB #30

Spending two months in your apartment without a job is a lot like visiting another country without a camera: It's great while you're there but then some time later, when you're back home, you start forgetting about all those good times you had and only vaguely begin to recall those magnificent sights you once saw when watching French films on TV.

My eight-week vacation had burned through all $2,100 that I had saved up. And since I had quit my previous job, or, to be more precise, *just walked away* from my previous job, I was again unable to get any money from the unemployment department.

I had to look for work yet again, and that next morning I was ready with a fresh pot of Starbucks coffee, the *Daily Variety*, the previous day's *L.A. Times*, and my laptop computer. By 10:20, I had already faxed and emailed eleven resumes to various positions that I thought might be of some interest, and called several other companies that I felt more than qualified for.

There were no callbacks by noon. No email replies by the third cup of coffee. Nothing. By 2:45 I was beginning to worry. Had I lost my touch? Was twenty-nine jobs the limit for one person? Was I going to have to borrow money from my parents or, even worse, get a retail job? Too many questions, at least on only three cups of coffee.

By 4:00 in the afternoon I was frantically emailing every job on four separate employment websites. There had never been this long of a lull before getting some type of reply from a prospective employer. I began adding even more variations to my resume, equipping myself with working knowledge of almost any position available. By 4:25 I was a qualified landscape technician, an executive assistant, a script supervisor, an office manager, and finally, a medical billing assistant. Still no calls. Quitting time for the day grew nearer, as did the worry.

Six o'clock did finally arrive, and just before I turned off the computer to pour a glass of cabernet, I noticed the job posting. Glowing in thick black print at the bottom of the *Times'* classifieds section—which I had stolen the day before from Starbucks—read: MORTUARY DRIVER NEEDED. GOOD MONEY, GREAT HOURS.

What luck, I thought to myself. I promptly called the phone number, and the woman on the other side of the receiver set up an interview for me that night.

The way I figured it, I had two kinds of experience in the mortuary-driver field: I was once a limo driver, and I was once arrested for breaking into a cemetery. Although I would omit the latter part of my experience, the limo driver bit would come in real handy. I just had to throw in a few past sales positions and maybe a summer job at a cemetery in, say, Colorado, maybe? No, Phoenix—a summer job gravedigging in Phoenix. *Perfect.*

Traffic was light that evening, and I made it to the small

Encino office in 20 minutes flat. I walked up the stairs to the second floor of the stucco building, and inside suite #11 sat Phil, the portly owner of the company, and Cheryl, the portly wife of the owner. They both swung their leather office chairs toward the sofa and asked me to sit.

"Basically, Brandon, we pick up *expired* bodies and take them to different morgues around Los Angeles," Phil explained very casually. "Now, sometimes these expired bodies are messed up, okay? Sometimes they're decomposed, sometimes they're infants or children, and sometimes they're just parts of bodies, and that's truly the worst! Hands or legs, but you have to remember, they're just empty shells, vacant vessels."

"Hmmm," I nodded, tapping my index finger against the cleft in my chin, taking it all in and yet having nothing to say.

"I'm not trying to scare you, all right?" Phil added. "I just want you to know what you're in for. Sometimes when you pick the bodies up, the pressure pushes out the body juices from their nose and mouth, and you don't want to get any of that on you."

"Don't want to get it on me," I repeated to myself.

"Are you a religious man, Brandon?" Cheryl chimed in and asked.

"I was a Catholic when I was a kid, even an altar boy," I replied. "But now, you know, now I read too much to be religious."

They both looked at me with confused expressions. Phil finally nodded his head, "Well, good then. So, you don't believe in ghosts?"

"My Catholic upbringing battles my better judgment, but I've never seen a ghost, so both yes and no on that one,"

I replied, ambivalence being my trump card in a baited question like that.

Phil and his wife chuckled to one another, and I knew I was in for a ghost story. "I ain't no religious man myself, but I've seen things that would freak even Geraldo Rivera out. This one time, when I was dropping off a body at a mortuary in the early, early a.m., I kept hearing laughter coming from this closed coffin, then something took my keys from my belt and threw them across the floor in front of me! I took a little shit in my pants that day, Brandon."

I wondered if Phil drank heavily. I raised my eyebrows, implying that I was shocked by his story, but I was really more shocked by the Geraldo Rivera reference.

"How does this type of job sound to you?" he asked me. "Would you like something like this?"

I didn't *like something like this*, but I liked a roof over my head.

"What's the position pay, Phil?"

"See, that's the tricky part. You get paid per body, around $11. So, let's say you pick up nine or ten bodies a day, you made yourself about a hundred bucks."

The idea of handling ten different corpses a day, every day, just to make a decent living was repulsive to me. I could make cappuccinos for assholes for half a day and make more than this job paid. But there were no cash registers involved with corpses. No customers—no *living* customers—to have to deal with. And I was hungry.

"Sounds real good, Phil."

"Great! Why don't you come in tomorrow morning and we'll get you started. We'll send you out with Matt for the day, he's about your age."

"Terrific." I left the stucco building and drove back

home to North Hollywood only to fall asleep early, wake up, and return to the office the next morning at 8:55.

I parked my car in the parking lot just as Matt, my new coworker, pulled up in the confidential white mortuary van and idled behind me. He rolled the window down and pointed two fingers and a lit cigarette at me.

"You Brandon?" he asked.

"Yeah. Matt, right?"

"Totally," he said and opened the passenger door for me.

We shook hands as I crawled inside, and he flicked open his wrinkled cigarette pack at me. I pulled one out and lit it. "Thanks." Matt was about 30, with a moustache and blond hair. A slight mullet crept down his neck. He was the type of guy in high school that would drive his old American car slowly through the parking lot blasting AC/DC.

"All right, dude, our first one is a residential in Hollywood," Matt explained while getting onto the freeway. He then clarified that "residentials" were people that died uneventfully and without criminal motive in their homes, not to mention a good bulk of the business. "You know, like old people and shit," he added.

We pulled off the freeway and backed our van into the driveway of the late Mr. Richard Fowler's house. Matt organized his clipboard and finger-combed his moustache in the rearview mirror before we walked up to the front door.

Before we had a chance to knock, we were greeted by a young woman with red eyes and a cried-out voice. She opened the screen door and escorted us to the master bathroom, where her 70-year-old father, the late Richard Fowler, had collapsed in the middle of the night and died in a fetal position in front of the toilet.

"Why don't you bring the gurney around to the back

of the house while I take care of the paperwork," Matt suggested.

After returning to the van, I pushed the gurney around to the back of the house and parked it by the back door. I then walked into the bathroom and pulled the blanket off of the corpse on the floor, and I was quite surprised to see that his eyes were wide open. They seemed to follow me wherever I walked, like an expensive doll's eyes. His mouth was agape, as if he was frightened—as if he had died of fright in the middle of the night.

Matt returned to the bathroom to find me in a trance staring at the deceased. He squatted beside me and pushed Mr. Fowler onto his back, his bent arms and crouched legs moving in one solid motion. I slid the white sheet underneath him—his eyes still following me.

"Using the sheet, we'll lift him and walk him to the gurney on one, two, THREE!" Matt said, and we lifted Mr. Fowler and carried him to the backyard.

The corpse had a serious case of rigor mortis, making it impossible to attach the gurney's safety belts around his crimped arms and knees. The white sheet ballooned out above the gurney as if we were attempting to cover a large tree branch. I suspected what was about to come next but still wasn't prepared.

"We're going to have to straighten him out," Matt explained. "You do the legs and I'll do the arms. Just grab hold of his ankle and push down on the knee."

Its cold ankle felt like a thawing turkey breast in my hand. But its knee felt somehow still human—I could feel its skin rubbing against the kneecap whenever I pushed down on it, making it nearly impossible to get a grip. I then pulled on its foot and pushed down on the knee in one powerful swoop, and the sound of old wood breaking erupted from under the sheet. I could actually hear the ligaments snapping in his leg, and my stomach instantly began to turn. My mouth started to salivate, and I knew I was close to vomiting. Thankfully, Matt pushed me aside and straightened the other leg for me.

We easily fastened the safety belts around the body this time and wheeled Mr. Fowler to our van in the driveway. "Okay, I want you to slide the gurney into the van, so you know how to do it for next time," Matt instructed. "Remember to pull up on that lever there by your hand when his head reaches the bumper. That'll retract the wheels."

"Sure," I replied, "I can handle this."

Mr. Fowler weighed about 150 pounds, so I was going to need to push the wheeled tray in with some muscle. As I pulled the gurney back then shoved it forward, the daughter of the deceased appeared beside us with two steaming cups of coffee. I was startled by her sudden presence and released the lever too soon. The sound was the most frightening part as Mr. Fowler's bald head smashed into the van's bumper and then fell to the cement with a hollow pumpkin thud. Upon impact with the ground, the white sheet had flown back, and Mr. Fowler's wide-open eyes now watched us all from under the back of the van.

"Oh shit!" I gasped. Matt and I kneeled down and lifted the gurney back onto its wheels and finally into the van.

We both turned around to apologize to the daughter for what had just happened, but all that remained of her was the sound of a distant slamming screen door and two steaming splashes on the driveway where she had spilled both cups of coffee.

After Matt apologized repeatedly to the woman, we

delivered Mr. Fowler to a mortuary in Encino and headed back to the main office, at my insistence. Back in front of those leather chairs, I explained to Phil and his wife that there was no way I could go on being a mortuary driver— not even for the rest of the day. That much reality just would not work for me. Phil and his wife chuckled then he pulled out a prewritten check for $11 from his wallet. "We didn't think you looked much like the mortuary type."

THE CITADEL OF
TOASTER OVENS

JOB #25

The phrase "Hey, take care of this" can be interpreted many different ways. When attached to a bullet-ridden corpse it would most likely imply burying it in the desert in the dark of night. But if someone said "Hey, take care of this" before pointing at a wounded baby bird that had fallen from its nest, it could have meant mothering the bald little creature back to health just as easily as it could have meant dumping it in a shoebox coffin. Those five basic little words could be construed many, many different ways.

So when a delivery of a hundred toaster ovens arrived on two wooden pallets in the center of the housewares department and I was told, "Hey, take care of this," I did. I took care of it. I drew up some crude blueprints for a glorious European cathedral right there in the center of the second floor of Robinsons-May Co. before taping off the neighboring kitchen appliance aisles as a "Warning: hard-hats needed" zone.

I started with the spine of the mighty structure I would call the Citadel of Toaster Ovens first, then I built walls and pillars so high they nearly touched the overhead fluorescent lights. Those rectangle packages made perfect bricks, and each one stacked so gracefully atop one another you'd think freemasons designed them. I was surprised it only took two hours of waving customers away to build the enormous stronghold, and by the end it resembled something any ten-year-old boy would love to have in his backyard on a birthday. There were lookout windows set at waist height, a tiny door that required stooping over to get through, and battlements and ramparts atop each wall. I even brought two fold-up chairs inside and attempted to stay hidden until lunch, but an old woman peeked through the open entrance and dangled two packages at me.

"Do you know anything about these?" the silver-haired woman asked from behind a veil of perfume. She was balancing two rival portable CD players in her hands, focusing on the weight of each instead of the brand names and bullet-pointed features written on the packaging.

I didn't know a thing about CD players. It was 1997, and I was poor. The poor still used cassettes and records. "The Quasar is far superior to the . . . to that one in your hand there . . . *that* one," I explained to her as I stepped out of the Citadel.

"This one feels better," she said after shaking the slim box, which also shook the walking cane that formed a crescent moon around her wrist. "Feels like a better product."

"Because it's heavier?"

"Lighter," she replied.

"That's interesting. Why?"

"A lighter product means more advanced technology, which means crisper sound and a longer lifespan," she answered, now reading the features and benefits on the winner. "And this one's got a shock absorber so the CD won't skip if I decide to use it while walking or jogging."

"That's interesting," I said. "And the other one doesn't?" With her glasses nestled at the brim of her nose, she turned her gaze from the winning device to the losing device. "It doesn't say so, which leads me to believe it doesn't. You'd think they'd really showcase a feature like that."

"Especially in a bullet point."

"Especially," she agreed. "Can you ring me up for this?"

"No, I'm just the salesman," I answered. "But you can take it over there beside the entrance and they'll ring you up."

"Thank you, young man."

"It was a pleasure."

I envied that old woman as I watched her walk across the sales floor, toting her small package in a big empty shopping cart with one wild wheel. And I was proud of her for entering the technological world of portable CD players that attach to belts, especially at her age. I imagined her going home to her little retirement complex with her new battery-powered music player, wobbling contentedly to the cafeteria at dinnertime with Tony Bennett crooning through her headphones. What a brave new world she would soon be entering. Baths would never be the same again.

I loosened my tie because it was beginning to make me gag and returned to the cash register at the center of the floor, my new hub for eight hours a day. I could have rung her up—I was *supposed* to have—but I still wasn't a hundred percent comfortable with these new registers that all the big department stores were beginning to use. No longer satisfied with mere cash, check, and charge, these new elaborate devices now accepted payments to the store credit card, calculated coupons and discounts through barcodes, issued store credit vouchers, and redeemed gift certificates.

My manager, who was a couple years younger than I, appeared almost magically beside me. He spent most of his paychecks buying new suits and ties to wear to work, leading me to believe that he was still in college and living at home or, at the very least, just living at home. He wore green contact lenses that looked like two neon buttons against his Filipino face. He pointed to my Citadel of Toaster Ovens just before those green eyes shrank to slivers, like the Hulk in reverse.

"We can't have a display like that," he decreed. "We can't have any display over four feet tall or someone could get hurt."

"But there were so many boxes, I thought I'd do something extravagant. It's a citadel . . . like a fortress. Like 'Fortress of a Sale' or something. Or 'We defend good prices.' I didn't know about the height thing. Next time."

"I'm going to need you to take that down right now, actually. The whole thing."

"Sure, I can do that," I answered quite happily knowing it would keep me away from the cash register for at least another hour; three full days out of training and I still had yet to ring up a customer.

I stood in the center of the Citadel of Toaster Ovens one last time and stared blindly into the hundred identical little boy-and-mom faces smiling deviously at me from the stacked boxes. On the far right side of every package, the giddy two were cooking a mini pizza and smiling at the ease of using a toaster oven—a mother and her son, Caucasian; she was a brunette in her 30s and the tot no more than eight. The pizza was pepperoni. Mom was fervently pointing at the warming meal behind the petite glass door, and the kid looked as if he was about to clap his hands or plan a cunning cookie heist.

Every toaster oven box I pulled down from the walls revealed a new layer of this mom-and-son relationship to me, over and over again. By the tenth box she was burning pieces of the absent father in the little oven; by the twelfth, Mom was showing Junior where she keeps her soul warm at night. On *this* box, Mom had caught her little scientist cooking the family cat, and that's why she was pointing at it so enthusiastically; by the twentieth box, the two were cooking a turd casserole together; the next few also involved feces-related food products, but eventually we saw Mom showing little Tommy how babies were cooked at 375 degrees until *done*, not made.

I was peeling away so many layers of this familial riddle that I was forced to begin writing these eye-opening observations onto the fronts of every other box I pulled down. The print was subtle enough to be purchased without notice, but definitely noticeable when opening the box at home. The most horrible of comments, too, ranging everywhere from the aforementioned turd casseroles and husband penises all the way to the World War II fairy-tale-themed caption, "Li'l Jewish-Born Fairy Oven: Cook 'em till they're magically delicious!" Eventually running out of heinous commentary to write down, I resorted to caption bubbles and colorful statements about poop and wieners for the last thirty or so. The Citadel of Toaster Ovens was finally dismantled and rebuilt into a bulky four-foot-high rectangle, with each of my sixty or sixty-five little scribbles neatly positioned out of sight.

"Excuse me." A much younger woman than before

tapped me on the back. I was squatting on one knee admiring my handiwork and she had sneaked up behind me.

"Hi," I replied.

"I need to get this; can you help me? I'm so late."

I escorted her back to my cash register and was surprised at how well I rang her up on a credit card sale. Activation button, enter my employee code, run the laser over the barcode, push the *Visa/Master* button, and cha-ching. I smiled proudly at my own prowess before telling her, "That'll be $114.40."

"And I need to pay $100 to my store card first." She was already holding out her Visa card, her Robinsons credit card, and a $100 bill, regardless of whatever her purchase came to with tax. I could tell she wasn't going to take no for an answer.

The transaction was already complete, according to the register; it just needed payment before it could move on. I wished she would have mentioned wanting to pay off her store card with cash before I rang her up on the credit function. There was a process to recall the last sale, but I couldn't remember it. I remembered that it was quite complicated to do, so instead of trying I glanced around the sales floor for my manager. He was nowhere to be found, and she continued to stare at me impatiently. Then she crossed her arms.

"Is there a problem?" she snapped.

"I'm trying to void out the first sale to add in the . . . the cash part," I replied. "But it's complicated."

"Just do two sales! God, this is why I go to Bloomingdale's now. Seriously." She checked her watch, and I felt my face grow red. "It's a simple request. It's not really deserving of my *entire* lunch hour. This really can't be that difficult."

I had to remedy this situation immediately but I had

two credit cards and a shitload of cash in one hand and no idea what to do with the other hand. She kept goading me on, so I pushed the *$100* key, pushed the *Payment* button, swept her Visa card then her Robinson's card, and hoped for the best. The register computed the transaction for a second before the cash drawer sprang open with a victorious rattle of coins. I knew I had fucked up somewhere in the process but I put the $100 inside and shut it nonetheless. I ripped off the receipt and tucked it into the bottom of her bag underneath the package.

Once she huffed off, I examined the store duplicate of the receipt for what had actually happened during the sale, but it still remained a mystery. The Visa card wasn't charged for the $100, and it didn't ring up as a cash sale either. The receipt clearly showed that $100 changed hands somewhere in the transaction, but the cash drawer readout stated the drawer tally still stood at the amount it was three hours prior, minus the recent credit card sale for $114.40. It was a conundrum. It was a conundrum that could probably get me fired. Although having extra money in the register was better than being short at most major department stores, it was still frowned upon at Robinson's. I could come clean about the situation and blame it on the jitters, but my green-eyed manager was looking for any reason to get me out of there. The debacle of the Citadel of Toaster Ovens would be nothing compared to this.

There was only one option I could think of to remedy the matter: That $100 was going to have to disappear. Like the whole thing never happened. But $100 was big time. I had stolen from retail jobs before, but $18 and a bottle of wine had been my maximum. But this wasn't *stealing*— focus on that. This was simply removing something from the cash register that was never supposed to be there to begin with. I could do this—I could get away with it. After all, what employee would steal $100 on his third day at a job? They'd *have* to think it was a mix-up in the accounting. I'd have to be smart, though, from here on out—remove the guilty cash before going to lunch then hide it in my car. That way, if they searched me at the evening shift change, I'd be clean.

Because of the overhead security cameras, I devised a way to open the register and remove the $100 by leaning over the opened drawer while pretending to straighten the sunglasses rack that sat beside it. To the camera, it would appear that I was just lazy, not thieving. And it was beautifully executed too, my opened blazer engulfing the entire theft from view of the cameras. With my empty right jacket sleeve tucked into my pants pockets, I surreptitiously grabbed the bill and slid it into my shirt and hurried out to my car once Green Eyes relieved me.

I hid the money in the seat springs, ate my sandwich, then smoked two cigarettes back to back before leaving my '81 Firenze. Upon my return to the cash register, however, was not the usual sight of my Filipino manager tapping his watch. Greeting me now was a 30-something female employee in a smart pantsuit, who turned in my direction as soon as my little manager pointed at me approaching.

My heart suddenly began to pound in my chest and my legs felt as if they were about to collapse beneath me—how had they discovered my thievery so soon? Was there another overhead camera that I hadn't seen? Did my manager count the money in the drawer while I was gone? Was that unpleasant female customer actually a shill on a mission from management to catch me stealing? Sweat was beginning to form across my forehead and the back of my neck, and my right hand fumbled to find a pocket. Would jail be involved? Did they have a holding cell in the basement like Disneyland did? The questions kept coming with every step closer to the register until finally I arrived with the sorriest example of a smile smeared onto my wet face.

"Hello there," I said.

"Are you Brandon?" Pantsuit asked, showing no sign of emotion.

"I am."

"Oh, good," she said and handed a small burgundy jewelry box to me. "I'm Rhonda, in Human Resources. We just like to show our friendliest salespeople that we appreciate their smiles, even if they're new to the store."

I opened the little felt box and pulled out the lacquered gold and bronze star tucked inside. It was no bigger than a cufflink, with a tiny earring-like shaft poking out from the back. I examined it closer then displayed it to Rhonda and my manager, as if it were some type of surprise birthday gift that they were anxious to get a look at.

"Thank you," I said. "I'll cherish it." I ran my fingers over the lapel of my coat trying to find the embroidered slit where you put things like whatever that star was, but Rhonda stopped me and tapped her fingernail on my plastic nametag.

"It goes on your nametag, so customers know you're a star."

"Oh, I see," I said and popped the bitty burgundy thing into the groove in the plastic, between the store's name and my own. "This is very sweet. Thank you."

"You don't need to thank us; thank yourself for being such a great salesperson. And thank the customer you helped buy a portable CD player this morning. She just couldn't stop raving about what a nice salesperson you were."

"The older gal? Really?"

"Yep, she even went down to customer service to sing your praises."

As Rhonda walked away, I glanced over at my manager to find him glaring at the new star on my nametag. He didn't have one on his nametag. That fancy suit, the silk tie and matching socks, the leather shoes, the year of employment there—all that and no star.

"That's got to feel pretty shitty, huh?" I asked him, still sore about having had to raze the Citadel of Toaster Ovens. He frowned, shook his head, and walked away without a verbal reply. He'd never say another word to me again.

Nothing ever became of the missing $100, although I'd like to think that having the bronze star on my nametag made me impervious to accusations like that. And when we got a big order of rice cookers in the following week, I rebuilt the citadel with no protest from Green Eyes.

MEAT BURRITO AND A SIDE OF BEANS

JOB #63

"We don't spell 'come' C-U-M here," Lauren explained while standing in front of my little Formica desk in the office which, one week prior, had been the Xerox room. "I know most other adult magazines do, but we don't. If you look up 'cum' in the dictionary, it means 'along with or in combination with.' It does not mean semen—male or otherwise."

"That's very true," I replied, glancing at the eleven highlighted *cum* references in the half-page column of text in my hand, which I was supposed to have proofread for those types of discrepancies. I leaned over my computer and handed the printout back to her. "It just feels so natural for it to come out as . . . as *cum* . . . the C-U-M version. Sorry about that."

"Nobody seems to get it right," she said. "Don't worry. I know it doesn't look right, but it's proper. That's what I'm most concerned with. Nobody seems to give a shit about the proper use of English these days, so I'm doing what I can to correct that. Even if it's just here in porn."

She was the sexiest boss I had ever worked for, with her pale skin, dyed pink bob cut, plaid miniskirt, and knee-high boots. And to see her standing before me, and to listen to her explaining her grammatical preference of euphemism for a man's ejaculate was a position that I had never dreamed possible. But there I was, the newest Copy Editor for three of the nation's biggest gay men's adult magazines, mistaking *cum* for *come* on my first day. For shame, self. For shame.

"But you really need to catch these things. It's all in the Style Guide that I gave you; all the acceptable spellings and punctuation points," she added. "And remember: no children, no animals, no forced sex. You need to send it back to the writer if you see any of those."

"I'll be sure and keep an eye out," I replied.

"Oh, and feel free to use other euphemisms for 'come' or 'cock,'" Lauren added. "You've got like . . . nine . . . ten 'cocks' peppered throughout this article. Readers get bored with reading the same name over and over. Try replacing some of these 'cocks' with 'dick,' 'prick,' 'meat-finger,' or 'shaft.' They're the Holy Four. They'll get a lot of use. And 'balls' too. 'Nuts' are fine, or 'sack' if you have to . . . just not 'testicles.' There's nothing sexy about the word 'testicles.'"

She definitely misread the expression on my face; what she must have thought was revulsion was really just pure and simple astonishment—astonishment at hearing such colorfully perverse words spoken so nonchalantly by both an attractive woman *and* an employer. "You're all right with this still, aren't you?" she asked with motherly eyes. "I'm not freaking you out, am I? That look on your face . . ."

"No, no, not at all," I replied. "It's quite the opposite, actually. This look is my thinking look. What about skin plums?"

"Once more?"

"Skin plums. Instead of testicles. Because they hang, like fruit."

"Ummm, not so sure about that one."

"How about meat-fruit? Like, 'this is my meat-fruit.' Or man-fruit might be pretty good," I added.

My references were getting more comical and less sexy, according to Lauren. She explained that it was probably due to some inherent mental safety mechanism which substituted humor for emotion when confronted with sex; she then asked if I grew up Catholic. She was good, but I denied everything. Then she suggested come-dumplings for the article, and I proposed man-yolk, but we both settled on cock-giblets.

My first week as Copy Editor at Sizzling Publications passed by rather quickly, and quite easily. My average day was divided into two tasks: (1) writing photographer and model credits across the bottoms of photos of men with 9-inch penises penetrating other men with nine-inch penises, and (2) writing red hieroglyphic code beside misspellings and grammatical errors in articles and fiction pieces for the upcoming issues. The proofreading language was an amazingly spirited vocabulary of symbols, once you memorized its thirty or so most-used characters—or once you invisi-taped a small cheat sheet to the bottom of your monitor. The swirls and circles and dotted lines looked like a primitive Hebrew language that had all but died out with the Old Testament, and now only a few highbrows and scholars knew how to use it correctly. And I made sure to explain it this way to most people when asked what I now did for a living, and always while rubbing my chin and nodding. Sure, any asshole could circle a word that needed to be capitalized, or find a location in a sentence that would be better served with a comma instead of a period. But find me one son of a bitch that can propose using a semi-colon correctly, especially in a paragraph about two men fondling each other's scrotums, and I'll show you a genius in the wrong line of work.

So I arrogantly inscribed my little red marks beside, below, and above every grammatical error, punctuation problem, and misspelling I could find, explaining to each and every staff writer—with my intellectually superior crimson code—that his use of "their" should have been a "they're," and his "cum" should be "come." Drunk with this newfound power, and only slightly to impress Lauren, I began to go above and beyond what was editorially necessary. Almost every "that" became a "which," "where," or "when." Semicolons were appearing everywhere; hyphens were popping up between "cock" and "sucker," but not between "cock" and "sucking," which was a totally different ballgame, according to the Style Guide—the whole noun-versus-verb thing, you see. My budding passion for the job helped me to realize that I had always been a proofreader at heart. I had just never really known it until I applied for a job as one.

But the question of my sexual preference never came up—not during the interviewing process and not as the weeks passed on. I guess they just assumed that any man applying for an editorial job at a gay men's porn magazine was either gay, really into man-on-man pornography, both, or none of the above and just needed a job. Falling into that latter category, I knew the laws had worked to my advantage in getting the position, because it was illegal to ask the sexual orientation of a person during the hiring process. I also realize that this law was usually reserved for the gay not the straight, but the sauce for the goose was the same for the gander, according to Grandma. But I thought for sure, by now, someone would have just asked me.

It took another week until I realized that I was literally the only heterosexual man in an office of over fifty male coworkers. I had a few solid paychecks in the bank and a brief understanding of the rights I had as an employee, so I felt it was time to let a little bit of the truth out. Nothing too damaging at first; just a few random comments to Lauren, then a few through the local gossip channels in the graphic arts department. Just enough for them to question my preference for the vagina or the penis, maybe even toy with the idea of "playing for both teams," at the very least. Then a three-day weekend found me in the arms of a woman named Brass McMann, who had taken it upon herself to blow into her cat's rectum while I was giving her oral, and I felt the need to relay this odd information to an editor named Michael that following Tuesday back at work. We worked for a porn magazine, after all, and I hadn't had too many recent tales to tell at the watercooler, so I needed something to share. But it was now finally out of the bag: I slept with women; I was a breeder. Much to my surprise, he complimented me on being so well dressed and well groomed for a "vagina preferer," then passed the news through a few of his own gossip channels. Well, his channels reached much farther than mine did, and by lunchtime the news of my heterosexuality had reached Sandy.

"You're straight?!" she charged into my office with a great big smile and announced uncomfortably loud. "I knew it! I knew you were straight! I had a bet going on, and I knew it! It's just you and me . . . and Lauren . . . but she's married. Everybody else here blows cock! Well, I guess I do too, and probably Lauren. But you sure don't! Wow! Great! That is so good to hear!" And at precisely that moment I knew I should have kept my mouth shut.

When you surround a single woman in her mid-30s with nothing but gay men and one straight man, you're looking at trouble. When you surround *Sandy* with nothing but gay men and one straight man, you're looking at an orgy and probably a lawsuit. She was the editor of the magazine *Young Guys*, which, like its name made clear, showed pictures of early-20-something twinks flirting with the camera in such scenic locations as pool, locker room, pool, and locker room. My first conversation with Sandy established that she was "very much" a single, heterosexual woman; healthy and disease-free; on several dating websites; turned on by male porn; "very much" a single, heterosexual woman again; that she preferred *cum* over *come*; and then a little joke about just preferring cum in general. After she flashed that devious, love-thirsty smile of hers, I knew employment at Sizzling Publications would never be the same again. My candor had severed the innocent unicorn's horn.

Sandy was graced with an enormous set of breasts, an intrusive personality, and a phone-voice that permeated office walls. And she seemed to have a talent for writing male-on-male pornographic prose, although she had the good sense to use manly sounding author aliases like Sherwood, SJ, and Sam for her articles—to keep the illusion alive for her readers. Her "Editor's Recommendations" page of the top-performing dildos and vibrators always had a tried-and-true quality about it, although I considered it a little devious to judge a vibrator's merit on vaginal stimulation as opposed to anal stimulation. But a good Copy Editor doesn't dare touch such topics out of his pay grade.

There are times when someone flirts and it's so subtle that the message goes unnoticed by the receiving party. And then there were Sandy's flirtations, which were always noticed, always seemed to take place over a desktop full of nude photographs, and consisted of comments like, "Look at *that* cock, will ya? God, I'd give anything to rub that sweet little pecker right now. Say . . . he looks kind of like you . . ." Or, "Do *you* ever just stand in front of a locker-room mirror like that and jack off? I bet you make a face like his when you blow your load on your own reflection? I have a big mirror like that at my place . . . we can find out." And yes, I agree, it's difficult to judge what truly makes a flirtation a flirtation when you're staring at a photo of a college quarterback masturbating, which also happens to be part of your job. But if you could have just seen that look in her eyes— like a wolf in heat staring at a rabbit that resembled both lunch *and* the last penis on Earth—then you would know what a dangerous situation I had found myself in.

"She's loud and obnoxious," Lauren would always say after slinking into my little office seconds after Sandy left. "I hate her. I really hate her. I can hear her from my office, and I'm way over there."

"She said I—"

"And she's a sycophant. And she's one of the leading contributors to the whole 'cum–come' debacle. I truly hate her. I'm going to ask Papa Legba to teach her a lesson. I really am. If she keeps this up, I am."

Papa Legba. It was moments after this precise conversation when I discovered that Lauren was a practicing witch. And not the hippie-mom, quartz necklace, Sarah McLachlan type of witch, but the Haitian voodoo type. The type that put themselves into trances, made strange little dolls, used powders made from dried bones, and swore oaths of vengeance on people they hated. Apparently, Papa Legba was her spiritual guide in the afterlife, and she made offerings to him weekly. He could only be reached by closing her eyes and chanting his name or something, which she did quite frequently in her office.

Papa Legba or not, the feud between Lauren and Sandy was escalating day by day, and I, like most of the other employees, was slowly being forced to pick a side or fall into the void between. Because, like any good grudge between female coworkers, it wasn't just *them* that you had to worry about; it was the legions they built around themselves. Sandy had her friends-turned-allies, most of whom were in the advertising and graphic departments. And Lauren had her supporters, who were upper management and Human Resources. The rest of the editorial department was split on their partisanship: *Follow the loud lady that talks too much, or follow the smart one who makes us spell "cum" as "come"?*

There was no decision on my part. Even though I was beginning to suspect that Lauren was a little crazier than I had originally assessed—be it the rattling drawer full of empty antidepressant bottles or the time she asked me to hold a tape recorder while she underwent one of her rolled-back-eyes trances—the alternative to her was a thousand times worse. Besides, Lauren had hired me. She had helped me to realize my true nature as a Copy Editor in pornography. She had also won my undying loyalty by introducing me to her medicinal marijuana dealer, who made weekly deliveries to the office. And, of course, I still wanted to sleep with her. So I signed the deed. I had her back, and she had mine.

Regardless of—or possibly as a result of—the feud between the two editors, my career in gay porn began to flourish. I was asked to write a few short articles about gay-related news events for an upcoming issue, which then turned into erotic storylines for a few picture sets. Within a week of the publishing of that second article, I was promoted to Associate Editor of both *9 Inches* and *Young Guys*, and given a bigger office and an assigned parking spot in the subterranean garage. Along with my new windowed view of Wilshire Boulevard and my pay raise, I also received health insurance and a healthy 401(k) package. I began writing more and more articles and fiction pieces for the magazines. And according to the letters to the editor, it was top-notch gay porn.

The best I could figure it, my porn succeeded where others' failed because mine was written from a different perspective than what most readers were used to—like the way S.E. Hinton, who was a young female author, had penned such an insightful, male-coming-of-age novel like *The Outsiders*. For Hinton, not knowing what it felt like to be a teenage boy somehow helped her to write about teenage boys. And for me, not knowing what it felt like to be *in* a teenage boy somehow helped me to write about being in teenage boys. For instance, instead of the typical storyline of "Bobby" meeting "Tony" under the college stadium bleachers to celebrate a football game victory with a hand-job and a finger up the ass, my plots dove into Tony's and Bobby's emotional and psychological sides. My character development was rich and deep, and exposed the true nature of Tony wanting to get hammered by the quarterback. You see, Tony was a lonely child; he burned ants with a magnifying glass when his mother wasn't around; he stuck candles in his ass as a teenager before going off to college to discover his true nature, his true sexuality. Now, Tony couldn't get enough cock, and Bobby the quarterback was more than willing to provide. Bobby, you see, loved the game of football so much that he equated the pigskin with the asshole. Climaxing was his touchdown and the field goal was the reach-around.

I even surpassed Lauren's "Holy Four" recommendation by creating my own long list of usable euphemisms for the three most overused terms in male pornography: cock, balls, and the ass. I had every corner covered with my new index. Need a good substitute for cock? Try a poker, meat-rocket, prober, porker, chunky finger, dong, the ripper, pork sandwich, Dr. Feel-Good, the thick one-eye, beef monster, meat enchilada, skin stick, vein burrito, bulbous bologna, and man-meat. Or for the uncircumcised I had the cloaked druid and the pig-in-a-blanket. Oh, balls, you said? How about meat plums, man-fruit, coin purse, candy sack, come-factory, danglers, love-nuggets, dingleberries, come-kwats, or little hairless fellas. Ah, yes, lest we forget the asshole . . . the cornerstone of any good bout of sodomy. Try one of these on for size: man-pussy, hot-pocket, brown-eye, the pooper, the pooder, the dingus, man-gina, my sweet ride, velvet cocoon, chocolate-pocket, raspberry starfish, pink balloon knot, meat sleeve, love-hole, man-hole, sweet meat, chili cup, the midnight gap, the meaty hollow, snack crack, and The Angus.

I had everything going for me those first few days until the other part of the new job duty surfaced: As Associate Editor, I was also supposed to work directly under the other editors, one of whom was Sandy. And she made sure to state it like that every time the issue came up in conversation: "You do a great job working *under* me," she would joke constantly. "You use your 'cocks' so powerfully under me." A few times a week would have been funny . . . for that first week. But it was a few times an hour, every hour. And always with the perfume, leaving a thick, scented trail between her office and mine every 20-25 minutes.

I started to dread hearing the clopping of her approaching high heels, and I would constantly pick up the phone and pretend to be in a conversation with a freelance writer or curious customer when she poked her head into my office. With my head angled down and eyes shielded by a tensed palm, anybody else would have simply placed their workload onto my desk and left, or come back in a few minutes. Not Sandy. When standing in my doorframe for five or ten minutes wouldn't grab my attention, walking in and leaning over my desk would. Her thick cleavage would pour out from her low-cut black top and steal the thought from my head—I was forced to acknowledge her.

Her advances and candor and perfume were escalating each day. Normally a smiley type of guy, I tried instead offering her blank stares and stiffened lips when spoken to, but that did little more than beg her to finish her long-winded stories. I tried another method, passing a bit of gossip around where I had finally gotten serious with a nice gal in Beverly Hills and wanted to settle down, but that still did little to quell the beast in the black skirt. So, I went for the Nagasaki number and attached a plastic dropbox outside my office door and sent an email around telling my department that they could simply leave their work for me in there if they so desired, thereby eliminating the time-consuming chore of having to speak with me. But that didn't work either. Instead, Sandy took it up a notch. As punishment for my dropbox idea, she began announcing over the office intercom, "Brandon, please report to Sandy's office *immediately!*" whenever she needed me.

An earlier version of myself, like the 1996 model for example, would have taken Sandy up on her advances and fucked her on a lunch break just to get her to leave me alone. And just to fuck her, too. But this newer model that I was now behind the wheel of, it had an extra decade of experience under the hood. And this newer model had also learned the hard way what sleeping with coworkers can do. Twice.

My allegiance to Lauren was growing stronger with every one of Sandy's attempts at getting to know me better. We started taking cigarette breaks downstairs at the lobby café, doing nothing but sipping, inhaling, exhaling, and grumbling about Sandy. It was amazing; our mutual hatred of "the loud one" was actually bringing Lauren and I closer together. Even in our weekly staff meetings in the conference room, Lauren and I would walk in together, sit together, and leave together in a conversation—replacing the old system of Sandy arriving late and pushing any available seat across the room and next to me. Needless to say, Sandy was not happy about this new seating arrangement. Then it started to get really complicated.

Sandy began leaving work exactly when I did every night. She would take the elevator down with me and ask if I wanted to meet her for a drink. I knew this because she had asked me that same question a dozen times or more already—at the front desk, in my office, in the elevator, in the lobby, in the parking garage. A man could not humanly have that many "prior plans" on his calendar, and my excuses were beginning to wear thin. So I started staying later at work, and then so did she. And when she couldn't find any work to do to warrant staying an extra hour in her office, she would sit in her car, parked beside mine in the parking garage, waiting for me to take the elevator down and attempt to leave. There would always be a little pile of cigarette butts at the foot of her car door—like a 1940s private investigator on a stakeout—giving away exactly how long she'd sat there for. I kind of felt badly for her, that she would have to go to these lengths just to get some guy to spend five minutes with her. And as I spied on the perfumed private investigator from my hiding spot behind the column near the elevator, creating my own pile of cigarette butts beneath me, I actually considered just walking over to her car and asking her out for a drink. How bad could it be? Just two coworkers blowing off some steam over a beer. But then I caught a whiff of her perfume seconds before I heard her car door slam. She had applied a fresh dousing of fragrance and was headed back up to the office, no doubt to search for me with an alibi of "forgetting something." I did what any person would do in my situation: I hid behind the concrete column until she entered the elevator, then I dashed to my car and sped off before she could come back down.

That was a bad idea, I learned the next day. A very bad idea. Sandy didn't even have time to take off her sunglasses before she stormed into my office and slammed the door behind her. She tore off her shades and shouted, "Why won't you go out with me?! I've been nothing but nice to you! What's wrong with me?! Huh?! Answer me! Answer me, goddamnit! What the fuck is wrong with this? This should be perfect! It's just you and me here!"

I was more than a little caught off guard. "Because we work together," was all that my three sips of coffee could put together that early. "That's just . . . and I'm dating some—"

"Oh bullshit!" she screamed. "You don't think I know you're single? Bullshit! It's written all over you! So you'd rather just be alone, huh? Is that it? You don't think I've heard that shit before, huh?"

Coworkers were beginning to walk past my closed glass door and not-so-subtly glance inside. Sandy must have looked like a bulldog pacing before its prey. Her stout little body, packed into a black skirt and blouse, waddled back and forth down the length of my desk. She was spewing out bits and pieces of complete thoughts that she must have rehearsed a dozen times on the drive to work that morning. Something this huge *had* to be premeditated. I really didn't know what to do, so I stayed in my seat and watched her face grow redder with every outburst.

"Phone calls! I called your cell phone three times over the weekend! And did you return any of my calls? Of course not! Why? I don't know! I'll tell you why! You think you're too . . . too . . . hot shit, don't you? Is that it? Well, you're not! I'm a good person! I'm better than you! Don't even return any of my calls! I made you! I gave you this position! I'll take that shit away too! Watch me! Teach you not to return my calls, mister!"

I started to run through my usual excuses for not returning phone calls before realizing that I had never given Sandy my phone number. I'd start there. "Hey! Easy, easy . . . First off, how did you get my number? I never—"

"What?! What are you whining about?"

"My private number. I never gave it to you; and now I think you can see—"

"Don't be such a pussy! You're on Google; everyone's on Google! You're not special! I can call whoever the hell I want to call! I don't need *you* to give me your number!"

She proceeded to shout at me for another 10 minutes before I finally reached my boiling point and demanded she leave my office. Nothing. I stood and pointed at the door. She folded her arms. Fine. If she wasn't going to leave, then I was. I grabbed my blazer, pushed her out of my way, and rode the elevator down to the lobby café for an espresso and a cigarette. I needed to think. I needed to do something. Employment there could never again be the same after that morning. I'm sure the entire place was by now afire with rumors and gossip of the two breeders' love quarrel, because that's exactly what it must have looked and sounded like to anyone within an earshot of my office. At that thought, part of me wanted to get into my car and drive the hell out of there, forever; they could mail me my last check. But then Sandy would have won. Everybody would have assumed that I was the asshole that screwed her and dumped her, or somehow broke her heart and spit on the pieces. Who in their right mind would believe that I was being stalked by a lady half my size? Who would believe that I was the one being harassed in this scenario? *Harassed.* The word kept repeating itself in my head. *Harassed.* Then the prefix arrived and changed everything: *sexual. Sexually harassed. Sexual harassment.* And just like that, I knew what I was going to do. I'll see your loud, humiliating outburst, Sandy, and I'll raise you a sexual harassment suit!

Four simultaneous conversations happening around the receptionist's desk halted the exact moment that I stepped out of the elevator. Eight pairs of outraged eyes were now fixed on me, none of them able to look away or even blink. I felt good, though, and I smiled at them—a mischievous smile, but still a smile. And then, instead of turning left toward my office, I walked around the right side of the receptionist's desk and directly to the Human Resources department. I sat down opposite the HR manager, and the first words out of his mouth were, "Yeah, I thought I'd see you in here this morning."

No city knew their lawsuits like Los Angeles; and no company took their sexual harassment cases more seriously than an adult magazine publisher. You put those two points together and you get one hell of a "Fuck you, Sandy!" It looked so good on paper, too: A boss intimating sexual favors from her assistant; stalking the assistant; threatening to fire him, etc. By the time I left his office 30 minutes later, a sexual harassment complaint had been filed against Sandy, and legal documents were being drawn up in the corporate offices in New York. They asked if I wanted to make it a legal matter, and they'd even provide the attorney, but I declined as long as I never had to work under Sandy again. Although I was angry enough to file a harassment complaint against her, I wasn't angry enough to ruin the next 10 years of her professional life—I just wanted it to be like that first month again, when she thought I was gay. So our offices were separated even farther from one another, and Lauren became the buffer between all oral and email communication between Sandy and me. I couldn't have arranged a better settlement.

And it was a great couple of weeks that followed before the remorse kicked in. Not necessarily remorse for what had happened to Sandy, but remorse for what it said about all of us heterosexuals. Like we were all pussies; couldn't settle something sanely and without attorneys involved. This big melting pot of a company, with fifty gay men and four lesbians living, working, and coexisting happily alongside one another in the eccentric world of hardcore sex—but it was those two damn straight people that had to take it too far.

Although I lost a few coworkers as friends because of

the event, Lauren, as well as the new glow on her face, were companions enough for me. She loved what was going on. She adored torturing Sandy, and now she didn't need to limit herself to simply *imagining* a world where Sandy didn't exist; she could now orchestrate it. Lauren said I wasn't allowed to write anything for *Young Guys* any longer, which left Sandy to write all her own articles for the upcoming issue. And her emails that asked for my help never made it past Lauren's draconian buffer—well, they did, but Lauren and I just laughed at them. I'll admit, at first I loved watching Sandy struggling to keep her head above water, and forced to stay late every night to get her work done. But as the weeks wore on with this same sad scenario, I started to feel really sorry for her. She was actually honoring the guidelines set up by the Human Resources department to keep her job, and she even tossed me a couple of apologetic smiles when we were caught in the elevator together. But what I really felt badly about was aiding Lauren in a voodoo ceremony, where I kept guard while she poured some type of mystical powder under Sandy's desk and cast a spell. And I felt even worse that next morning when Sandy came in with her arm in a cast after some "crazy homeless guy" attacked her while she was walking her dog the night before. Lauren was ecstatic; I was freaked out.

Every night I left at 6:00, and every night I would see Sandy's car still in the parking garage—no piles of cigarette butts under her door, no perfume, no Sandy. There was a little part of me that began to miss that, and I didn't know why. I had never been the object of someone's fanatical adoration before, and I guess I'd always assumed that if it had ever happened to me it would register as some feeling *other* than infuriation. I began toying with the idea of all the other scenarios that could have played out had I been a bit more imaginative to Sandy's advances. I could have turned it into a secret sexual partnership where *I* was the boss; maybe make her my love slave and act out all my secret perversions; perhaps I could have used her to bargain for a better position in the company; forced her to never speak to her relatives again; maybe even have sex with an animal. I could have probably turned her crush into almost any twisted thing I desired. And it was that last thought which made me realize that I had changed. I had always been sort of a dick, according to close acquaintances, but now I was getting vicious. I was actually considering more ways to hurt someone just to mask the guilt of hurting them in the first place. I could blame the porn all I wanted for my sudden lack of empathy—staring at photos of sweaty, hardcore sex all day would desensitize anybody after nearly a year—but the real fault fell upon me and me alone. Because I had allowed it to affect me. I had left my moral door ajar, and the dick walked right in.

I made a vow to myself; I was going to change. At work the next day I said "Good morning" to Sandy in the lobby, and she smiled kindly. I then offered to write an article for her after lunch, and she thanked me graciously as she handed me three photos of an uncircumcised 8-inch cock, and with no innuendo. When I left Sandy's office to return to my own, Lauren grabbed me by the arm and yanked me into the kitchen.

"What the hell are you doing?" she demanded. "You're not . . . you can't help her! We've got her right where we want her! She's going to quit soon! Papa Legba confirms this. I heard around that she's calling up other magazines for jobs, but no one wants her. Don't help her anymore!"

"I . . . there's no one to write the . . . I just wanted to help her out with an article," I replied. "I feel bad about all this, and I had some free time."

"Bad?" Lauren snapped. "Papa Legba said to be strong. The homeless guy attacking her was just the beginning. She's going to pay for being such a . . . such a cunt! She will pay. And don't stand in the way of Papa Legba or his retribution."

Fucking Papa Legba again. God, I wanted to be a gay man at that moment. If this was how breeders acted— voodoo curses, sexual harassment lawsuits, punishing coworkers—then I wanted nothing to do with the vagina any longer.

I got back to my office and knew what I had to do. There was only one remedy to this situation. I had been happily welcomed into the jovial kingdom of gay men's porn, and I shat upon the rug in the warmth of its glow. I would have to remove myself from this fertile kingdom, to save Sandy's job *and* possibly her life, and to again level the playing ground that the two female editors had shared before I arrived. Although porn had been very good to this professional gypsy, it was time for me to leave.

Not knowing who else to talk to about my decision, I traced my cell phone's incoming-call history and found Sandy's phone number from several weeks back, and I rang her that night. We talked for a solid hour about life, about the sexual harassment complaint, about the magazines, about Lauren, and then about me quitting. Although she was against me leaving the magazines, she knew that it would be beyond weird for me to resume working there, and be friends with her, with the Human Resources department and Lauren keeping tabs on us both. Before I hung up, I informed her that Lauren was out for blood and had been putting magical powders under her desk, and she promised to start locking her office door at night.

That next morning was a Friday. I walked into the HR office and, after lifting the harassment complaint against Sandy, I offered my two-week resignation. They asked if it was due to Sandy, or if she had threatened or coerced me in any way. I laughed a little, which probably wasn't the most professional thing to do when resigning, then simply explained that the pornography had finally begun to affect me. I guess that was a common thread among quitters in the adult business, because they offered to let me vacate my position as Associate Editor one week from that day and still leave with a good recommendation.

So that's exactly what I did. That next Friday rolled around, and I packed all my belongings into a cardboard box and said good-bye to all of my coworkers. Sandy was the only one that offered to help me carry my stuff down that afternoon, and we stood and smoked a cigarette in the parking garage.

"God," Sandy remarked with a grin, "all this because of a crush. I'm really sorry it came to this."

"Kind of snowballed, didn't it?"

"*That's* an understatement," she replied. "I promise from here onward, I'll never try and fuck a coworker again. No matter how much I want to."

We both giggled a bit. Then there was a brief patch of silence while we individually debated what to say to one another next. Then a weird bit of eye contact. It was obvious that both of us wanted to say what was really on our minds, but we were still a little gun-shy from the whole harassment thing. So I unlocked the back door of my car and threw the box onto the floor. She remarked on how big my backseat was, then how dark my tinted windows were.

"Technically, we're no longer coworkers," I said. "Just two people smoking cigarettes in a parking garage."

"So, getting into your backseat and lifting my skirt wouldn't be grounds for termination?" she asked jokingly.

"I don't think that would, no." I replied. "But if you, let's say, touched my man-fruit or rubbed my glazed beef-cicle, then that probably would . . . if I still worked here."

"You mean your meat burrito and side of beans?"

"My little Vic Mackey and his dangling backpack."

"Vic Mackey?" she asked.

"The bald guy from *The Shield* . . . Michael Chicklis . . ."

"I *so* would have fired you for that one."

And with that, Sandy crawled into the backseat of my old '97 and pulled up that black skirt of hers just like she said she would, and I promptly followed her in. It was a quick and dirty bout of sex, but it was one of life's more memorable ones because of the closure aspect. That backseat romp was our apology to one another. It was our good-bye to one another. And it was our act of contrition for defacing the good name of heterosexuality.

McPLUMBERS

JOB #20

No one knows for sure when the toilet was first invented. It seems like every country has its own unique "discovery" of a device that politely and sanitarily collects and removes waste from under a squatting position. Some parts of India were using water-based shitters as early as 3100 B.C. The Egyptians were dropping deuces in water closets almost 3,800 years ago. Even the Scots shat in toilets around the same time, but the true originator of the toilet as we know it today— as well as all modern plumbing—is the Roman Empire. Nearly 4,000 years ago the Romans were using aqueducts made from enormous stone blocks to bring in fresh water to their palaces and cities from rivers miles and miles away. By the fourth century, the city of Rome boasted 11 public bathhouses, 856 private baths and 1,352 public fountains and cisterns. The Romans are actually where we get the name "plumber" from. *Plumbus* in Latin means "lead," which was what they used to make their pipes and faucets. Plumbers were celebrities back then. They were indispensible. They were the most sought-after craftsmen and artisans for as far as the Roman Empire reached.

This is no longer the case today. In today's world, plumbers are basically the guys that unplug toilets and touch human shit for a living. And from my first six days as a plumber's assistant for one of the bigger "Rooter"-suffixed plumbing companies in Los Angeles, I would have to whole-heartedly agree with that assessment. Thugs, dropouts, drunks, and convicts—guys that you would never let into your house under any circumstance other than an iconic van parked in your driveway and brand recognition. We were McPlumbers—the guys you called not to lay the pipe but to unplug the shitter.

A plumber's *assistant* was what they called the new trainees—the handful of us who had answered the ad in the paper and passed the written exam, and who were now getting a paid week of on-the-job training in courses like 1) How to handle irate customers; 2) How to use a motorized, coiled drill-thing to unplug a pipe; and 3) How to no longer eat food with your bare fingers. Ah, but god bless the paid training, though—a solid week of a salary for just a little bit of work. We were supposed to be gaining valuable experience from the veteran plumber we were partnered with. And I use the term "veteran plumber" quite loosely here. You see, I was partnered with a husky chap named Pedro, who looked like he'd seen a few years in jail before fathering a handful of children from several different obese women all named Maria. And his behavior over the past six days was the stereotypical Mexican figurine of a sombrero and a set of knees—the only thing this guy did was sleep in his driver's seat when not on a job.

But I can't blame Pedro too much. Being a plumber wasn't the type of occupation your teenage self envisioned your future self having. Being a plumber in 1994 was a consequence of every bad choice you made *before* 1994. It was the type of occupation that your probation officer suggested would keep you out of trouble. We had no learned skills or years of education in the craft of irrigation; we simply had the vans and tools and "Rooter" name. We were franchise plumbers. Our only saving grace was that we could be at a client's home in 45 minutes. We only got the emergency calls, which usually meant a toilet had overflowed and poured gallons of sewage water across the tiled bathroom floor. You then had to kneel in it to properly push the coiled metal cord of the electric snake as far down into the toilet's pipe as possible. And with your knees then stained and soiled, your canvas-gloved hand submersed in cold filth, and your face as close to a brimming bowl of someone else's urine and excrement as you ever thought imaginable, you turned on the motorized snake and tried to hold on to its gyrating cord and guide it down the pipe as it jumped around in the bowl and splashed your neck and chest with soupy beige water. The worst was when you felt a stray drop hit your lip but your hands were too dirty to do anything about it. It sickened you that there's a drop of what might be someone else's shit on your bottom lip, and it must stay there until the job is finished. You fight yourself against the urge to use your sleeve or your shoulder to wipe it away because you know it won't be a clean wipe; you know you're going to get some of *whatever* that is in your teeth or on the side of your mouth. And you focus all your available mental energy on making sure that you don't absentmindedly bite your bottom lip or, heaven forbid, lick your lips. And this wasn't a rare occasion. This happened nine out of every ten calls.

We sat in the van in the parking lot of a Wendy's and listened to an oldies station as we waited for our next call.

As Pedro dozed off with his feet up on the dashboard and his head on the hand rest, I reflected. I recollected. I reminisced. I pondered my family legacy, then its sudden demise at my hands. I had been very good this past week about not dwelling on the Consolidated Film Industries job—or, to be more precise, the ending of it—but here I was now, listening to some old, dead asshole singing about doing the twist while I dwelled on one of the monumental failures of my 23 years of life. It had been a short-lived spectacle and my only real taste of union life, but it should have been my birthright—my fate. Like British royalty, I was born into it.

Growing up in Hollywood, you either worked in the film industry or you served the people who worked in the film industry. Not much else to do outside of that. I came from a long line of Christophers who had nestled into the laborious, behind-the-scenes underworld of Tinsel Town and stayed there. My dad was a film cutter in the editing department of Consolidated Film Industries for 36 years; my grandfather was that same company's accountant before that. Then it was my turn. A union job, with a starting pay of $23 an hour! I hadn't broken the ceiling of $9 since calling it quits on an associate's degree the year before.

I remembered my first day working there, weeks before this plumbing job was even a thought. It was like a family reunion at C.F.I.: Every adult I had ever known growing up was suddenly my coworker. Each person I ran into in the halls stopped and asked how I was doing, how my mom was, if my brothers were still all right. There were more union-guaranteed breaks than actual work. Employees all drank beer at lunch, snoozed at their desks, and engaged in hour-long conversations about quarterbacks and horse races.

I could do this, I had assured myself at the time. I could give up my dreams and aspirations of sovereignty and struggle for this lifelong cushy ride into retirement. These people all did it; it couldn't be that difficult. To hell with breaking new ground in the literary world; I was going to be a unionized film cutter and make lots of money. I would be able to buy a house, a new car, maybe a racehorse or a yacht. Even though cutting strips of film was about as exciting as combing your arm hair while conversing with your own reflection for eight hours a day, every day, it was a career—an actual career—and not just another bullshit job. It was a life choice.

Although I was then certain of my newfound path after only that first day there, fate was not and suggested otherwise. The moment I arrived at Consolidated Film Industries for my second day, I was called upstairs into the foreman's office. It seemed he had just that morning received the news of my failed union drug test, even after I drank one of those $35 bottles of cleansing liquid that were guaranteed to make you pass. It was horrible. I wasn't fired on the spot, but I was immediately "unhired" on the spot. No one made eye contact with me as I left the office and walked down the long hallway to tell my father that I would no longer be working alongside him. He nodded his head and seemed to be waiting for me to blurt out, "Ha ha, just kidding!" Or maybe I was expecting him to say it. But nothing followed but a pat on my arm and a, "Come by the house and see your mom this weekend." I nodded and apologized for any embarrassment I might have caused, then walked to my old Camaro and drove to the movies. I then drank wine for three days straight before finding the ad for the plumber's assistant job with no experience required.

The CB radio in the Rooter van severed me from my nostalgic regrets. After a squelch and a clearing of someone's throat on the other end, the antiquated plastic device on the dashboard informed us of our next call up on the expensive side of the Encino hills. It took us a solid 20 minutes driving to the top of the huge hill in our clunky van, but we arrived to find another of our vans parked there at the head of the small mansion's circular driveway.

"We're assisting on this one," Pedro said as he parked right beside the other van.

"Sounds good."

A younger version of Pedro approached my Pedro at his opened window. "Hey bro, we got a good one this time." They smiled at one another.

Pedro had me drag a large aluminum-covered box from the van to the back of the house, where a shallow hole had been dug at the center of an acre-long garden descending down a hill. The silver box was heavy and looked like something a ventriloquist would keep an expensive dummy inside of. I could have used a hand from either Pedro bringing it over, but a glance back at their precariously huddled conversation behind the vans made it pretty clear that they had needed a private conversation away from me.

I squatted behind the silver box and watched Mini-Pedro introduce the silver-haired homeowner to the other Pedro. A few papers were passed between them before Pedro pointed to the hole that I was crouching inside of; then they all suddenly looked at me. I quickly jumped out of the hole then pointed at the hole. The old man covered his mouth as if catching a word from coming out midway. He paused then softly nodded his head, finally acquiescing to the two Pedros and their seemingly bad news. Then two chubby, tan-skinned smiles in blue short-sleeve shirts strutted from the patio to me and my hole.

"See, I told you!" the younger Pedro exclaimed to the older Pedro once out of earshot from the homeowner. "The whole thing, man! He said he'd go for it. All of it. This shit's from the '50s . . . he doesn't know. All the way down the mountain, bro."

"*Dios mío!*" Older Pedro grinned a real devious set of pearls.

"We'll split the commission, right down the middle." Little Pedro noticed me leaning in to hear. "Sorry, new guy. This is all me and Pedro. You're still in training anyway. You don't get shit, bro."

"But you see how you can make real money doing this now, right?" my trainer asked with two fingers into my shoulder.

"Find an additional Brandon?"

"No, bro! Customers believe whatever you tell them. You're the plumber, bro. They believe you. You can tell them anything and they usually go for it."

"I was just . . ."

"You'll figure it out, bro."

Little Pedro opened the silver box and pulled out a large coil of rolled black cord and handed it to me. He wiggled what looked like a tinted lightbulb attached to the end of the roll of insulated wire and said, "Slide this end down the pipe slowly. We need to see what's clogging shit up."

As I squatted over the ditch and fed the bulbous black head of the cord down into the pipe, I looked back at the Pedros to find them flipping buttons and turning knobs inside the opened silver box. It looked like some type of NASA portable operations center: a small video screen, joystick, wires, blinking red lights. I leaned over and examined the green images awakening on the video screen when Big Pedro said, "There's a small camera at the end of that wire, so we can see down the pipes."

"Infrared?" I asked.

"No, it's always just green like that."

I pushed the cord farther down the pipe and watched the oval display across the screen like a first-person miniature view of someone walking through a dark tunnel. It was a smooth, clean ride for a minute or two before the obstruction came into view about 60 feet down. A tree's root had broken through the ceramic pipe and formed the blockage. I quickly surmised a logical approach to the most effective way of fixing the problem. I turned to the two Pedros and explained.

"What if we mark the cable right here, then we'll pull it all the way out and measure it down the mountainside. Then we'll know exactly where that root broke the pipe. We can dig up that spot and repair it. How about that, huh? That'll save the old guy a bunch of money."

They looked at each other and laughed. "Bro, that's like a $300 job. I'm not sitting here sweating my ass off for $300. We're going to tear this whole fucker up! All the way down the mountain. The old guy thinks it's all fucked up."

"It's like a $9,500 job. That's almost $1,800 commission . . . for Pedro and me. That's how you make money at this."

"He's rich, bro!" Little Pedro added, "He doesn't care. Look where he's living, bro. He's probably got millions tucked away. Fuck him."

I started pulling the cable out of the pipe as the Pedros hatched their plan. They had a pretty good point about the homeowner being able to afford the costs, but I kept imagining the old guy as my father—the type of man who believed in honest plumbers and would take what these guys said as gospel.

They walked back to the patio for negotiations with the old man while I dragged the silver box back to the van. I snuck in a quick cigarette and watched the old man shaking his head as Pedro raised his shoulders, as if to say, "There's nothing I can do about it." I walked to the steps of the patio and eavesdropped on the rest of the conversation—partly for training and partly to be nosy.

"Yeah, it's damaged clear on down to the street below . . . never seen anything so bad before," Big Pedro said proudly.

"Ah, no, no, no . . ." the old man shook his head. "But $10,000? Seriously? There's nothing else I can do? That's . . . that's $10,000! Can't we just fix part of it?"

"No, sir. You've got root damage from that hole there all the way down. We're going to have to take all that old plumbing out and replace it. All the way down the hill, sir. But we've got a special goi—"

"Oh cripes . . . oh cripes . . . I did all this myself back in 1957 . . . '58. Arlene and I just bought the place . . . just got back from Korea. We put everything we had into the mortgage . . . didn't have two dimes to rub together after that. I did all this plumbing myself. Took over a year . . . poor Arlene had to shower at our neighbors' place for most of '59 and '60. She never—"

"Yeah . . . so I'm going to need you to sign here and initial this and this, authorizing us to get started." Pedro handed him a pen and held the clipboard for him as he signed.

"God rest her soul . . . if Arlene knew I was paying $10,000 now for what cost us about $500 back then . . ." The old man's nostalgia was growing thicker, buying him some temporary happiness until writing a one followed by four zeros on the check. "She'd bring me down lunch and coffee every day, clear on down the hill, the farther down I got. She even fell on several occasions but didn't complain one bit."

"That's messed up," Little Pedro offered his condolences and shook the clipboard.

The old man finally initialed everything and signed the check, and the two Pedros hustled giddily back to their vans to call in the order for a small bulldozer, 100 yards of PVC pipe, and some day laborers. It was just me and the old man on the patio now, both of us staring out at that big blue sky ahead of us.

"That sure seems like a lot of money to fix some pipes. I think I'd even squirt in a bucket to save that kind of dough," he said, though it seemed it was more to vent his frustrations than to clarify the scenario for me. "That's almost what we paid for this house! But I don't want to leave this hassle for my kids when I'm gone."

He was staring at me when I glanced back at the two Pedros, both of whom were still on their phones but probably now telling their wives about all the fancy shit they were going to buy for them when they got their commission checks. I felt for the old man, which was a natural instinct for me. Empathy had always been my Achilles' heel. I hadn't realized it until we made eye contact. I wanted to tell him to seek a second opinion on the plumbing matter; to call up any plumber in the Yellow Pages outside of the "Roto"-prefixed variety. I wanted to point down the hillside to where the one and only root had broken through the pipe and tell him that's all that needed to be fixed. It was the right thing to do, and every fiber of my moral code was fighting my tightened lips and new career choice. But if I did happen to change his mind, the Pedros would have known it was me that did it—they would have known it was me that transformed their $1,800 commission check into a $38 commission check split two ways. I would have been fired, possibly beaten up, maybe even killed.

I began thinking of different ways that I could surreptitiously tell the old man this without either Pedro catching on. Then, for some strange reason, I started thinking about what the Pedros would buy with their $900 apiece. A new nightgown for Maria, a pitcher's mitt for little Julio, Dodgers tickets, schoolbooks, perhaps some new fire decals for the open-hooded Camaros permanently parked in their driveways. Then I started thinking about what I would buy for myself if I got an extra $900 on my weekly paycheck. I'd definitely buy a new television and replace my VCR with a laserdisc player or one of those new DVD devices. I thought of how cool I'd look showing up at a client's house in a tailored blazer and silk scarf. I could treat myself to a month of steak dinners at Musso & Frank; take every other month off from the job to work on a novel; take a vacation in Italy. Italy.

What would the Italian plumbers of yesteryear do in this situation? Would the Romans screw over their fellow countrymen for a profit? Of course they would. I glanced back to the old man, who was now staring off into the clouds, probably mentally subtracting the cost of this plumbing job from the dwindling savings he was surviving on. He shook his head repeatedly.

"You have a beautiful home, sir." I told him.

It took him a few seconds before he replied. "Thank

you. It didn't always look like this. You should have seen it when we first moved in . . . just a shack standing here."

"I'm sorry to hear about your wife."

He nodded his head and continued staring off into the blue sky. But his wife's passing was not the most important factor running through his mind at the moment. "Does $10,000 seem right to you? That seems really high to me."

"I just started this job," I answered. "I'm in training. I'm not too sure about how much things cost yet."

"Yeah. Yeah, I suppose I'm just from a different generation when things didn't seem to cost that much."

"Don't you have a neighbor that can come over and take a look . . . maybe they might have some insight."

"*My* neighbors? Oh, no, no, no. The people who live around here are all movie producers and stuff—bunch of rich people. They don't know anything. Besides, those guys you're with are professionals, right? You guys work for a big company. I see the vans everywhere."

He had opened up another perfect opportunity for me to tell him to get a second opinion, but something inside me prevented my mouth from saying anything. I had a rush of thoughts about my own self-preservation now that I was without my union job. I had my whole life ahead of me to worry about. This moment would be the turning point in my life—the period where I shed the empathetic feelings of youth and became a man—a man who put his own self-interests above the feelings of others—a man who wouldn't disgrace his father's good name because he couldn't bear not to smoke a joint with friends the night before his big drug test. Today I would grow up, no matter how painful it would be for me, or for others. Today I would grow up.

"Arlene always said I was too trusting. But what kind of life is it if you can't trust people?"

The Pedros were on their way back to us, and I knew that all I had to do was keep my mouth shut for a few more seconds and I'd be home free. I glanced back to the old man but saw my father standing there instead, telling me to come by on Sunday and see mom. It felt like one of those moments in a political thriller when the protagonist had to let one innocent man die so that a million other innocent people would be spared. I couldn't bear to look at him again, but I did—I had to. But when I saw the old man this time, I saw capitalism embodied and not my father. I saw the way business worked; I witnessed how success worked. Then it spun around and I saw myself in him. I saw that I was very much like this old man in that I was too trusting and didn't question what I should have questioned. I wanted to punish myself for letting my father down and humiliating him in front of the people he had spent half his life working with. I wanted to teach this old man what happened when you let down your guard and trusted a fat plumber like Pedro, or a 20-something plumber's assistant with little moral direction. I wanted to be mean to make the shame dissipate inside me. I wanted my heart to callous over and bury the empathy under layers of uncaring, inhuman selfishness.

But I couldn't. I couldn't do what Pedro and Pedro could do. I couldn't kill one innocent man to spare the lives of a million others. I just couldn't. I didn't have a family to feed, or children to put through school, or a mortgage on a house. I didn't possess those fundamentals that produce a triumphant, successful man who's willing to do almost anything for a buck. I only had a handful of blossoming morals and some jaded decency to build a career upon. And as jaded and blossoming as they were, they were all I had.

I looked back up at the old man to find him still staring, waiting for me to put words to the gaping mouth below my confused eyes. But the words didn't come out. The caveat never came. Then I felt Pedro standing beside me. He was happy and smiling, and he patted my shoulder proudly. Pedro looked the way my father had looked on my first day at C.F.I., before I got fired. He was proud; proud of the big job he had negotiated; proud of himself for doing it; and proud of me for being a part of it. I smiled back at him because I knew that was what he wanted to see—and maybe that was what I wanted to see. I couldn't bring myself to look back at the old man after that. That part of me was now over.

The small bulldozer and day laborers arrived about 35 minutes later. Big Pedro and I left after the old man disappeared into the house and 50 feet of his garden had been torn up. Back at the main office, Pedro recounted the story of the overpriced plumbing job to several coworkers, including the branch manager, and several cans of congratulatory Budweiser were then handed around. Pedro patted me on the back again and explained to his fellow beer-sipping plumbers how I had helped swindle the old man out of a small fortune, even though I was still in training—that I was a born plumber.

As I punched my timecard for the day, the branch manager handed me another half-filled plastic cup of beer and said, "Great job, kid. You've passed your training. Pedro said you're ready for your own van. You keep this up and you could make a lot of money. How about we send you out on your own tomorrow? Commission on whatever you do! How's that sound?"

"Yeah, that would be nice."

After he patted me on the back, I walked into the bathroom and poured my beer into the toilet. I would not celebrate this moment. I was a bigger sucker than the old man for letting this happen. Before returning my timecard to the wall, I wrote above my typed name: I QUIT. PLEASE MAIL PAYCHECK TO ADDRESS ON FILE. And I left. I went by the folks' house on Sunday and stayed for dinner, but things just weren't the same as they were before either of those two jobs. I had learned some things about myself over that three-week period, things that I didn't know were in me. But they were out now, alive and functioning on their own. I vowed to be a better man from that day forward, but it took a few more years and a few more disappointments before it really sank in.

LITTLE GENERALS

JOB #39

I had been living next door to Scott for longer than most marriages lasted. We'd been friends since high school and sort of gravitated together when the adult years found us. And when a vacancy came up in his sleepy apartment complex on a dead-end street in North Hollywood, I had naturally grabbed it regardless of the crazy white trash family in the house across the way. Seeing each other every day kept us both young, grounded, tethered to immaturity like two brothers constantly racing for the front seat. No matter how many years passed us by, or how far high school stretched behind us, seeing Scott jingling his keys into his door from across the woodsy courtyard at night made me feel like my teenage self was always handy in my back pocket.

Like any two fully grown, teenage-minded men, Scott and I made a competition out of everything. It started with chess, then Scrabble, then Gin Rummy. Then watching *Jeopardy* on TV, where the competition evolved into keeping wagers and scores on writing tablets. From there we competed with women we slept with, amounts we spent on dates, quickness of hand-eye reflexes, names of actors in movies, and home furnishings. But it wasn't until about my fourth year at the complex when the competition took a perilous turn.

I'm not too sure which one of us bought the first BB gun, or even why, but the fourth year at the complex found us both with CO_2 compressed air pistols, itchy trigger fingers, and keen eyes. The warzone was our U-shaped two-story complex, where a 10-foot by 30-foot courtyard of dense fig trees and foliage separated our two sides of the battleground. I'm not sure really why it was, but I remember taking the first innocent shot at him as I watched him sorting through his mail on his way up the stairs. From the vantage of my second-floor balcony, I was nearly hidden from sight. The fig trees between us were enormous, and their massive, flopping leaves practically walled me in. I could make out each step his black slacks took through patches between the large leaves, and once he reached the top step I released the safety on my pistol and fired. It was only a leg shot, but I heard a loud yelp just before his screen door slammed open and he jumped inside his apartment, slamming the door behind him. I couldn't help but laugh harder than I'd ever laughed before, which I'm certain reverberated within the U-shape of our serene complex and carried itself straight into Scott's front window to console him as he rubbed out the sting in his thigh.

I felt a great sense of accomplishment, and I lit another cigarette on the balcony as I waited for the impending phone call asking why I had taken up arms during such a peaceful time. But that phone call never came. Ten minutes had passed since that first shot rang out, and as the sun slowly set on our little Gaza Strip I couldn't help but wonder why Scott hadn't called to either chew me out or demand a truce. But a silently slid-open window and a tiny, noiseless tear in his screen soon quelled my concerns. A BB zipped by me and into the wall exactly one second before another pinged me in the shoulder. The elusive bastard had been watching me, and because he didn't have a balcony of his own he improvised and sniped me through a window. I got to my knees and crawled into the apartment, slid the drapes closed, and assessed my wound. He had gotten a good shot in, and it stung like the dickens. A welt was beginning to grow right below the deltoid. Another BB hit my balcony screen before I returned fire with a pop at his front door. It went on like this for another 40 minutes or so, until the night came and took away our vision. But I knew that he was watching, waiting for me to let down my guard and take my customary drive to Del Taco for dinner. I knew he'd be standing at his window with his gun drawn, ready to spray down copper rain at the back of my head when I ran to my car. And he knew that I'd do the same to him if he dared try. We could have called a truce, but we never did. We just both went hungry that night and learned to pick up our drive-thru dinners on the way home from work.

That taste of combat had sparked awake some type of warfare gene inside me, and I began romanticizing the hell out of my BB gun. I spent my evenings with the pistol tucked into the back of my pants, even as I cleaned dishes, watched TV, and did my push-ups. And every day at work I'd miss that cold metal feel of it jabbing me in the lower back. Luckily, the days passed by rather quickly at Dales Jr. Mini-Market, and before I knew it I was back home again each evening—gun in the back of my pants and cabernet breathing on the kitchen cabinet, eagerly awaiting the first shelling of the night.

It was that next Thursday that changed the course of the

war for me. It was a typical day at work, stocking the beer and wine shelves then jumping behind the register when a customer came in. Dales Jr. was a small liquor-store-turned-market that specialized in European beers and kitschy local wines as well as basic grocery necessities and lotto tickets. The majority of people who came in walked there from any one of the hundreds of nearby apartment complexes, and most were semiworking TV actors with a few musicians and alcoholic deadbeats thrown in.

It was Studio City and everybody knew everybody by name, except for the 300-pound black man who walked up to my register with a single can of Budweiser on that day. He gave me $2 and asked for a little bag to put his beer in. Upon giving him the folded bag, he opened it, returned it to me, and calmly said, "Now fill it." My blank stare must have been enough for him to realize I hadn't seen the silver .38-caliber pistol pointing at me from under the cuff of his shirt, so he wiggled it for me. I saw it then.

"Put the money in the bag," he calmly said again, glancing anxiously over his shoulder at the two women in line behind him.

My own safety didn't register right away; my initial concern was that I hadn't deposited the majority of the cash in the drawer into the drop-vault under the register, which I was supposed to have done every time the tally reached $200. And as I grabbed handfuls of bills from the drawer and shoved them into that little brown bag, I realized that this son of a bitch had come at the perfect time and robbed the perfect employee, because he was going to be walking away with close to $600—about $400 more than he should have been, had I been doing my job correctly.

Strangely, he said thank you before walking casually

out the door. As I hammered the silent alarm button beside the register, the 40-something woman who was next in line placed a four-pack of wine coolers onto the counter and cupped the mouthpiece of her cell phone.

"Just that," she said and went back to her call.

The adrenaline finally kicked in when I realized she hadn't seen a thing, and my heart began to race at the thought of coming that close—unnoticeably—to getting a .38-caliber bullet in my stomach. As I plucked a wine cooler from the four-pack on the counter, I thought it peculiar that the entire robbery had happened so coolly and only now, a full 10 seconds later, was I beginning to feel the galvanizing energy of the adrenal glands kicking in. And as I charged out the front doors with the glass wine cooler bottle in my right hand, I could feel my rational mind constricting and the animalist, adrenaline-fueled rage beginning to take over. I owe the terrible aim of that hurled wine cooler to the adrenaline fury, but its startling velocity and blazing impact against the concrete wall beside the getaway car somehow made up for it. The 300-pound assailant glanced at the wet explosion then at me before crawling into the passenger seat of that little Corolla and speeding out of the parking lot.

The police came about 20 minutes later and filed a report. My boss came 30 minutes after they left and demanded I finish the remaining three hours of my shift, which I did before stealing $25 of my own plus Canadian cigarettes and a bottle of Polish vodka. That was my compensation for nearly losing my life for $8 an hour.

When I got home, I brought the vodka and a two-liter of Coke out onto the balcony and chain-smoked cigarettes until I was good and drunk. Scott's lights were still off and I assumed he was out on a date somewhere, most likely spending more on dinner than I ever had, just so he could spite me. I wanted nothing more than to tell him about the day I'd had, and how I had come closer to dying than he ever had—and how I had won *this* particular competition. I laughed a little out loud and accidentally splashed my drink onto the plastic patio table beside me, where the BB gun still laid from last night. My eyes instantly fixated on the weapon, and I saw it differently than I ever had before. What was the allure of a weapon like this? Why were combat and crime and causing harm so inherent to human nature? I wondered if the 300-pound robber ever sat on his balcony with a vodka and Coke and *his* pistol sitting next to him on a table. Did he think about stuff like this? Did he question himself? Did he question his ability to take another life? Would he really have killed me if I hadn't given him the money? Did he play with guns as a boy? Did every boy play with guns growing up? How could a species be so indifferent to death and hope to function? How could a species survive with this sort of nonchalant mentality toward taking a life?

Headlights then appeared from the driveway before extinguishing into the courtyard of fig trees. A car door opened and shut. Black slacks began to walk up the steps to the second floor, illuminated in the midnight ambiance by a yellowed overhead floodlight. I had every intention of reaching for the phone to call Scott and tell him of the robbery the moment he walked in his front door, but I picked up the BB gun and shot him in the thigh instead.

THE GRILLED CHEESE EPIPHANY

JOB #28

I couldn't stop thinking about the way Ruby positioned her nipples above the bra cups instead of inside them. It wasn't for any seductive or provocative reason; she just didn't know any better. But there they sat all day, every day: two brown, knobby silver dollars behind gossamer cotton, resting atop buckling bra fabric that bulged out almost as far as her small, perched breasts. She was a mousy Vietnamese woman with a thick accent and an online bachelor's degree in business management, and she sat facing me in the desk five feet from mine. Somehow, at the age of early-30-something, she had never received proper instructions on wearing a bra.

There were two older women who worked in the small office with us, and neither of them had ever tried to correct our accountant's camisole disclosure. And I knew they had noticed too; I could see them glancing at her visible nipples almost as frequently as I did. And I think the only reason they didn't say anything to her was because our office didn't receive any outside people—no clients, no customers, no walk-ins of any kind. It was just the four of us in that room, and they didn't want to deal with an awkward situation like that if they didn't have to. Or perhaps they thought it to be some type of Vietnamese couture.

I kept thinking about those nipples in that camisole when I should have been more focused on how I had departed the job. Because I just left. Never called, never emailed, never went back. I had showed up for work on Monday then disappeared on Tuesday. I had spent six months with that little family-owned fruit-powder company as their shipping and receiving manager, dispatching their delivery trucks to health-food stores across the state, and I had left without so much as a "good-bye" or an "I quit" or a "fuck this shit." I had taken the coward's way out, even with *my* own loose termination standards.

And it's now been a week since leaving them without a word, and I vowed today would be the day I would finally extinguish that guilty, glowing red "14" on my answering machine by calling them and explaining exactly why it was that I left and never returned. But I had no explanation—a week later and I still hadn't come up with an articulated reason for leaving. I knew *why* it was that I left. It wasn't just a whim or a wild hangover; my disappearance was a premeditated action, debated for hours and hours in the mental courtroom. I had weighed the pros and cons countless times with coffee, with wine, with *Friends* on TV, and with friends watching TV, but the verdict never faltered—I had to get the fuck out of there. My life had changed due to the responsibilities of that job and I didn't like where it was headed—something drastic needed to be done. There was a scalpel option and a machete option, and the courtroom voted for the latter. I was in my late 20s and saddled with a blossoming career that could have easily swept eight or ten years under the carpet in the blink of an eye, and I just couldn't willingly let that course unfold.

Life had become the repetition of an average Wednesday, playing out over and over again. My psyche had actually ingested the workweek schedule into its natural body clock rhythm, and I would wake up seconds before the alarm clock rang and be shaving before I even realized what was going on. I had my Monday button-up shirt and my Tuesday button-up shirt and so on; don't park on the south side of the street on Thursdays, bring cash for the taco truck's breakfast burrito on Fridays. I would go into the same diner every day on my lunch break, watching the same unhappy faces watch me. I could smell their fat, unhappy families at home, their mortgage worries, their cholesterol problems, their restless leg syndromes. The faces always ordered the same Cokes in Styrofoam cups, the same chiliburgers and sandwiches, the same salads, and they always reviewed their checks each day looking for any discrepancies in the waitress's addition of $5.49 + $1.69. I could see the quelled aspirations and dying dreams hovering above their chewing heads, crying out for me not to let myself become like one of them.

"It's the Grand Trap."

"Adult life's not like it is on the TV."

"If I could I'd do it all over again . . . and not have kids."

"We tied our own nooses, boy. Fuck retirement."

"Get out while you can. Disappear!"

"This new Honda has replaced my soul."

"My house is just a cot on a sinking ship called S.S. *America*."

"I loathe my wife but I don't know how to live without her."

"Don't strive to be middle class, strive to be middle *classy.*"

The "14" blinked brighter and brighter from the answering machine, yet I was still no closer to making that call. There was no way to explain to my boss about the epiphany I had had in the diner. There was no way I could sculpt into words exactly how I had felt when I heard a dozen imaginary voices telling me to quit my job and pursue a life that I believed in before it was too late. I suppose madness was as good a reason as any to terminate one's own employment, but it wouldn't explain why it took me a week to return their repeated calls asking for a simple reason why.

I should have been thinking about the hardships I had put upon those four people in the office, and all those deliveries that were due to go out and didn't, and the disregard I had shown the boss who was just beginning to treat me like a son. But all I could think about was Ruby and those nipples poking up over her bra, and how I would never again see them glaring at me from across the office.

MOVING IN PLACE

JOB #50

Another week had passed in an unemployed limbo, with no good interviews in sight. So I was forced to have to take a job that was well below my standards, according to the playbook that I had established a few years back. It was 8:35 in the a.m., and 95 minutes ago I added "Professional Mover" to my canon of career endeavors.

There comes a point in your 30s when you realize that your prime has been in full bloom for quite some time already, and you know you're either really close or already beginning the descent down the other side. I realized this as I was carrying a large suede loveseat from our client's house into an enormous storage truck parked in her driveway. My hair and shirt and pants were soaked in my own sweat, and the loveseat that I was struggling to carry now had a perfect stained imprint of my chest and arms and face across its expensive tan fabric. It looked like a bust version of the Shroud of Turin.

Only an hour and a half into this job and my back already ached, my legs quivered, and my balls felt like they had crawled up and hid in some deep cavity of my groin. I could hear myself wheezing at every step; and I had to pee 40 minutes ago, but the urge had somehow completely disappeared somewhere between the last two loads.

"If that guy dies," the attractive blonde homerenter shouted from her porch, "I'm not going to be held responsible, fellas." She pointed at me, and the two muscular movers that were supposed to be training me now turned around and laughed at me.

"I . . . just . . . I just had a flu shot," I mumbled from inside the half-filled trailer of the truck. "I guess I'm still a little winded." My soft clerical hands hadn't lifted anything but cigarette after cigarette to my mouth for years now. Manual labor was one occupation I never thought I would see myself in, especially not at 8:45 in the morning.

"Just watch the chair, will you, please?" she asked nastily before crossing her arms and walking back into the house.

Jesus, the brawniest of my two new coworkers, made sure she was safely inside the house before he jumped into the truck trailer and violently pulled the loveseat from my trembling arms. "Never drag the shit in front of them, bro!" he advised while effortlessly lifting the enormous chair and placing it atop the matching sofa using nothing but his tattooed forearm and thigh. "Bro, you gotta be cool when the clients are around. When they see us being cool with their shit, then we get the real cash—the tip, bro."

"I'm just a little out of shape, Jesus." I replied. "I'll bounce back by the next load."

"You're a skinny fucker, aren't you?" Jesus remarked after I lifted the bottom of my T-shirt to wipe the sweat from my eyes.

"Yeah. The salad days. Well, the side-salad days lately."

"You don't eat meat?" he asked. "Eh, *this* fucking job will put some meat on you, bro. Toughen your *guero* ass up!"

"Cheap-ass Erik Estrada," I mumbled after I was sure he jumped down off the bumper.

I lugged a cardboard box of albums and a rolled-up rug into the truck before returning to the house for the next round. I paused for a few seconds in the secluded hallway between the bedroom and the bathroom to catch my breath when I overheard Jesus talking to the client in the now-empty den.

"So, why you moving, miss?" he asked as he easily picked up a huge box of books and rested it onto his shoulder.

"Well, Julio, I was working at Paramount when I got this place," she replied, "but it's just been so slow this past year. Everything's going to Canada because it's so cheap to shoot out there. Everything's going to Canada but me. I can't afford this place anymore."

"Well, don't you worry, miss," Jesus said. "We'll get you moved real quick. Three hours tops. I could tell you're worried about the hourly rate. We'll get it done as *in-ah-spensedly* as we can for you. Don't you worry, miss." This was Stage 2 of Jesus' ploy for getting the big tip later; Stage 1 was *being cool with the client's shit, bro.*

"Actually, I'm not too worried about *that*," she replied. "I'm more worried about that skinny guy you brought. I don't think he's going to make it through the day."

"Yeah," Jesus agreed, "he just started today. We get a lot of these guys who think they're tough enough to do this. I don't think he's going to work out." Jesus and I saw eye to eye on that one. I tiptoed into the bathroom and flushed the toilet, then returned to the stack of albums and CDs near the door and got back to work.

After another hour of moving, the entire house was finally empty. My arms and legs were useless to the situation now, so Caesar, the other muscular mover we came with, jumped into the trailer and anchored all of her possessions to the walls with some type of elastic rope. Jesus leaned against the porch column and flirted with the client as she locked her front door for the last time. I watched all three from the street with a cigarette.

She gave us directions to her new, and much less expensive, cabana apartment on the other side of town, just blocks from where I lived. I knew she must have really dropped off the Hollywood radar to move from a house in the hills into a one-bedroom in my neck of the woods. You see, my new neighbor and I resided in the "old Russian immigrant" part of Hollywood, where the neon lights and glittered streets of Tinsel Town converged with the color gray.

"But follow my car down the hill because it gets tricky near the bottom of the canyon," were her last words as she drove off. And we didn't follow her directly, and we did indeed get lost at the bottom of the canyon road like she foretold, and she never looked back in her rearview mirror to see that we weren't there. We were a huge truck storming down a small hillside road, crushing tree branches and spilling trash bins on both sides of us, and we had managed to elude her.

"Hey, grab the wheel, bro!" Jesus said to me as soon as we got off the winding road and onto Laurel Canyon. I reached over and grabbed the rattling steering wheel as he dug into both of his pockets with both of his hands. Several seconds later, his right hand emerged holding a wrinkled little joint. He smiled and lit it up, then took back control of the steering wheel.

Sitting between Jesus and Caesar in the cab of the truck, I automatically became "the passer." I had intended to only take a puff or two to relieve some of the aches and pains I had coursing through me, but that option really wasn't up to me as soon as Jesus heard the Rolling Stones on the radio. By the time we reached Sunset Blvd., my face felt like mint ice cream and the realization that I was in the company of a Jesus and a Caesar became remarkable to me.

"Because Jesus . . . the Jewish one, with a strong 'J' . . . and Caesar were enemies back in the Bible," I tried to explain, but the concept didn't translate from mental dialogue to verbal dialogue very well. "Like two opposing pillars of . . . difference. And you guys . . . are friends. That's good you worked that out. Pontius Pilate."

The cab went quiet for a few seconds before Jesus changed the subject and said, "Check this out . . ." He sat up closer to the windshield and gingerly rested his hands atop the steering wheel, so that both he and his fingerless gloves were very visible to the lane of cars driving toward us. "Okay . . . here we . . . GO!" he shouted and flung both hands across the top of the steering wheel to the left, which looked, to an oncoming car, like he was turning that huge truck directly toward them at full force. He wasn't, of course—his hands were only cupping the wheel—but it was the sudden jerk of his entire body and that crazy wide-open mouth that sealed the deal for the oncoming traffic. The first car skidded to a halt from 35 miles per hour; the second driver screamed and covered his face before blindly swerving into the next lane over, nearly killing a bicyclist; the third car did a complete 360-degree turn right in the middle of the road.

Every time a horn blared or tires screeched, Jesus, with

his red eyes and sloppy grin, would cheer and glance at me or Caesar for our reaction. I'm not sure about Caesar, but I was too busy clutching the dashboard and wishing I had a seatbelt to give a shit about accolades.

"Man, I'm a total DUI right now," Jesus admitted as he drum-tapped the steering wheel and yawned.

"Just keep it together and try and find that lady's car," Caesar replied. "I don't know what I did with her address, but she said her place was right around here somewhere. I think she said that."

I had nothing left to offer this job. I was spent. And I was freaked out. And I was high. I hoped we would never find her car so that we could just go back to the office and chalk it up to experience. But the second time around the block revealed the client's Audi with its hazard lights on down a side street. Jesus decided to park the enormous truck right there in the middle of Fountain Avenue, which was one of the busiest streets in Hollywood at that hour. Once we got out of the cab and walked to the rear to open the back doors of the trailer, a huge pile-up of cars had already begun forming behind us. Our truck was so wide that, not only did it completely block one full eastbound lane, it also went several feet into the only other eastbound lane next to it. All east-going traffic on Fountain now bottlenecked right at the back doors of our truck. Drivers had to inch into oncoming traffic just to get by us, and each and every one of them had something colorful to say about it. And even worse than having to now remove from the truck every box, table, sofa, and chair that we had just loaded into it, was having to do it by way of the 15-foot ramp at the rear of the truck, which jettisoned straight into the traffic jam. It was like being on a model's catwalk, but instead of camera flashes and paparazzi screaming, "Look over here," we had aspiring actors in beat-up VWs shouting, "I'm going to kill your fucking mom, you retard!" Anonymous insults were one thing, but to face your insulters and receive their threats for a solid 15 feet was an entirely different affair. There were fists shaken, trash thrown, and coffee hurled at us. Lit cigarettes and *fuck yous* were tossed our way unrelentingly. And most cars even went so far as to honk before giving us the middle finger when they finally passed by, just to make sure we were looking in their direction for the insult.

It was somehow less agonizing moving her in than moving her out. It only took about an hour before that last loveseat and box of records were gone from the truck and in her den-turned-office. I was completely drenched in my own sweat again, and thought I heard my lungs blow a valve as I got back into the cab of the truck.

We returned to the Pack & Go headquarters a little before noon. When I stepped out of the truck, my jeans and T-shirt had completely dried, giving them a crisp, ironed feel. My legs didn't take to walking too well after sitting down for nearly 20 minutes. I stumbled over to a bench in the parking lot just as my legs gave out and seated me.

"Hey, kid," the portly owner of the company approached me with a clipboard. "You just got back, right?"

"Yeah," I gasped, "just a second ago."

"Okay, I want you to go with Ken and Duke on this next one," he replied, pointing to an older black man and a younger white guy, both built like Greek statues on steroids. "I got a small business for you guys, so it'll be chairs and desks and shit like that. Probably a good four hours, so you can thank me later."

Fours hours, I thought to myself. At what they're paying

me, four hours equaled $28. There was no way. There was no way that I could do again what I had just done. There was no way that I could continue working for this company, not even for the rest of the day. I couldn't tell him this but I couldn't go on working either. I had to think quickly.

"Okay, but can I grab a quick bite first?" I asked him. "I'm hypoglycemic. I'll just run to the taco place across the street and be back in 10 minutes."

The boss frowned and looked at his watch. "Ten minutes, buddy! I got these guys waiting for you." He jotted something down onto his clipboard and walked back to the office.

I hobbled across the street to my trusty old Volvo parked at the painted white-then-yellow-then-white-again curb. After unlocking the door, I collapsed into the driver's seat and devoured the ham and Velveeta sandwich that I had prepared that morning. I was completely and utterly exhausted. The logical side of my mind tried everything in its power to convince "us" to get out of the car, walk back to Pack & Go, and continue working for the rest of the day. Rent was coming up, and I was a few hundred behind. But I then realized that the side of my brain that constructs logic was not as persuasive in the mental courtroom as the other side—the side that's lazy and preferred watching *Magnum P.I.* reruns on weekday afternoons—not to mention the side that preferred having both of his testicles intact. It was a good back-and-forth for awhile there, with both sides of the brain offering up some compelling litigation points. But only one side was walking out of this tribunal unscathed and victorious.

I fumbled out the damp $20 bill from my pocket that the client had given me as a tip and tucked it into my wallet,

right behind the three ones. Jesus was right about that one—
being cool with the client's shit, bro paid dividends. I listened
to some BBC news on the radio for a few minutes before
admitting to myself and to both litigators that I would not
be going back to work as a professional mover. I started up
my Volvo and headed off to a better horizon, but ended up
back at my apartment, three blocks down from where the
client now lived. Job #50 was short-lived and awful. Job
#51 had to be better.

Realizing three days later that my back still throbbed,
my knees still buckled, and my balls still hadn't dropped
back down to their standard elevation wasn't the worst part
about the whole sad Pack & Go affair. Three days later, the
worst part of my half-day of being a professional mover was
calling the company—after disappearing midway through
my first day on the job—and asking them to write me a
check for the couple hours that I had worked.

And after going in later that afternoon to pick up my
check for $21, I had to explain to the boss with the clipboard
why I never returned to work that day, and how I sat in my
car from across the street and watched him looking for me.
And I told him that I normally wouldn't have the audacity
to come back there with my head down and my tail between
my legs asking for the $21 that I almost died for, but a cer-
tain insurance company wanted payment to insure a certain
someone's Volvo for the month of July, or that certain someone couldn't legally drive anymore.

He looked at me as if I were crazy. Then he looked at
me and realized how serious I was about needing the money.
He paid me the $21 in cash out of his pocket, and I left and
never drove down that stretch of Sunset Boulevard again.

THE BROKEN TOYS OF HOLLYWOOD

JOB #53

It starts with the dishes. When you're always at home you're always eating at home, which makes for a lot of dishes. Then the hardwood floors. The hardwood floors of this apartment blanket themselves in dust every chance they get. Had I known that four months ago, I never would have ripped up the carpet, especially not without the landlord's consent. Now it's just perpetually dusty wood. And then after you clean the floor you look around and see that the bookshelf could use some dusting, because your collection of three softcover Vonnegut novels doesn't scream out like it used to. Then you move the lamp and end table closer to the cleaned bookshelf to show off your handiwork, and then, of course, you must move the small ornate rug closer to the end table, to help it all flow together. By then it's 3:00 in the after-noon and you haven't yet eaten breakfast, and you're starting to get the shakes from too much coffee in a hypoglycemic stomach. And the laptop still sits on your desk idling, with its little spinning blue circle telling you that your $39-a-year antivirus program still hasn't found that particular virus which prevents you from going online to send out resumes. But all that's okay because you've been unemployed for four months and a few more days aren't going to make much of a difference. And the apartment is now clean. Again. Third time this week.

The job leading up to this odd period of orderly fixation was one of the better ones from my canon. Among all those retail gigs and cash-register careers, I had lucked out and scored a job as a manipulator of foreign television entertainment for a shoestring production company in Los Angeles—a scriptwriter, they called it. But being hired to "write" TV documentary scripts really didn't involve the act of writing at all; at least not at Pungent Productions. Within that boxy two-story building, it was more a matter of perusing the film vault closet and sifting through a few hundred hours of handheld camera footage from Hollywood press junkets, movie premieres, red carpet footage, and celebrity interviews, and hopefully finding a couple hours' worth that didn't have a copyright attached, or at least didn't have a recognizable TV interviewer on-camera. Sometimes Pungent Productions paid for the rights to use the footage, but most times they just illegally recorded large chunks of it and hoped for the best.

Then it was time to piece together a decent 46 minutes' worth to illustrate some semblance of a celebrity's rise to stardom. And then the actual writing part came in, when you were able to compose little segue-sentences like, "But then tragedy struck the young actor . . ." You then tell the video editor to slide that foreboding segue-sentence in between footage of Keanu Reeves at the premier of his breakout role in *Bill & Ted's Excellent Adventure* and the audio track of the 911 phone call of close friend and actor River

Phoenix overdosing on Sunset Blvd. That's the magic right there. That's Scorsese style.

Those TV documentaries we made were the cheapest products ever produced, with a good portion of them literally costing us $70 and an afternoon to make. But to basic cable stations in Canada, Yemen, and the Czech Republic, our programs were star-studded red carpets right into the glitzy celebrity world that was Hollywood. They were also the same shitty DVDs for sale on Amazon.com for $4.29, promising to reveal never-before-seen footage of Elvis Presley's secret love life or Leonardo DiCaprio's undiscovered early years. But they never do. They just showed the same old shit from every other TV documentary out there. And sometimes they actually *were* the same old shit from every other TV documentary out there—our boss was known to record programs right off his TV, from the History Channel and PBS, then have his graphics department add our own logo directly over the other station's logo at the bottom corner of the screen. Then he, of course, would package and sell the show as his own. Seriously. If you've ever bought a celebrity biography or *Beverly Hillbillies* box set off the DVD rack at Ross Dress For Less, then you may have been duped by my old boss. And you'll know one of our documentaries when you see it. Words are usually misspelled on the cover, proper apostrophe usage is rare, and the phrase "This DVD is neither endorsed nor authorized by the (fill in the name) Estate" always rests somewhere near the bottom of the plastic cover. Our shows had a constant one-star rating on Amazon.com, and "Biggest pile of sh@t ever!" was a recurring mantra in the customer reviews section.

You see, Donatello, the president of Pungent Productions, was a con man who was once chased out of Brooklyn with just a suitcase—at least that's how the story went. He was a swindler, a grifter, and the self-appointed Executive Producer for every single show we made, whether or not he even knew we were making it. He didn't care too much for all the bad reviews, or for little things like legalities. He knew his shows would rarely be seen by American audiences, so issues like copyrights and trademarks and logos were of little concern to him. And these shrewd filmmaking practices were also a major part of the rest of his business structure, especially the hiring process. Donatello knew that if he only hired the dregs of Hollywood—the alcoholic editors, the drugged-out writers, the Spanish-speaking-only producers, and the still-in-college legal team—he could both save a fortune with shitty take-it-or-leave-it salaries *and* employ workers that would never question his copyright ethics. We were the unemployable outcasts and pariahs of the entertainment industry—a few of us on the way up, but most on the way down. Cigarettes, porn, and poor work ethics filled our days, and cocktails and karaoke filled our nights. We were the Bad News Bears without the Walter Matthau, and much older.

As piss-poor as Donatello's approach to filmmaking was, it also had its perks for us, the people who made the documentaries. The shows were pieced together at such a rapid rate that they were rarely proofed or checked over by anyone other than the aforementioned alcoholic editors or drugged-out writers. We had complete autonomy in content and direction, and we could shape the show any way we pleased, whether factually or fantastically. If someone brought some good pot or decent cocaine into the editing bay, then you could be damn sure that a Beach Boys show would have a strange four-minute freak-out montage, or a narration diatribe comparing Keanu Reeves's film career to Jesus' resurrection from the cross, or possibly even a shoddy reenactment of Elvis dying on the toilet.

A perfect example of this would be the once-serious documentary *African-Americans in Cinema*. I use the term "once-serious" because it was the first time that Donatello had actually paid a genuine TV writer/producer to make a substantial show about the rise of the black actor throughout Hollywood's history. Three weeks later, that genuine TV writer/producer abruptly quit because all of Donatello's checks bounced. The half-finished script for *African-Americans in Cinema* then landed on my desk, attached to a Post-It note saying, "Make this work fast, kid." All of the semicelebrities and film historians had already been interviewed on-camera, and most of the needed film clips had been procured; it was just the narrator's dialog that was only halfway written. So all I had to do was write up a dozen or so little cinematically historical segue-sentences about particular black actors from the 1930s on up to 1989.

We stopped at 1989 not because it was some centennial year in filmmaking, but because there was a stricter copyright involved with movie trailers made after that year—at least that's what our college sophomore legal adviser explained. The past 12 years of Spike Lee, Denzel Washington, and Morgan Freeman, all erased from the glory that was *African-Americans in Cinema* because Donatello didn't want to spend a few bucks. Regardless, as I was writing up my little segue-sentences I realized that my name would never be in the film's credits. The previous writer, the genuine TV writer/producer that quit, would get full billing. This left me with a whole new world of freedom in which to change the plight of African-Americans in cinema forever.

The script wasn't too bad in its current form; but that last third—after I got through with it—was where it got weird. Seven solid minutes of that 52-minute program now celebrated James Earl Jones being the voice of Darth Vader, including as many film snippets, movie stills, and poster zoom-ins that I could convince the editor to throw in. Then I focused the last few minutes of the documentary on the Blaxploitation films of the 1970s, mostly because all those film trailers were in the public domain and free to use. And they showed tits too. But that was that—no Spike Lee, no Morgan Freeman, no 1990s, not even much of the 1980s other than an Apollo Creed reference and a film snippet of the Russian boxer killing him in *Rocky III*. If you should happen to watch a documentary about the history of black actors and wonder if it's the one I wrote, simply look on the menu screen for the show's fourth chapter. If it's titled *Chocolate Dreams* then you're in for a James Earl Jones treat.

Then like any good thing in life, it had to end. The poor quality of our products as well as the multiple cease-and-desist lawsuits from the Elvis Presley Estate, the Sinatra Estate, KISS Music Licensing, and a few others finally caught up with us. In one big sweeping week, 70 percent of the company was laid off with promises to be rehired once "that lawsuit thing" was resolved. That was four months ago—when I had carpet.

I have now spent spring and much of summer within the confines of my apartment complex, spying on neighbors and watching the bougainvillea on my balcony come to full bloom. Judge Judy and Judge Alex, and even Judge Millan from *People's Court*, have given me so many valuable insights into our judicial system that I feel adequate enough to represent myself if those documentary lawsuits should ever find their way to my front door. But I've been cooped up here for so long that I'm starting to feel like Martin Sheen from the beginning of *Apocalypse Now*, when he's stuck in the hotel room and falling deeper and deeper into insanity until finally breaking the full-length mirror while drunk and naked. I've been waiting too long for my next mission; my mirror moment is coming, I can feel it. I even started waking up in the mornings muttering, "Saigon . . . shit."

But the apartment is clean now, and the bougainvillea blooms an electric pink at sunset, and the world will forever have a permanent reminder that Keanu Reeves's film career is as glorious and monumental as J.C. getting the cross job. All thanks to a con man from Brooklyn hiring a drugged-out writer from North Hollywood, and the butterfly flapping its wings.

THE ELECTRIFYING
CASE OF THE BROKEN
WINDSHIELD

JOB #44

Only an American woman—a salon blonde in her straight vodka 50s—would correct a vacationing Frenchman on the proper pronunciation of his own French language. Her crisp, new blue L.A. Dodgers shirt and matching windbreaker jacket were a dead giveaway of her own holiday status and vacation highlights—no detectable accent, though, but hearing her every word from clear across the bar was indication enough that she was from the East Coast somewhere. But that's the beauty of drinking in a hotel bar in Los Angeles: You imbibe beside all types of people, from all over the planet. Put a few overpriced Blood Marys in them on a Friday afternoon, and each one is buddying up to any asshole within two barstools or earshot.

As I watched all this from my own barstool, I was thinking about Natalie and the offer she had proposed to me earlier in the day. Nat was a cute English bird that had an accent like calligraphy on silk, and when she asked me to join in a threesome with her and whatever lesbian we could drunkenly dig up on a Saturday night, it was as if I was being bathed in that silk. It would be my first time being invited into a threesome, although I think Nat just wanted to get laid and having me as a wingman increased her chances of *something* happening.

Penis had always been off Natalie's agenda due to some weird events from her childhood, but she'd led a colorful and full life in spite of never coming into contact with one. She had spent a few years as a personal assistant to Cher before coming to the States. The aging Bono-less singer then brought Nat to L.A. on a work visa just months before the job went south and she got kicked out on her ass in Malibu. Nat bounced back by meeting the nearing-40 granddaughter of the legendary Liberace and moving in with her. The two had only been dating for a few short months when the granddaughter suggested Nat marry her brother—the drugged-out, still-living-at-home *grandson* of the great Liberace—to get a greencard. Nat did just that, then grew to despise the pair of them and moved out on her own some months later. Invigorated with her newfound citizenship and bachelorhood, she found a cheap studio apartment (a "flat," she called it) in Sherman Oaks and her first official American retail job. That's how I met her. We were coworkers—floral arrangers—at a very posh flower store in The Valley. And the reason I knew all of this personal past history about her after only two months was because she talked a lot.

But this leads me to why I'm drinking a German beer in a hotel bar in downtown Los Angeles during business hours. When I wasn't assembling floral bouquets and taking phone orders at the store, I was out making deliveries of lavish $400 flower baskets and $600 tulip-filled vases to various film producers' offices, Beverly Hills mansions, and the occasional hotel lobby. The Dodgers lady then began squeezing the mouth of the Frenchman in order to correct his pronunciation of *oui* to more of a *wah*, and I knew that was my cue to get the hell out of there and back to work.

I returned to Mark's Garden to find Nat talking to a customer and Joel, our third and final front-counter coworker, smiling at me from behind the cash register—his bleached yellow hair violently gelled into a raspy pompadour. He resembled a futuristic and very porn*ish* Roy Orbison, with his thick black wayfarer glasses, leather pants, and sleeveless button-up shirt. And it was hard to fathom, but that was his daytime disguise—the incognito workday outfit. Because the nights and the gothic clubs knew Joel as Fate Fatal, the not-quite-yet-legendary singer of the band The Deep Eynde, who crooned onstage in skintight outfits and chains.

At the back of the store were a dozen anonymous European designers, each with their own floral skillset and colorful accent. But up front at the counter it was just the three of us. Our two work-worlds were separated by at least a hundred bins of various fresh-cut flowers kept in a chilly, rustic, almost fairy-tale environment—canvas-less antique picture frames hung nakedly from walls, wrought iron shelves and tables supported flowering orchid plants and topiaries, and stacks of different-sized terra cotta pots peppered the floor. And each colorful aisle of tulips, roses, freesia, and lilies had its own candy fragrance wafting around in the air conditioning current above it. And tethering this entire mystical environment together was Vivaldi's *Four Seasons* playing on endless repeat. It was truly a magical place to work. It was our little rabbit hole of employment; our job behind the looking glass.

"I heard you and Nat are going to have a big night tomorrow," Joel said with a proud grin when I tucked my delivery receipts beside the register.

"She told you?"

"Of course! Why wouldn't she?"

"I don't know," I replied. It just seemed like something you'd keep between the parties involved. Until after.

Joel glanced around then leaned in closer to me. "You have to be cool, let them do their thing for awhile. Help out, but pace yourself. Pace yourself. It's more of a viewing spectacle than a sex act for you. OK, I've said my peace, I've gotta split. I've got a show tonight. You guys coming? We're playing at the Mint at 11:45."

"I'll do my best," I answered, but we both knew what that meant.

For all intents and purposes Joel was our manager, though he never acted like it. He really loved working at Mark's Garden, and he put his heart into every bouquet he made. Nat and I loved the place too, but in a slightly different, more-realistic way. As soon as Joel went out the back door I sidled up to Nat and waited for the wink. Once she finished the worst looking bouquet ever made in that store, she glanced over and flashed me the eye. Then a little smile. I tapped a few functionless keys on the cash register, which made a series of *beep* sounds but little more. The wink was our signal for a cash-paying customer.

"I'll just ring you up for that, sir, since Natalie has her hands full," I said to the older man who boasted a bewildered expression at the sight of the two dozen tulips peppered with baby's breath and sunflowers, which he was about to purchase. "Say, that's beautiful, Natalie. The *Tuscan Sunrise* is really quite a masterful creation. Natalie is one of our finest florists."

"It's like my fingers are dancing when I make it," she replied in that chirpy accent.

Two more taps on the functionless keys then, "Oh, darn. This thing is jammed again." Natalie wrapped the bouquet up and I flashed a quick peripheral scan of the store for any other coworkers in view. "Well, it's about $65 with tax . . . but let's call it $60 for the hassle."

He begrudgingly handed over three $20 bills and Nat gave him the aborted fetus of Mother Nature's offspring. He'd never come back again; all three of us knew it. As soon as he left I opened the cash register and exchanged one of the $20s for two $10 bills then divvied up the loot between the two of us. We chalked it up to our cost-of-living increase and lack of paid overtime.

"We can get a little charlie with this and have a *real* good time tomorrow night," she said tucking the money into her pocket. I learned a few weeks back that "charlie" was an English euphemism for cocaine. Not sure what kind of aphrodisiac it would make, though. "You still in for tomorrow night? Did you think yourself out of it? I'll understand if—"

"I'm still in," I snapped. "Very in."

* * *

I awoke early Saturday morning to a chill in the air and in the stomach. I had spent the prior night recording myself shaving my chest then most of the early morning setting that footage to classical music. I went downstairs to get my customary weekend drive-thru breakfast only to find that my beautiful 23-year-old Cadillac Fleetwood Brougham—a hulking, silver, finned beast of a car—had been molested in the night. Much unlike the previous evening, its windshield now had a thick crack running from the top to the bottom of the glass and the drivers side mirror sat on the asphalt beside the front tire, with its electrical wires splayed out around it like severed arteries. Some weeds and rubble had pooled on the hood. My face grew red and heated, first due to being victimized followed then by pure rage. I scanned the apartment windows around me, hoping to spot the perpetrator peering out at his wrath of destruction below, but saw nothing. Both directions of the street were desolate, quiet; a couple of birds chirping but nothing more. The only person awake at that ungodly hour of 8:20 a.m. was an older man with a gas-powered weed-whacker roaring away the unwanted greens surrounding his lawn. He watched me as I approached with my side mirror in hand. He was my prime—and only—suspect and I was going to make sure he knew it.

"What's up?" he asked, letting the weed-whacker idle quietly.

"Someone busted up my Cadillac's windshield," I stated. "Were you weed-whacking over there this morning? Something you want to tell me?"

He shook his head, frowned his lips, and continued whacking. I pointed back to my car with the hand holding the mirror. "There's some dirt and grass left on the hood; something you might see if a weed-whacker had been involved."

"Whoa, easy, buddy! Don't make an accusation like that on me. I had nothing to do with your windshield," he said, very clearly angered by the allegation. He idled the weed-whacker again and turned it upside down so the whirl-ing plastic coils were buzzing between our faces. I thought he was going to use it like a weapon to drive me away, but he instead raised his hand and tapped it against the circular red blur twice, hitting spinning plastic each time. Then he showed me his reddening but uninjured hand.

"This thing can't break a windshield! It can't even break skin!" he clarified. "And my lawn stops right there," he pointed to the far side of his driveway, which was a good 15 feet from the front of the Cadillac.

He had two very valid points, but I wasn't ready to remove him from my list of suspects just yet. I walked back to my Cadillac and assessed the scene of the crime as thor-oughly as any CSI agent on television. Just below the center of the enormous crack in the windshield was the point of impact, where a finely shattered indent—about an inch in diameter—told me that it was a blunt instrument that did the damage, and not something with a point.

I took the side mirror back up to my apartment and doodled some diagrams of my Cadillac's angled windshield, the street directions, and the most likely trajectory of what-ever blunt mystery object hit the glass. I analyzed multiple scenarios, various directions, and numerous theories, but it was nearly impossible with only two dimensions to go on. I needed three dimensions. I needed three dimensions to fully grasp the recoil of the blunt object. What I needed was a crime lab, but all I had was a picnic table that I used as a writing desk.

It was already early in the afternoon when I thought up the plan to find a plastic car model with the same angled windshield my Cadillac had and run some trajectory tests on that. I drove to a hobby store and found a 1:32 scale model of a 1975 Monte Carlo, with nearly the same type of long, rounded windshield and spent another two hours building it. I probably could have forgone painstakingly gluing the headlights and chrome details on as well as spray-painting it silver just like the Caddy, but I wanted the most factual representation of the incident as possible. Once it dried I set it onto the table then pushed the table up against the window, so I had a crisp, clear view of the actual silver car facing north on the street below and the plastic silver replica facing north on the table right in front of me. I gathered a handful of tiny pebbles and flung them one at a time at the plastic windshield, from every angle. Only one direction provided a clean hit at the center of the windshield then to the driver side mirror, and that was if it was thrown from the passenger side. So I could rule out a drive-by rock thrower. My list of suspects now stood at three: the backseat pipe swinger, the remote-but-still-possible weed-whacking neighbor, and some asshole who just walked by with a big rock and smashed the windshield then the mirror then walked his big rock away.

Natalie called just as I was about to start testing the drive-by pipe theory, and she asked what time I'd be picking her up.

"I thought the plan was for 6:00?" I asked.

"Yes, it was," she answered sharply. "And it's 6:20."

The clock said she was right, and I told her I'd be there in 40 minutes, to which she loudly exhaled. I wasn't going into my first threesome unshaven and unshowered—the night was young; we had all night to find our concubine.

* * *

Natalie and I were sitting in the dark booth of a dive bar in Sherman Oaks, drinking pints of beer at a lacquered wooden table that our forearms stuck to each time we lifted our glasses. She had put her brown hair into two braids that arced out from each side of her head like a 12-year-old, and her tight T-shirt hugged her little pudgy tits and exaggerated her pierced nipples. I had taken account of her nubile naughtiness on the drive over, but the two lines of cocaine we did in the parking lot had sent my brain into an entirely different direction.

"So, it must have been some type of a steel pipe, like a plumber's pipe, with a knobby blunt edge to it, right? And this guy, he . . . he must have swung it at the windshield, right? Boom! Breaks the windshield! Boom! Recoil sends the pipe into the side mirror, knocks it clean off, like some madman with a Viking axe taking swings at . . . at a palace door. No reason for it. No reason for it. Malicious! Yes, I'd label this just plain old malice. Full asshole move. No reason for it."

She was watching me talk but I could tell her mind was fiddling with six to eight things she wanted to say as soon as I shut up. And like a game of musical chairs, whichever of her chance thoughts I happened to silence on would surely launch straight out without hesitation nor connection to the statement before it. I was analyzing all of this very diligently while my mouth continued to spew out theories about the Cadillac, like two separate machines working in tandem. Conscious and subconscious dialogue happening simultaneously, parallel to one another. It was actually like there were four separate conversations running around our table: my inside and outside voices, and hers, then all four acknowledging one another in some weird psychic-cocaine phenomenon.

". . . but it's those little pale pebbles that have really stumped me on this case."

A second of silence then *boom!* "What are you going to do? Tonight! Watch? It's so weird! I'm nervous! Tonight! Let's get drunk first!" I was wrong—all her boiled-up thoughts had rolled out into one big blob of words, wide eyes, and flashing teeth. She took another quick gulp, flashed a gaze around the near-empty bar and spun back to me. "I've only been with one lad. When I was a teenager. My first time. I didn't like it. At all."

"You know, we never set any ground rules for tonight," I interjected. "We're both new to this . . . to a threesome. We should discuss the . . . I don't know if . . . I mean . . . do I put it . . . do I put it in you both? Is there some proper system to this? We should discuss this."

"Hmmm, good idea. Good idea. Okay, let's figure this out now." She took another swig before leaning forward and interlacing her fingers. "I think you could—and if only tonight happens, not like just us two—but you could do oral on me, and I could do it to you a little bit. And fingers and stuff. And do whatever you fancy to her, and so will I. We should just focus on shagging her! *That's* what we should be thinking."

"Yes! That's it! That's good! Focus on her. All things point to her. A little doodly-doo on you but focus on her. This is going to be awesome. I'm going to show her things even you don't know about yet!" The reality of the situation had already left the table and filling its void was another swallow of a Coors Light and two eager smiles.

Natalie then slid her closed hand across the table and

deposited a rolled $1 bill and a thumb-size bag of "Go Yeah" powder between my empty glass and fiddling cigarette hand. "Do a bump in the loo and get us a 'nother round, yeah?" she proposed. "We'll take turns."

There's nothing as rock 'n' roll as doing cocaine in a bar bathroom—it's like a lyric-come-to-life of any number of Rolling Stones songs. The rounds of Coors kept coming, and the lines on the toilet paper dispenser kept getting snorted—first every 30 minutes, then about every 15. Hours had passed with this same reckless rotation in place until the bravado of the drugs and alcohol had reached its prime, and our pick-up strategy couldn't get any finer tuned. We both looked around the bar to find that it had filled up nicely by the eleventh hour—a perfect time to put our threesome plan into action:

Step One

Natalie scoped out the barstool area—where the heaviest concentration of lesbians, transgenders, and full-on butches meandered into one big herd—until she found her prize.

Step Two

After another quick toot in the bathroom, I sidled up to the lanky woman with the blonde flattop, who Nat had nodded at, and I ordered two Coors. She was pretty decent looking for a woman with a square-shaved head: light southern drawl, on the easy side of her 30s, cute smile. We made a little chit-chat, then it was time for Step Three.

Step Three

"Hey, so ma friend and ehhhh are eeeerrrr on a special . . . sssignment," I drunkenly explained. I could think clearly and in perfect sentences, but the dialogue coming out of my mouth was warbled and chewy. "She wants essss . . . with you and . . . she's looking at you. She's . . . say hi." I pointed toward Nat with my beer hand and spilt suds across the floor. Then I spilled again when I signaled for Nat to join my new flattopped friend and me over at the bar. Smiling, Natalie sauntered over and the two began talking. I wasn't intentionally trying to eavesdrop but they were right there beside me, playing touchy-feely with one another as they shouted over the jukebox. She said her name was Ty, which was lesbian for Teresa. She was on leave from the Navy and housesitting her friend's place a few blocks away. Natalie was shit-faced, and I heard her shout to Ty that I was her long-lost American brother and we were into some weird things. Ty then bought me a beer and asked if we wanted to take the party back to the house where she was staying. I couldn't believe it, and neither could Nat judging by the relieved expression on her face: Our plan was actually working.

I left my Cadillac at the bar and we piled into her '90s Camaro, which reminded me a lot of Knight Rider. And I kept speaking into my pretend wristwatch communicator and telling KITT, "I need you, buddy!" the entire three blocks to the handsome blue house.

I remember Ty showing Nat and me the refrigerator full of food, the cupboard full of wine and booze, and the kitchen drawer with a bag of grass and rolling papers in it. I remember her telling me how nice it was for a brother to care this much about his sister, then she suggested I make a drink, roll a joint, and find a movie on cable. It was the most amazing recommendation for a plan that I had ever heard, and I quickly accomplished all three in the span of a minute or two. I remember Ty saying she was going to show Nat the rest of the house as I gnawed on cold pizza in one hand, sipped from a rum and Coke in the other, took a few puffs from the smoldering joint in the ashtray, and watched the beginning shoot-out scene from *Terminator 2* on the TV. Then I faded.

When I came to a short time later, Schwarzenegger was being submerged into the vat of molten metal and giving the thumbs-up to little John Conner. The mix of drugs, alcohol, more drugs and alcohol, and, finally, food, had taken over and temporarily shut down headquarter operations. It felt like I had only closed my eyes for a second, but almost an hour had passed, judging from the scenes in the movie. I glanced around the living room but there was no sign of the two ladies. I stood up and steadied myself against the wall before stumbling into the hallway with my drink. "Nat," I whispered into the darkness, but no one answered back. I was sure they were in the thick of romance somewhere in this house; my only hope was that I hadn't missed it entirely by passing out.

With my hand grazing the wall at my side, I Frankenstein-walked farther down the dark hall until hearing soft moans and pants coming from a bedroom door left ajar. It was pitch black inside but I poked my head in and clearly heard the ground zero of sighs. This was the place and, judging by the sounds around me, I wasn't too late. I couldn't see a thing when I walked in, but I felt the presence and warmth of the two coiled lovers on the carpet at my feet—I was standing right above them. I tossed my shirt off, kicked off my boots, and let my jeans fall to the carpet in a jingle-jangle of loose belt buckle. I stood there right next to them, naked as the day I was born, with a boner planking directly above them like a street sign to Horny Ave. I was close enough to hear pubic hair rustling against pubic hair and feel the exhaled warmth of orgasmic groans across my bare shins. I must have stood there for a solid minute listening to them grind together, hoping one of them would just reach up and pull my pecker down into the mix. But neither of them did. I deliberated several strategies on how to get myself involved—should I just lie down and work my way in? Announce my arrival with something like, "Did somebody ask for sausage on their pizza?" Start making my own sounds? All were decent options, but I went for a more direct approach: I licked my middle finger, blindly traced someone's arched back and simply inserted my digit into the first hole it touched—anus, vagina, Ty or Nat, I had no idea, but it went right in up to the knuckle. Very wrong approach, and definitely very wrong hole. It was instantaneously obvious and quite loud that Ty didn't like having a male's finger inserted into her ass because she screamed with all her might, "Get the fuck OUTTA HERE!" Her anger clinched her rectum and shot my finger right out like a magic trick.

Once the shock wore off, I fumbled around the floor and quickly retrieved my jeans, shirt, and boots and rushed out the door. I hurriedly dressed to the closing credits of *Terminator 2,* gulped down my drink, and let myself out the front door. I was much drunker than I was in the darkness of the bedroom and staggered down the sidewalk trying to find my way back to my Cadillac at the bar, but I had no idea where I was. I hit a car bumper and fell on someone's lawn before stumbling back to my feet. That three-block drive in the Camaro turned out to be the most elusive journey an American car had ever made. But I found a liquor store at the next corner, mumbled something into a payphone about "a taxi" and "home," and 20 minutes later I was jingling my keys into my apartment door.

* * *

It was a painful Sunday spent under the covers, and the only reason I got to my feet all day was to take another taxi back to the lesbian bar to retrieve my Caddy. With my throbbing head and trembling hands, the busted windshield and broken side mirror didn't seem like too much of a problem anymore. We matched now. We were both torn up and slightly damaged from a night that got away from us, but we both still started up and made it home.

The cocaine-and-booze hangover wasn't much better on Monday back at Mark's Garden, even with a full two nights of sleep under my belt. Nat looked like shit, too, but she had the cherub glow of a freshly laid woman to mask it. She asked where I had disappeared to Saturday night, and I explained the whole finger-in-the-angry-hole tragedy to her. She had no idea; she didn't even remember me coming into the bedroom that night. We joked about trying a threesome again, without cocaine, but we both knew that plan would never come to fruition—both the "threesome" part as well as the "without cocaine" part. Once you do a particular thing on coke, it's never as much fun to do it again without coke.

After making six of the worst bouquets my dulled senses and watery eyes had ever witnessed, I knew it was due time to put that Monday to rest. Tulips should never have to go through that sort of punishment. As I circled my block trying to find a parking spot big enough for the Brougham I happened upon an open patch of street directly behind where I had parked Friday night—the night of the incident.

I took the spot, and as I walked past the new Lincoln Town Car parked ahead of me, which was sitting exactly where my Caddy had been assaulted, I noticed an all too familiar sight: Its windshield had been cracked at the center, too. There were no grass blades or concrete pebbles on his hood, and its side mirror was still attached to the door, but a long, straight crack ran from the Lincoln's roof straight down to its glistening black hood.

It was an odd feeling I got from seeing it—a trace of anger, a surge of empathy, but mostly a feeling of relief knowing that someone else's car had been damaged like mine. It took some of the sting away, and I'm not too sure why. Our mutually broken windshields made us brothers—like sibling victims of the same abusive father. Neither of us was unique in our persecution. We were simply the prey of some stupid asshole who liked to break windshields on that particular side of the road. Twice.

Twice. Twice *could* be a coincidence. But twice could also be a good hiding spot. Twice could be a good vantage point. Twice is confidence. Twice is a reason. Two windshields. Two identical cracks. Same place two nights in a row. Someone wanted that parking spot; that's why our windshields were cracked. They were warnings for us to keep our distance. I glanced around and noticed a large, beaten RV parked precariously in front of some trash cans down the street—too big to fit properly in the spot that could easily fit three cars. I remembered that same RV had been parked for an entire week right here, where my Caddy and the Town Car now sat. I remember its enormity had taken up the entire allowable parking section on this side of the street, leaving the red parts of the curb to bookend each of its bumpers by mere inches. The old RV had wanted his perfect spot back—it must have been his elusive white whale, that perfect parking spot. And he would go to any lengths to frighten away would-be takers, including smashing their windshields. It all made perfect sense.

Once it grew dark enough out, I moved my Cadillac to the next block over and snuck back to my apartment through the alley. I knew the Town Car would also be leaving soon—its owner was a chauffeur, and I heard him getting ready next door. It wasn't more than five minutes after the Lincoln pulled out when that big behemoth RV chugged its way up and eased right into that long, open spot. Its headlights extinguished and the engine gasped before silencing. All the drapes were drawn but I noticed a small TV flicker awake in the back, unsuspectingly. I had laid out the cheese and he had fallen right into my trap.

With my apartment lights still off, I grabbed my pellet gun and opened my kitchen window. I cut a small slit into the screen and slid the barrel of the pistol through. Camouflaged behind the blossoms of the tree just outside, I began firing little lead rounds at each of the RV's side windows. I heard about a dozen *tinks* of pellets bouncing off glass until recognizing that one unmistakable sound of a window shattering. A big one near the back, by the sleeping quarters. And it was going to be a cold night, too.

I felt immediate gratification at breaking his window and hopefully sending glass shards all over his warm bed. His little TV stopped flickering, and he was presumably now glancing out from behind his darkened drapes trying to find his RV's assailant. But he would not find me. And the next day he would disappear to some other street forever. It turned out to be one hell of a long, electrifying investigation, but the case of the Cadillac's broken windshield had been solved.

THE GRAND DISILLUSION

JOB #1

I had just graduated from high school with the most solid of "C" averages to help guide me into adulthood. There was a strange electricity coursing through me during that sweltering August of 1990—school was finally finished forever and I could now, legally, start the exciting adult life I had always dreamed for myself. It felt like a whole world of possibilities was dangling right there in front of me, like fruit for the picking, and all I had to do was reach out and grab it.

Eighteen years old, living in a tiny pool cabana in the backyard of my parents' house, with an old Underwood typewriter my best friend and confidant—I thought I had it made. For a few years, at least. But Dad thought differently. My plan to become a novelist had been set in stone since my sophomore year after reading *The Old Man and the Sea*, but my father had a very different agenda in store for me now that I was officially a grown-up.

"Get a job or sign up for community college," were the first words out of his mouth once he sat down at the dinner table. "We haven't seen you in almost a week . . . been holed up in that damn room out there. You've got to do something with your life."

"But, pop, this is a really pivotal time for me. I'm just now finally beginning to hone my skills as a writer. Hemingway was—"

"Oh, horse shit! *Hemingway* . . . you need to get a Heming-fucking-job! And get a haircut while you're at it. You look like that . . . Henry Fonda from that . . . Peg, what was that piece of shit?"

"*Easy Rider*," Mom replied. "And it was Peter Fonda. His son. But you do need a job, honey. Even Peter Fonda had a job before he made it as an actor."

"Peter Fon—where did Peter Fonda come from? I'm not trying to be an actor! I'm a writer." There was a brief pause while everyone was chewing, so I added, "And writing *is* kind of a job, if you think abo—"

"Oh, horse shit!" Dad blurted out in mid-swallow. "As long as you live under this roof, you'll be gainfully employed. Since you don't want to enroll in community college, that's the way it is. Job time! You need to live life first before you can write about it. And doing that requires money, which requires a job."

Wow. My god. He was right. My dad was absolutely fucking right. Up until that dinner, the highlights of his 18 years of sage advice had been 1) Always bet on the horse that takes a shit just before the race; 2) Let the garbage disposal run for 30 more seconds; and 3) Dog shit doesn't pick *itself* up. But then from out of nowhere springs a statement so profound and so uncommonly logical as *I need to live life in order to write about life.* So simple yet so philosophical—existential, even. My father, the Buddha of North Hollywood.

But then he grabbed another spoonful of peas and added, "The bill's in the mail for that gem. Just get a fucking job."

That next morning, once my folks had already left for work, I came into the house to get my cup of coffee. The pot was unusually full and still hot, and taped to the tiled kitchen counter was $15 beside a note that read "Haircut today! Then job hunt!" Dad knew my routine. He knew the coffee pot would be my first stop.

But it was that second cup of coffee that gave me the idea to cut my own hair in the bathroom mirror by grabbing a handful of my ponytail and blindly chopping several inches off the bottom. And then just like that, I was $15 richer. I put on the best shirt and slacks I had then bought a pack of non-generic cigarettes and some cheap sunglasses from the corner market.

I walked the streets of Burbank and analyzed the various businesses with "Help Wanted" and "Now Hiring" signs in their windows. I wanted a job that paid well, but also one that I could actually perform, and that would also hopefully provide some colorful new experiences to put in my novel. I was starting to get excited about joining the workforce and making some real money finally. It was time to start living life. It was time for autonomy and independence; it was time for self-sufficiency; it was time for *my* own roof over *my* own head. And having a paycheck would provide all of that, and probably better drugs too.

I filled out an application at Circuit City, because there was something so sinisterly cool about being a salesman. But the manager explained that a knowledge of stereos and televisions was mandatory, long hair was unacceptable, and the wearing of sunglasses during an interview was unappreciated. Strike one. Lesson learned. I walked out and decided to follow the direction of the sun next.

I strolled around for some time until coming across Warner Brothers Studios, and I explained to the security guard that I was interested in a career as a film screenwriter and wanted to apply inside. He shook his head from inside his little security shack and pointed back toward the street that I had just come from. I saw my own reflection in his mirrored sunglasses and wished to hell I had used that $15 to get a real haircut instead of smokes and shades—it looked like there was a blonde helmet sitting crookedly on my head.

I decided to call it a day after my first two rejections in order to reassess my whole job-hunting strategy, but as I was walking home I discovered an eclectic-looking thrift store tucked between a little plumbing company and a neighborhood bank. But before stepping inside Ritzy's Vintage Finds, I pulled my hair into a ponytail, removed my sunglasses, and unbuttoned my shirt to the third button down from the collar to give myself a breezy, wayfaring, drifter sort of look. It was the type of style, I imagined, that all thrift-store salesmen had. They must have all been world travelers and fashion nomads, I concluded, to find such a wide selection of vintage clothing and Hawaiian shirts, and to be able to offer them at such bargain prices.

"Can I help you find something?" a pasty, middle-aged woman with dreadlocks asked from behind the counter. I hadn't even noticed her sitting there behind all the hanging Mardi Gras beads, feathered boas, and fuzzy rearview-mirror dice.

"Ah, yes. Good afternoon to you," I replied as professionally as I could; I even clenched the arm of my sunglasses between my teeth, like my dad did when he was speaking to someone in a serious manner. "I was curious as to your employment . . . to your needs of employment . . . if you might be in need of some employment . . . for an adult that—" and then my sunglasses fell from my mouth and hit the glass counter; I left them lying there between us and clarified what I had been trying to spit out all along, "Are you hiring, by chance?"

It took her a few seconds to absorb everything that had come out of my mouth, and after she handed my sunglasses back to me she answered, "Well, we could use someone to help out around the store. It doesn't pay much, but we need the help."

"Really?"

"We were just going to put a sign out for summer help, but you beat us to it."

"That's just . . . that's just great!"

"Why don't you come back tomorrow morning about nine. You can meet my partner and fill out the application and stuff. He's better at that sort of thing."

"Great! I'll see you tomorrow morning! And thanks a lot."

I walked home congratulating myself on finding not just a job, but a great job, and on only my first day of searching. I wasn't just going to be a salesman of exotic, one-of-a-kind clothing and costume pieces, I was going to be the best god-damn salesman they'd ever seen. When I got home I started leafing through all my mom's fashion magazines and familiarizing myself with styles of dresses, names of fabrics and prints, proper skirt lengths, and which colors were this season's hottest. I typed up mock conversations with fictitious customers and finessed my educated answers over and over.

Why yes, ma'am, this blouse was made in a small Cuban village by talented artisans. It's yesterday's couture at today's low prices!

At the dinner table that night, I boasted about how easily I had found a job in the lucrative world of pre-owned clothing, and what interesting literary experiences I would collect by being a salesman. I explained over Mom's Mystery Goulash that once I saved up enough money I would get an apartment of my own and officially begin work on my first novel. I then crowed a bit about probably being sent to Paris at some point to search for next season's vintage fashions, and how I might just end up staying in the City of Light because of its amazing literary scene. Dad nodded his head, politely placating me. A thrift store wasn't exactly what he had in mind when he had told me to get a job, but I think he was just happy that I wouldn't be spending the entire summer getting stoned with the pool man.

The following morning I perused Dad's closet for the sharpest blazer he had, slipped on my freshly polished "Grandpa's funeral" shoes, and walked the mile up to my new place of employment. The woman I spoke with the day before, whose name I learned was Ella, introduced me to the owner of Ritzy's Vintage Finds. His name was not Ritzy, I discovered after introducing myself. It was Robert. Plain old Robert, and he looked nothing like the jet-setting apparel connoisseur I had imagined. He wore a wrinkled Hawaiian shirt and a Gilligan hat over graying hair, and he reeked of body odor, stale beer, and mothballs.

"Hey, buddy. Heard you're starting today. That's good, we could use you," Robert said. "You might want to lose the blazer, though."

"Is it too much?" I asked.

"No, it's fine. I just don't want you to get it all dirty."

"Ah, gotcha." I took off the cream-colored coat and draped it over my forearm like a fancy waiter with a cloth napkin. "Ella said something about some paperwork I need to fill out?"

Robert took the coat from my arm and flung it onto a chair beside the counter. "Naw, don't worry about it. We're going to keep this on the down-low, if you dig it? It's better for both of us that way."

"Oh, sure," I replied, "that's cool."

"Ella told you we're going to start you at $5 an hour, right? And that's a tax-free $5 an hour. But keep that between us, yeah?"

I glanced at Ella behind the counter, thinking he meant the "between us" was to keep this information from her. But she was barely three feet away and staring right at us. There was no way she couldn't have heard every word we said. But I looked back at Robert and gave him a subtle nod.

The bell on the front door then rang and a 40-something woman and her teenage daughter walked in. The girl immediately pointed at a white nurse's costume hanging on the back wall, and they both navigated through countless racks of multicolored clothing to examine it up close. My previous afternoon of fashion research immediately kicked in, and I whispered to Robert, "That'd look great with some black Mary Janes. Very authentic. Would you like me to go handle this?"

"No, that's Ella's department," he replied. "I need you for something else. Come on, follow me."

As we coursed our way through brimming racks of shirts, dresses, and jackets designated by different decades scribbled onto cardboard pieces, I couldn't help but wonder what exciting task lay ahead of me. Would he start me out in

1920s apparel then let me gradually progress to the '70s? Or perhaps a little tutorial first about coordinating blouses with skirts, or which colors truly complemented a houndstooth print? The further into the store we walked, the more eager I became.

"Wouldn't this scarf look just terrific with that maxi dress over there?" I asked him, trying to show off my blossoming expertise.

"Kinda," he said without even looking at it.

We made our way into a back office, past a bathroom without a door, and then finally to a two-car parking lot directly behind the store. Although technically outside, the 10-foot by 10-foot asphalt patch was surrounded by two cinderblock walls and a large, metal trash dumpster. An opaque piece of ribbed green plastic covered the entire enclosed area, showering us both in an eerie, spearminty glow.

"See those bags up there?" Robert pointed to several bulging canvas sacks lying on some filthy crates, each big enough to satisfy Santa Claus. "Why don't you go ahead and pull those down for me?"

The task required climbing on top of the crates and using every bit of strength I had to haul each hundred-pound sack down from its resting place of what looked to be years. Dust, leaves, and rat shit pellets rained down on me with every yank. By the time I pulled down the eighth and final bag, my white button-up shirt and ironed tan slacks were drenched with sweat, soiled with muck, and stained with suspicious brown spots. I collapsed onto the final bag to catch my breath, while Robert unfolded his arms to toss me a can of spray paint.

"Now aren't you glad I told you to take your blazer off?" he asked. He noticed me examining my newly polka-dotted slacks. "That rat shit should wash right out. Give it a good soak."

He slid on a pair of leather gloves from his back pocket, opened one of the canvas sacks, and pulled out an old, tattered pair of black combat boots. Two rats shot out from the sack and bolted under the trash bin exactly one second before I leapt off that same sack and landed several feet away in the *Karate Kid*'s crane stance.

"Holy shit!" I barked. "Did you see that?"

"Yeah," he replied casually, "don't let 'em bite you. It's not fun."

He smacked the two boots together to shake off the dirt and rat pellets then turned them over to show me their soles. "You see here, these are both size 12 and in pretty good condition. This is what we're looking for. I want you to spray-paint a little dot onto each sole when you find a good pair like this, then clean 'em up a little and stack them over by the wall."

"Is there a specific number of good pairs you're looking for?" I asked, already knowing the answer I was going to hear but hoping for a different one.

"As many as you can find!" He snapped back. "There's eight goddamned bags there. Should be a couple hundred good pairs."

"And what about the not-good pairs? What should I do with them?"

"Seriously?" he asked, his red eyes squeezed together. Then when he realized that I was serious and still waiting for an answer, he added, "You *don't* put a red dot on them. I thought that might be a given."

He turned and was about to walk back inside when I asked my follow-up question: "Is there a pair of gloves I can use?" He stared at me for a few seconds, looking almost offended by such a request. Then he pulled off his left glove and tossed it to me.

"One should do you fine. And don't get paint on it," he said before slamming the metal door shut behind him.

I was amazed at how many pairs of boots those canvas sacks held. I had pulled out, cleaned off, and spray-painted the soles of at least fifty pairs before the first sack was even empty. And that's not even counting the obliterated boots that didn't receive a red dot, or the rats that skittered out into every direction. By my calculation, I had spent about an hour and a half on that first sack, so I lit up a cigarette and took a little breather before starting on the second. Halfway through that Camel, I discovered how blackened my right gloveless hand had become, and I could only wonder how much of it was dirt and how much of it was rat shit. As I took another drag with that same filthy hand, I thought about all the health hazards of putting those feces-stained fingers that close to my mouth. But on the flip side, I also now understood the actual labor involved in being able to afford a pack of real cigarettes like Camels. The pros outweighed the cons on money versus disease, so I smoked that cigarette right down to the filter, but as carefully as I could.

The second bag was just as arduous and disgusting as the first, but I learned to pass the time by imagining the lives those boots had led before ending up at Ritzy's Vintage Finds. Some were from the German military, some Asian, but the most ragged pairs came from one of the Arabic countries of the Middle East—at least that's what language the "100% leather" on the boot tongue looked to be written in. Then I thought about how many soldiers might have died while actually wearing these very same boots, and if Robert had gotten a discount in price for something like that.

He came out again just as I started on the third sack, and he made a little joke by asking when I'd found the time to change clothes. I glanced down to find that my tan slacks were now completely brown and my dressy white shirt was a blend of beiges and black smears.

"And you got my fucking glove all filthy, man!" he added, and quite seriously.

I decided not to respond to that and instead asked when I could take a lunch break. He looked at his watch and replied, "As soon as you're done there."

"But I'm not even . . . I'm not even through the third bag yet," I exclaimed. "There's like five more bags to go."

"Then you better get cracking," he said and returned to the store.

Get cracking, I thought to myself as I pulled out the next pair of boots, wiped a rag over them, and spray-painted the red dot onto their soles. *Get cracking*. I'll *get cracking* on you, Robert! I'll *get cracking* on you and your stupid vintage thrift store. I'll *crack* your stupid head open and fill it with these rat shit pellets.

A big rat then shot out of the bag and actually ran up my sleeve before launching itself into the rows of cleaned boots by the wall. I fell over backwards and could only muster the energy to spray-paint the air in its wake as well as part of my glove. That was the last straw. That was all I was going to take from Ritzy.

I got back to my feet and threw off my one glove. I was going to march right into the store and tell Robert what he could do with his stupid, rat shit job. I hoped the place was full of customers, too, so they could all hear exactly what was on my mind. But when I went to open the door, it wouldn't budge. He had locked it—he had locked me out there in that little rat-infested, boot-filled chamber. My eyes darted around for any sign of an escape route, but the place was fortified with debris and wire at every corner. A dash of fear then mixed with my anger, and I used all the strength I had left to try and push the back door open again, but it still wouldn't move. I felt like one of the rats trying to get out of the sack, and I bounced around from wall to wall looking for any way out. I finally put my back against the big metal dumpster and pushed it out enough for me to fit through, and a cool gust of fresh air rushed in and stirred up the dust.

I was free! Free from that green-roofed prison cell, and free from that stupid job! And the sweet air of my liberation smelled like blooming jasmine and fast-food burgers as I stepped out into the sunlight, and several rats followed suit and skittered off to a new life away from canvas sacks and combat boots.

But I only got a few steps toward the alley before realizing that I couldn't just walk away without giving Robert a little piece of my mind first. He could keep the damn $15 or $20 he owed me—that wasn't what I wanted. What I wanted was for him to remember me. What I wanted was for him to have a permanent reminder of the aspiring novelist who had said enough was enough.

Not wanting to circle the entire city block just to shout "I quit!" through the front door and run away, I instead grabbed the can of red spray paint and wrote my departing message in five-foot-tall letters across the cinderblock wall of the boot chamber. My lanky-lettered, crimson-colored "I QUIT" would be the first thing that slave-driving Robert would see once opening that back door to look for me. And it would be the same thing he would see every day when he took the trash out until he finally painted over it, or paid some other chump $5 an hour to paint over it. But I felt avenged.

Then I grabbed the best pair of size 12 boots I could find and got the hell out of there. Of course, I realized several blocks later that I had left my dad's blazer back at the store, but I considered it an acceptable amount of collateral damage for such a triumphant end to Ritzy's Vintage Finds—to my first job.

That night as the family gathered around the dinner table, Dad asked how my first day of work had gone. And then he asked if I had a time frame for when they were going to fly me to Paris, so Mom knew when not to include me for dinner. And without acknowledging his clever sarcasm and timely wit, I calmly explained that a good education was probably just as vital to a writer's growth as self-sufficiency and an income, and that I'd like to go ahead and take him up on his offer of enrolling in community college.

He smiled and nodded his head without comment. I think that had been his plan all along.

OPERATION HOT FUDGE

JOB #6

8:51

The Camaro started up like a lion cub at dawn. Which was good because I was running late—not *oh shit* late, just *come on, come on!* late. I had to make it from Sherman Oaks to Studio City—about six sporadically traffic-riddled miles—in just under 10 minutes. It was doable but highly unlikely for a Thursday.

9:02

The freeway was a truly bad idea. I took advantage of the standstill in traffic and removed my T-tops without removing my seatbelt—just reached up, unlatched, and threw them behind me into the backseat. It was already sunny and nearing 90 degrees, which was made worse and stickier by the low-lying cloud of trapped exhaust simmering atop the fresh asphalt sea surrounding me.

I loved my Camaro. She was a classic 1979 model with the aforementioned removable roof and an air-compressed device above the rear wheel axle that raised or lowered the entire back end of the car by several feet. She could go from gaudy hot rod (like it was now) to ghetto low-rider with just a few seconds of bicycle tire air at any gas station. And as cool as that feature was, it wasn't even my idea—I had traded this car straight-up for my 1973 Monte Carlo, which my Grandpa left me in his will. Sure, there was some sentiment involved in the trade, and my Dad wasn't too keen on losing his late father's beloved car in the handful of months since the funeral . . . but, shit, this was a Camaro!

And yes, it's true, the Camaro wasn't the most efficient car for a full-time courier to have, but it had class. It had balls. It had panache.

9:14

The elevator doors opened and Aldrena, the born-again Southern receptionist, told me that Edgar, the company's lead art director, wanted to talk with me as soon as I got in. I walked into the back, through a huge bullpen of graphic artists, copywriters, and art designers darting from cubicle to office to cubicle, and found Edgar leaning against a desk nodding to a new concept for the *Sniper* film poster. He was a portly man in his early 40s, who looked like he would be an abusive asshole after a few drinks. I had never really spoken with him before that day—I was AdZoo's courier and always spent my time on the road delivering ad concepts and mock-up designs to film studios. Being a courier was the life. From 9:00 a.m. to 6:00 p.m., Monday through Friday, it was just me and my Camaro cruising the streets of Los Angeles. It was the decade right before emails and online file sharing and affordable cell phones, so things had to be delivered in person, and at the timely discretion of the driver. It was awesome.

I grabbed a stack of papers along the way and approached Edgar from his side. "Good morning, Edgar. Aldrena *just* said you wanted to see me. I was . . ." I wiggled the papers then rolled my eyes, implying that Aldrena must have forgotten to give me the message until just that moment. She had just become my fall guy by default.

"Oh, good. You've already started."

"How so?"

"OK, maybe not. I need you to help out in the studio today; we're behind schedule. We can hire a service for deliveries. We've got two films for Paramount, a VHS cover . . . and some fucking horror movie with that kid from *Terminator 2* all due today. I need you working in here until it's done."

"But I'm the courier. I belong out there."

"Being a courier is how you get your foot in the door . . . then you learn something and move up. This is your chance to learn something. Most people would give their left leg to have the opportunity I'm giving you. You've been here for close to a year, right? And you're what . . . 30? You've got to think about your future . . . your future at AdZoo."

"I'm 21. And my only aspiration is to be this company's courier."

He shook his head with more irritation than dispute. He exhaled loudly and pointed to a Xerox machine beside a table holding several stacks of paper. "You're not a courier today. Today you're this company's errand boy. I need you to make forty copies of each of those stacks, collate them, and staple them into presentations. They're our concept designs for the poster, so make sure they look good. Don't fuck me over on this. This is big time. This is Paramount."

11:51

I had been copying and stapling for damn near three hours before Edgar popped up beside me and startled me out of my automatic assembly. He was straightening his tie and looked like he had just washed his face.

"These almost ready to go? I need to be out of here in an hour."

"Pretty close."

He picked one up and flipped through it, grimaced, and flipped through it again with a much more scrutinizing eye. He launched his head back and shouted, "Are you fucking serious?" Then he looked straight at me. "What the fuck, man? These aren't in order!" He slowly flipped through the pages of the thin presentation so I could see. "Two, three, eight, another two I think, six, there's a one . . ."

"But there's no page numbers—they're just pictures. There's no order to them."

"I had the *stacks* numbered, genius! Didn't you see the fucking Post-It notes all over the place? They're square and yellow with things like 'one' and 'two' written on them! That's why I said to *collate* them! Do you know what the fuck 'collate' even means?"

"*Yes*, I know what 'collate' means! I just didn't think Post-It notes would have anything to do with it." In hindsight, I had no idea what "collate" meant, nor had I ever heard the word used before. I actually thought it was a setting on the printer for richer, crisper images. Nevertheless, Edgar had taken his frustration too far by questioning a blossoming writer's command of the English language, even if he was right. And the fact that everybody in the bullpen was now watching me getting reamed by the art director didn't help matters much. Edgar had crossed the line.

"Unstaple everything and start over!" Edgar slammed the presentation onto the table. "No, that'll look like shit. Damn it! Xerox everything again and start over. And *collate* them this time! Page one, two, three, four, five, six, seven, staple! One, two, three, four, boom, boom, staple!"

"See, I heard 'collate' on that one. Now I understand."

He shook his head and snarled his lip before walking back to his office. And I started the entire process over from scratch, but assembling them correctly this time. I was never one for direct confrontation—I preferred the more passive-aggressive approach to retribution. And in that near-hour of copying and stapling I devised the sweetest act of vengeance my two decades and change had ever conceived. Edgar was going to pay dearly.

12:47

My grin was devious and silent as I walked the stack of collated and stapled presentations into Edgar's office. I laid them on his desk, and he shooed me away with the hand that wasn't holding the phone.

Edgar had no idea what was in store for him. But I did; that was why I left so cavalierly. Because I knew what was coming for poor old Edgar and his big condescending mouth. He would rue the day he chastised this company's courier. Because I had a plan—a damn good plan. I was going to take a dump on the hood of his brand new Mercedes-Benz right before his big meeting.

12:56

I passed by Aldrena on a phone call and motioned that I was going out to lunch. Edgar was finishing up the project then heading straight over to Paramount studios, leaving me about 13-15 minutes to put Operation Hot Fudge into effect. I got off the elevator at the second floor, where there were no surveillance cameras, and took the stairwell down to the P2 level, where that shiny new Mercedes lazed in the corner under a flickering overhead light. I approached casually, glancing through every windshield along the way to make sure no one would be bearing witness to my act of vengeance. The coast seemed to be clear, so I walked up to Edgar's Mercedes to scope out my "drop" angle. I had envisioned taking off my shoes and squatting with my back against the windshield, so as not to damage the car in any other way than defecation degradation. But seeing the actual distance from the sloped windshield to the hood made that theory moot—I would have only nailed the windshield wipers. I debated reversing my approach completely, where my hands would grab hold of the roof while my ass dangled over the hood of the car—what you might call a "free fall." That seemed logical enough until I saw the faint red glow of a blinking light coming from the car's dashboard. I hand-visored my eyes from the fluorescent above and gazed inside to verify what I already suspected: fucking Edgar had set the alarm.

Operation Hot Fudge just got a lot more complicated, and time was ticking down. I was going to have to take this shit to the next level, and fast.

1:08

One bad move and the alarm would go off, jeopardizing the entire mission. Anything to do with putting my weight on its hood or roof or windshield was now out of the equation. Lunchtime for most employees was 1:15, which meant in the next seven to eight minutes there'd be hungry civilians, not to mention Edgar, all over this garage.

I'd have to put Plan C into action. It hadn't been fully fleshed out, but it was going to have to do. I hustled over to the stairwell, stepped in, and shut the metal door behind me. I found a 24-ounce Carl's Jr. fountain cup, threw off the top and straw, and positioned it four inches away from the bottom step of the stairs. I held my breath for a second to silence my heartbeat and listened for any voices or footsteps entering the garage, but it sounded empty. I had to be certain—if someone opened the door, how in the hell could I explain taking a shit into a cup in a stairwell? There is no logical or even illogical explanation for something like that.

1:11

I lowered my pants to my ankles, spread my legs as far at the unbuttoned waistband would allow, and eased myself down until my ass rested on the precipice of the step. I used my internal eye to guesstimate where my anus was, and moved the Carl's Jr. cup back an inch toward the step. That seemed about right. I squeezed my innards but this new squatting elevation changed my entire shitting dynamic. I was hunched much lower than my toilet at home and my waist was pinched; and that normal feeling of inner movement was nowhere to be felt. Plus, I was nervous and on a heavy time constraint, and everyone knows you can't achieve a clean dump when there's a time limit involved.

But I pushed, and I grabbed the stairwell and elevated myself a few more inches, and I pushed even harder. The moving gears of the elevator hummed from behind the concrete wall beside me, and I pushed even harder. The muffled sound of a woman's laughter echoed from the first parking level, and I kept pushing. Then finally I felt the puckered seal of the anus widen, and that deuce of vengeance eased its ugly way out and dropped into the cup with a thud. The operation was so rushed that I hadn't even considered the toilet paper aspect, but the leaver of the cup had also left some used napkins and a wrapper, both of which worked just fine.

I buckled up, composed myself, then retrieved the cup. It was quite heavy, heavier than I would have expected poop to be. That's something you don't get a chance to know unless you defecate in a cup. I slowly opened the door and peeked out; I didn't see anybody but heard two sets of high-heel footsteps getting closer. Operation Hot Fudge was now in full bloom. I ran back to the Mercedes with the warm cup extended in front of me as far as my arm would stretch. I took one last look overhead for any cameras that I might have missed, then flung the weighty contents of the cup across the golden hood of that German automobile. It rolled briefly before coming to a halt in a crescent moon position, leaving a dotted trail several inches long in its wake. It looked surprisingly larger lying on the sparkling metal than it did in the cup. It kind of looked like a small bear napping on a frozen lake reflecting the stars overhead.

I had a difficult time pulling myself away from the sight of it, knowing it was I who had done that. It was like something you would see in a dirty alleyway.

1:19

I ran back up the stairwell, got off on the second floor, and hopped onto the elevator going down. I rode it to the lobby and exited through the front doors, letting the surveillance camera capture me checking the contents of my wallet—a sure sign I was innocently going to lunch. The beauty of Operation Hot Fudge was that, for all intents and purposes, I had left documented proof of leaving the fourth floor on the elevator and arriving in the lobby from the elevator—everything in between was just lost in the works. Aldrena wouldn't remember the exact moment I left—she was on the phone—so she was unknowingly my accomplice in this operation. She was my alibi. She was my fall guy and my alibi.

2:11

I had had a subconscious craving for Carl's Jr. and didn't know why, but that was where I went to kill 40 minutes and add the factual "lunch" anchor to Operation Hot Fudge. I returned to work still sipping from my fountain drink cup just when the source of that subconscious craving for Carl's was revealed, and I tossed the cup into the trash can just outside the elevator doors.

Aldrena didn't say anything as I passed her, so I walked back into the bullpen to find my supervisor Jennifer's cubicle and hopefully retrieve a delivery order. I asked her if Edgar had made it to his meeting on time, and she said that he had arrived a little late because of my collating fuck-up as well as "something weird that came up." But she wouldn't go into specifics.

She handed me a manila envelope and a pink carbon copy of a receipt, then told me to take the package to Pacific Palisades for a signature. If reality was my copilot, that would have been an hour-and-a-half delivery. But reality had never been my driving companion in the Camaro. Accompanying me on my journeys instead was a stack of

AC/DC cassettes and a stash of pot in an ashtray with a false back. So, this delivery was most likely going to run out the rest of my workday.

4:52

The signature was obtained from Pacific Palisades without problem. I had already made it back to Studio City but found myself too stoned to return to work, so I drove around until finding a park. I read the newspaper, braided a lock of my hair, and daydreamed about being on *Happy Days*.

5:35

I returned to AdZoo Advertising well prepared to be fired and ready to quit. Edgar must have returned from his meeting by that point, and who knew how far the backlash of Operation Hot Fudge stretched. I passed Aldrena and went back to Jennifer's cubicle and gave her the signed papers. She looked at her watch, said it was too late to send me out again, and told me to see if anyone in the office needed help until 6:00. All that meant was walk around and stay out of sight until Miller Time rolled around.

5:58

There was nothing so sweet as adding elements of confusion and arrogance to an act of retribution, so my wandering around the bullpen ended at Edgar's office. He must have assumed I did it, but knowing I had proof of my innocence emboldened the hell out of me. And, more than anything, I wanted to know how he removed the ogre from his hood in such a hurry. Did he use the same Carl's Jr. cup I did? Did one of my presentations become his shovel? Did he simply drive away and hope it rolled off on the freeway?

But I could not and did not ask him about that. Nor did I ask him how it felt to fuck with the courier. His dour yet still-not-certain expression said enough. The only thing I said to him was, "Sorry about the miscommunication earlier." And his only response was, "Glory is fleeting, courier."

THE THESPIAN LOSES HIS COAT

JOB #11

To grow up in Los Angeles is to grow up in The Industry, in one form or another. Perhaps as someone's assistant inside one of the dozens of film studios; maybe working in a warehouse full of movie props and stage settings; or possibly driving a bus full of tourists around Beverly Hills while narrating into a microphone the film history of a certain celebrity whose mansion you happen to be driving by. There are hundreds of colorful career avenues to walk down when entertaining a life in the City of Angels, each with its own unique twinkle of that golden Hollywood magic. But no vocation is as revered, as cherished, as treasured, as that of the actor.

Actor—the most coveted occupation in all of Tinsel Town. To act is to live. To perform on a film set surrounded by big hulking cameras, soundmen holding long fuzzy microphones, assistants with clipboards, and powerful stage lights—that's what it is to be alive! And when the assistant director pats you on the back and tells you that you're needed on set for your big scene working alongside the film's star, then you know you've succeeded where hundreds of thousands of others have failed. Because to act is to live. To stand alongside the likes of Sir Laurence Olivier and Richard Burton and Marlon Brando is to truly write your page in the cosmic book of history.

And *just* beneath the actor lay the true silent heroes of film. The very fabric that weaves a movie together is not the recognizable person speaking in front of the camera nor is it the beautiful cinematography or CGI effects. The true cornerstone of a film—of *every* film—is the person walking by in the background. The cute but plain couple dining at a café table directly behind the movie star and the soon-to-be movie star. The shocked bystander walking out of a department store. The guy in the trench coat across the street hailing a taxi. These silent, forgettable, unnoticeable people are the true keystones to every movie ever made.

That's right, we're the extras: the noiseless, action-less actors for hire at a daily rate. You can just call us "the background." We were living props that painted the backdrops of scenes in public places. We spanned the spectrum of all walks of life and age, and we had mastered the art of the pretend conversation.

While working with Marty on a gig that night, I realized I wanted to specialize in party and crowd scenes and only party and crowd scenes. Oh, look at me . . . calling him *Marty*, like you'd know who I'm referring to. In The Industry, we have darling little nicknames and abbreviated monikers for everyone. People probably call me Brandy, but I can't say for sure. But I'm talking about Marty Short. You'd probably know him better as Martin Short, the little goofy actor from a bunch of mediocre shit in the 1980s. But I worked with him, so I refer to him as Marty.

We were standing in the center of an enormous rented

mansion in Malibu for a big dance scene, just Marty and me. Plus the sixty or so other extras around us and between us. But *I* was the closest to him. The scene called for Marty, who was playing a child and dressed in a little schoolboy uniform, to be dancing within an anonymous group of much taller people, to make him look even more like a child. And this went on for hours. And without any music. That's one thing the average person doesn't realize when watching a TV show or a movie: When all those people are dancing at a party or a concert, and the camera pans by them rocking out to the blaring music, shaking their heads and throwing their hands into the air, well, it's really just silence minus the sounds of a few shoes scuffling. They add the music in later. And it's really creepy dancing without music. It's like being a ghost forced to relive some last morose moment of life over and over.

But that's what we were doing: not talking, but looking happy, and dancing to silence. Some much better than others, too. I couldn't dance even if there *were* music playing, let alone to the sounds of shuffling feet. So I resorted to the crimped-arms-at-the-waist rocking action and only put some effort into the "happy face" when the camera rolled by. Little Marty was in the center of us throwing around some wildly goofy dance moves, most of which must have hurt his 40-something physique. But he was a born entertainer, that Marty. The lack of music didn't slow him down one bit. He had danced himself clear on over to the other side of the room and stayed there. I considered nonchalantly following him over, but the shelter of the floor lamp beside me was one that I was not willing to give up.

Midnight finally rolled around, which signaled the end of our eight-and-a-half-hour shift. That was one of the beautiful things I learned about working on a film set: Everything ends on time or they pay you time-and-a-half until it's double time. We then stood in line to show our IDs and receive our checks for $98. Before I left the set I stole two plastic ice cubes from the kitchen scene. I just couldn't believe the absurdity of creating completely realistic ice cubes that would never melt and always look like actual ice when real ice does the same thing, and real ice is basically free. It wasn't like using a dozen trays of real ice for a single scene was going to add thousands of dollars to the budget. It wouldn't even cost a quarter. But I'm pretty certain those plastic ice cubes cost about $30 apiece.

While trying to find the freeway entrance out of Malibu, I ended up driving into a part of Los Angeles that was not intended for Caucasians. At least I thought it was still L.A., but it could have been Long Beach by that point. Or Tijuana. I pulled over at a well-lit gas station, got directions back to the freeway, but made the mistake of using the shitter before getting back on the road. I had hoped the flimsy door of the stall I was sitting in would offer some protection in case anything happened, but the latch was missing and the only thing keeping it shut was my thumb. That's when a pair of feet walked in and their owner knocked at my stall.

"Hey, bro!" the raspy voice said with a jail languor. "My friend likes your jacket. He's crazy, bro. You better just give it to him. I can't stop him. I said I'd ask you for it nicely before he went crazy on you. Why don't you just give me your jacket, and I'll give it to him?"

I stayed quiet for a few seconds hoping he would take that as a no. But he didn't. He washed his hands and kept talking about how crazy his friend was, and how much he liked my jacket. But I liked it too. It was black leather and had the metal tops of two dozen Bic lighters pressed around the collar. It was my first real leather jacket, and it always gave me a Fonz moment whenever I slid it on. The Fonz wouldn't put up with this shit—he wouldn't give up his jacket for anybody, let alone some gangster thug throwing around ambiguous threats in a gas station shitter. I really wished there was a latch on the stall door, though; that would make all the difference in the world. A simple latch. Where did it go?

"You're fuckin' pissing him off, bro!" he slammed on the door this time, and it briefly opened enough for him to see me with my pants down and me to see him with his tattoos and shaved head. Then something metal and pointed tapped on the hollow metal door. "You know what this is? I didn't want to pull this out, but it's out now. Just give me the fucking jacket, bro."

I was rational enough to pull out my cigarettes and lighter before tossing the jacket over the stall door to him. He ran out and I heard him laughing and shouting that he got the jacket, then a motor accelerated before disappearing into the night. I sat there on the toilet and pondered the whole idea of getting robbed without even really being robbed, because that's basically what happened. What he said to me was both a threat as well as a warning for my own safety. His friend was *crazy*, after all; the guy in the bathroom was just the liaison. And what I thought was a big sharp knife tapping on the stall door could have very easily been a car key or a penny. It was a reflection of a robbery that could have been, and yet it *was* that robbery. It was a suggestive stick-up. The more I thought about it the more I realized what a perfect crime it was. Maybe there was a crazy friend waiting outside and maybe there wasn't, but all he did was suggest that I hand over my jacket to save myself some possible misfortune. He was offering insurance, in a way: Pay me and I'll protect you from the real bully. Illegal, no, not really. Unethical, very. Uncool, hell yes. But illegal, I don't think so. It was committing a crime that wasn't against the law—the uncrime.

Then I pulled out the two plastic ice cubes from my pocket and fumbled them around in my palm. A crime that wasn't a crime and ice that wasn't really ice. I found no irony in that fact, nor the fact that something had been stolen from me on the very same night I had stolen something myself. But the events and the plastic ice did help me discover that there were some strange similarities between the façade of filmmaking and the guise of criminality. It's not that it's all fake, but that you, the viewer, have to help the suspension of disbelief move along as much as the perpetrator of the crime or film has to. A movie doesn't work if you, the viewer, don't let yourself believe it—it's just images being flashed across a screen at twenty-four frames per second. But if you let yourself believe it, that same film can become as authentic and genuine as any real-life scenario. And the same can be said for crime—I could have mumbled a foreign language or laughed maniacally from within the stall, and probably thwarted the stick-up and kept my jacket. But I didn't. I went along with the story; I let myself suspend my disbelief. I handed over my coat and enjoyed the rest of the movie. I was now an extra, after all. It was my duty as a performer to be robbed as authentically as possible.

THE RISE AND TRAGIC FALL

JOB #37

It was a little after one in the morning when the car horn went off. I had just settled into bed in the thick of the warm summer night when the howl of the honk tore through my apartment like a crowbar slowly forcing open the lid from a wooden crate. My apartment windows, like most of my neighbors,' were wide open and eager for a cool breeze. But nobody on Huston Street got their chilly gust of wind to fall asleep to that night. Instead, every resident in a three-block radius got the endless hooooooooooooooooooooooooonk of some asshole's car to cool us down.

As I lay there in bed and waited for the car's owner to arrive and fumble out his keys to finally mute this heavy, hollow screech, I deliberated whether hearing the more melodic sound of a traditional car alarm, with its varying themes and *doo-doo-wha-wha* diddies, would be more *or* less unenjoyable than this unwavering blast of a monotone horn. Both were terrible; but would one be less terrible than the other? And since we're on the subject, why would any car alarm maker even offer the option of a straight, endless, unbroken beam of a honk over the more traditional short, rapid bursts of honks? What car was so damn valuable that it required a steady palm-on-the-button horn for an alarm?

Six minutes was well past the maximum amount of time that an owner of a car was allowed to not recognize his own alarm—especially when one was as distinctively annoying as this one. I jumped out of bed and walked across the hardwood floor of my studio apartment to the wall of windows and pulled back the drapes. I searched the street below for the telltale blinking headlights or flashing brake lights, but the street was dark and showed no signs of unrest. It was actually serene down there, almost picture-perfect. The blaring horn was the only evidence of something not right—as if the wrong audio track had been mistakenly used with the scene. I tried turning my head from side to side in an attempt to pinpoint the direction of the noise, but both sides sounded equally loud from the window. That would mean that either I was directionally deaf or the loud car sat directly below my window, with only a thin layer of blooming magnolia trees as a buffer between us. That's just perfect, I mouthed to the drapes. Just perfect. Right under my window.

By minute fifteen, neighbors had started coming out to the street in their bathrobes and sleeping shorts. Angry tenants from my apartment complex as well as from the fancier complex across the street stood united in their hatred for this car making all that noise. They clung in little packs before merging into one big mob at the center of the street. Shaking heads and waving fists quickly became pointed fingers at the car hidden under the trees right below me—I knew it! Then two people from the crowd of a dozen noticed me watching from my window and pointed up at me, and I showed my solidarity to their cause by glancing at my naked wrist, shaking my head, and, finally, crossing my arms. It wasn't quite windtalker code but it did convey that I was equally as pissed as them, and it wasn't me they should want to kill.

It was now a quarter to two in the morning—Tuesday morning—and the steady honk still flowed. It had grown maddening. There was a point around minute 26 where my brain somehow muted out the noise for several seconds by awakening some type of auditory self-defense mechanism, but it was quickly overcome and incapacitated by minute 27. The mob on the street had grown to 20, and just about every apartment window in sight was now lit up. People had gathered around the blameworthy car underneath my window, and they were beginning to pound their fists against its hood and kick at the doors. Good for them! Whoever this ignorant asshole was, he had to pay for what his car had done to us. I imagined all of us out there with pitchforks and burning torches, ready to castrate the bastard as soon as he ran out with his keys jingling in his hand and an apology on his lips. The crowd below had grown furious, so much so that you could hear them cussing over the horn. One gentleman even picked up a good-size rock and hurled it at the car, but it did nothing to make it quiet again.

But the flung rock did get me to remember that *my* car was parked somewhere down there, probably not too far from the loud car being attacked by the neighbors. What if they grew so angry that they began destroying *any* car near the car with the alarm? What if my car—my car that I had just bought the day before—was being sat on or molested in some way by these irrational, pissed-off neighbors going berserk below? Sure, she was just a shitty 13-year-old Celica with more rust than white paint, but she was *my* shitty

Celica—my *new* shitty Celica. Then the possibility suddenly crossed my mind that perhaps it was my own Celica's car alarm going off; but then that notion left just as quickly as it came once I remembered that its alarm, stereo, and battery had been stolen prior to buying it—making the Celica's $600 price tag ideal. But then that realization prompted even more speculation.

Although the lack of a car alarm eliminated the possibility of that 30-minute honk being my *car alarm*, it did pose the question of it still being my horn. You see, I could afford to replace the car battery, which I did earlier that afternoon, but I couldn't afford to replace the stereo or the alarm. So, in place of the stereo I used a portable CD player and headphones. And in place of an alarm, I secured the steering wheel firmly in place using The Club steering wheel lock, which I had found lodged between the backseat and hatchback. I remembered the event very clearly; I remembered fiddling with the key to make sure the steel mechanism still locked and unlocked properly, then I remembered forcing the rubber-gripped talons of The Club across both sides of the oddly shaped steering wheel until it firmly and unquestionably locked the entire steering column in place. I remembered the event so vividly because I tried to unlock it a few seconds after locking it just to see if I had attached it correctly in the first place. And it wouldn't budge—it was locked so firmly in place that it was stuck. And every additional time I tried to yank The Club loose from the steering wheel it somehow pushed against the horn button, startling me as well as several dog-walkers each time. So I left it, figuring if I couldn't remove it then a car thief couldn't remove it either.

Upon this recollection–turned-self-indictment, my face

went numb seconds before turning as red as the color of guilt. I flung the drape closed, dropped to my knees, and backed up against the wall. The honk seemed much louder now knowing it was most likely mine. Every time I peeked out from behind my drapes, more neighbors seemed to be pointing up at my window. I had to somehow put a stop to this—there was a brand-new battery under that hood, which meant the horn could go on for several more hours. But I couldn't go down there, especially after letting this go on for the last 40 minutes. The mob had already seen me standing in my window directly above the guilty car, and I had crossed my arms, checked my invisible watch, and shook my head at them out of solidarity. But if I walked down there now, all the crossed arms and head-shaking theatrics would look like I had done all of this out of spite. Pure malice. Why did I have to cross my arms so fervently? Why did I pretend to check a wristwatch that wasn't there? My showboating was going to be my downfall.

As I slouched there under the window, I deduced all of my options and came to only one conclusion: wait it out until dawn. The sounds of the waking city might drown out the horn or, at the very least, most of these neighbors would eventually have to leave for work. So I was prepared to crouch there under that window for the next four hours like a marine under duress, but luck soon intervened. And it did so by way of a shitty new car battery that was on sale. I will never question my own frugality again.

The 45-minute brick of uninterrupted horn finally started to show signs of weakening. It began with a warbling echo of toots right before a series of deep sighs, then deafening silence for a few seconds, then full-on horn again. But it was dissipating. Gargling ripples of horn-like sounds then replaced the toots and sighs and, a minute later, it petered out completely. It grew so quiet so fast that the silence seemed louder than the horn ever was.

I waited until about noon the following day before checking on the Celica. As I had witnessed from above, they had beaten the shit out of it pretty good. But the neighbors were at least civil enough not to break any windows or spray-paint *cocksucker* on it; just some fresh kick marks in the door, a semiremoved windshield wiper, and a couple of rocks and a beer can on the hood. I pushed the debris to the ground and opened it up for a look.

"So it was you!" A male voice accused me from behind.

I leaned out from under the hood expecting to see the mob from last night with pitchforks and torches, but instead a husky middle-aged man in a black suit and mirrored sunglasses stood staring at me. My first thought was that he was FBI, and my eyes immediately flashed down to his belt to look for a handgun or a badge. But I assumed that a lot with new people, though. "*What* was me?"

"Your car," he answered sternly. "Your car horn, to be more precise. Hell of a way to meet a new neighbor."

"But I've lived here over a year," I replied.

"No, me," he answered. "I just moved in. I've seen you in the hall. I moved in right next door to you."

"Well, welcome home. Sorry about the horn last night. I . . . wasn't here when it went off."

"Yeah, I assumed that. I'm Tony, two-oh-two."

"Brandon. Two-oh-three."

We shook hands and both lit Camels. I was still a little wary of my "new neighbor," but it's hard not to admire a man in a black suit. Tony leaned back against a black Lincoln Town Car parked in front of my Celica—total government car; tinted windows and everything. I wondered if this was all an elaborate plan—the horn, the Celica purchase, the neighborly small talk—to enlist me for some covert operation. Or to make me disappear. Perhaps there was some shady CIA station chief in the backseat of his Lincoln watching me right now, studying my facial tics to see if I was nervous, see if I was hiding something, see if I was ready. I had to play this one real cool—just act like we're civil neighbors, nothing to suspect, nothing to conceal. Just be cool, bro.

"So, you off to work?" I asked casually.

"No, not till later," he replied gruffly, cigarette dangling from his lip as he turned around and opened the trunk. "I need to wash my car first."

He pulled out a bucket, a bottle of dishwashing soap, and a towel and, after filling the bucket with water, proceeded to wash the entire Lincoln Town Car—rims, whitewalls, and bumpers included—without getting a single drop of water or soap bubble onto his suit. The whole bathing process couldn't have taken longer than 70 seconds. I unlocked my door and sat down behind the wheel, keeping an eye on Tony as I slid the key in and turned the ignition over. I wasn't sure how, but the Celica started right up. But when I glanced back up, Tony was standing right beside me with his elbow resting on my opened door. He nodded his head to every rev I gave the engine.

"You take good care of your car," he said. "That's a good trait."

"Thanks. You too. Impressive wash job."

We glanced at each other a few times and nodded to the variation of each new rev but, for the most part, there was just an odd silence between us. He had definitely exceeded the nonconversation time limit for creepiness. But he stood there between me and the car door, preventing me from closing it, and staring at me with those mirrored sunglasses. It was as if he was waiting for me to say something, to confess to some crime I had committed, to disclose some secret New World Order theory that I had devised. The cops on *Law & Order* approached suspects this way when they knew the perp was guilty beyond a reasonable doubt; they wanted them to sweat a bit first. That's what this Tony was trying on me, but I saw through his little plan. I had been training for this moment since I was 14 years old. I was going to call his bluff. If he wanted to arrest me, or even assassinate me, then I wanted this son of a bitch to know that I had seen it coming. His undercover skills were juvenile at best; real grade-school job. Apparently my reputation at CIA or FBI headquarters didn't precede me. It would take more than a simple business suit to fool me. Get ready, fucker, cover blown!

"So, are you . . . Secret Service? Or Homeland Security?" I asked, my right hand gripping the stick shift readying for a fast getaway.

"Neither," he replied with a scowl. "Limo driver."

A limo driver? A limo driver. That made sense. Made more sense than the rogue government agent theory. And it would explain the Lincoln Town Car . . . and the tinted windows . . . and the quick carwash . . . and the mirrored sunglasses, too. A friggin' limo driver—I did not see that coming.

"What do you do?" Tony asked.

"Kind of seeing what's out there. I'm in need of a new career direction."

"Want to be a limo driver?" he asked.

"Isn't it difficult?"

"Not really."

"Sure, OK."

And that's more or less how I became a chauffeur. That was the new direction my career compass took. Tony drove me up to his boss's house in the Hollywood Hills that evening, and the interview process consisted of Marv, the boss, blurting out various landmark locations around Los Angeles and me explaining how I'd drive there. After he was satisfied with my completely fictitious shortcut to the Los Angeles airport, Marv handed me a boxy cellular phone and a set of car keys.

"Remember, that Lincoln is for work use only; no personal use. I keep track of every mile on that motherfucker, so I'll know. And save all your gas receipts or I won't reimburse you."

"Completely understood."

"And wash that fucking Lincoln every day. Tony'll show you some tricks. And no smoking in it."

"Okay."

"And . . . do you have a black suit you can wear? Green's not really going to work."

"I'll take care of it."

"Good. Do it today," he replied. "You're on-call from here forward. You're like a paramedic. That Lincoln is your ambulance. So park it close to your apartment, and be ready at a moment's notice."

"Will do, Marv."

I shook his hand and rushed out to his driveway where two new Lincoln Town Cars sat glistening side by side in the setting sun. I felt like I had just won a free car on *The Price Is Right*, and I giddily pushed the "unlock" button on the key fob to find out which one would be coming home with me. It would be the Town Car closest to me—license plate MARV12—and I tenderly reclined into the black leather seat and eased the door shut. Reality outside ceased to exist once that tinted window separated our worlds. When I started the gentle purr of the motor, it was as if I had sat down inside a luxurious spacecraft. The entire instrument panel was digital and quite colorful and illustrated every mile-per-gallon and rotation-per-minute in crisp, electric numerals; the gas gauge actually displayed onscreen exactly how many miles I would be able to drive before I had to fill up again; the heater and air conditioner were not the typical on/off and defrost buttons but digital thermostats equipped to set different temperatures for different seats. This car was my KITT and I was its Michael Knight. Everything had a button or an illuminated red gauge or a fitted leather sheath. It was only 1998 outside this tinted window, but to me it looked like the twenty-first century had already paid a visit to Lincoln Motors. I adjusted the side mirrors before running my hand over the polished black leather dashboard and then the black leather passenger seat. She was like a shiny, sophisticated shadow car, with a seat more comfortable and comforting than any sofa I had ever sat in. This car was all class.

I drove to the Salvation Army and pieced together a black suit for $14, then took a shortcut to my side of Hollywood so I could drive by a few of my friends' apartments, call them on the cell phone, and have them look out their windows at their classy friend in a classy Lincoln driving by. When I got home, I parked the Lincoln right behind my Celica then stood in the middle of the street and compared them both like a father standing over a firstborn and a bastard. I checked to make sure The Club was still securely on the Celica's steering wheel—albeit much looser this time—before shaking my head disapprovingly at it and walking up to my apartment for the night.

* * *

Marv called me a couple of days later and gave me my instructions for picking up Ed Warding from the airport. After getting into my mostly black suit and hustling out the door, I realized that my fabricated route to the airport would never have worked in the line of duty. It provided a decent, traffic-free tour of the coastline but did very little else in getting me to my intended destination. Luckily, Mr. Warding's flight was delayed, so I arrived right on time to retrieve him. I used a white piece of paper from my clipboard to write MR. WARDING in big bold letters, and I waited between the arrival gate and baggage claim with my sign at my chest. A well-dressed man in his late 50s walked over and handed me his two suitcases. What an asshole, I thought to myself. No "Hello" or "Good to meet you," just two armfuls of his clothes.

I had already forgotten his name by the time I ran back to the Lincoln and brought it around to the curb to pick him up. I searched my clipboard and pockets after lifting his suitcases into the trunk, but found no clue as to whom I was driving as well as to where I was supposed to be driving him. Then I remembered that the piece of paper that I had used to write his name on in big bold letters was the same piece of paper that contained all of that relevant information. Then I remembered crumpling that information-laden piece of paper into a ball and hastily tossing it under the car parked next to mine in the parking garage. And I remember feeling kind of bad about littering but not bad enough to bend down and pick it back up. I suppose justice was served on that one.

I closed the trunk and deliberated what to do before beginning this voyage of mystery. I couldn't ask the client what his name was and where he wanted to go; I would look as unprofessional as they come. And I couldn't call Marvin or he'd probably yell at me and take away my new Lincoln. KITT would know how to handle this—I was half-tempted to speak into my wristwatch communicator to remotely access KITT's hard drive and have him activate his brain-wave-perception device to read the mind of the anonymous client in the backseat, but I was a grown man and I was in public, so I decided against it.

No, I'd have to sort this one out on my own. This is adult time. Alright, let's start with the client's name first: Warren . . . Warren Harding . . . Warren Harren . . . Ward . . . Harrington Ward . . . Harrington Ward might be it. Or Warren Harris. Warren Harris might be it. Damn, I had drifted too far from shore—too many possibilities had tainted the whole pot. Alright, let's just nod a lot. Or, even better, I could just go with "Sir." Sir was perfect! I was sure he would appreciate being called "Sir." Now I just had to remember where I was driving him to . . . a hotel . . . the studios . . . some fancy home? Where was Sir going to . . . ?

At that point, the backseat window rolled down and the client stretched his head out until he found me leaning against the back of the car and staring up. His eyes were red and tired, and he loosened his necktie with a quick, angry tug. "Hey, buddy, come on! We gonna do this thing? Jesus Christ . . ."

"Yes, yes . . . just . . . checking this out," I quickly replied. What an asshole. I'd be damned if I called this guy

Sir now. Calling someone Sir was a sign of respect, and this chump hadn't earned my respect by rushing my thought process. Sure, I'll drive you around in my new Lincoln, but I won't be calling you anything remotely near Sir. As a matter of fact, if "buddy" is good enough to call me, it's good enough to call you too. Issue resolved, buddy.

The Lincoln started up with a soft, elegant shudder, and we eased into the herd of cars exiting the airport toward Beverly Hills. The odds were in my favor that he was headed somewhere in that city. Now I just had to finesse an exact address out of him.

"There's a *USA Today* on the seat back there," I offered with a glance of my sunglasses in the rearview mirror. Catch more flies with honey, I surmised.

He ruffled the already-opened Business Section and snapped, "Yeah."

What a dick. I needed to try a new angle. "Is there anywhere new on the agenda? Or just . . ." I let it trail off at the end hoping he would fill in the blank.

"Just take me to whatever address my office gave you, alright!" He replied with a tone and flair that more than implied that he wasn't going to say another word without it coming out as a shout.

"Sure thing . . . buddy." I had paused too long between "thing" and "buddy," and I heard the newspaper descend loudly to his lap. I chose to ignore it and didn't look in the rearview mirror, but at least now I had established that I was the type of chauffeur that called his fares "buddy" instead of mister or sir. I could probably call him buddy again and again now, and instead of being rude I was just being weirdly courteous, like a bereaved grandparent living in the spare bedroom.

I was going to make another attempt at getting the address again but the boxy black cellular phone rang from the passenger seat beside me. I flipped it open and answered it.

"Yes, this is Brandon."

"It's Marv. How'd it go? You got him?"

"Oh yes, fine, Marv. Everything's fine."

"You got him there with you? He's there?"

"Yes, the client and I are heading to the destination as we speak."

"Good, good," Marv replied after a lengthy pause. "So everything's fine then, and you're taking him to his . . . destination then?"

"Affirmative. And . . . just to verify, what address do you have there, Marv?" I asked with just the perfect blend of concern and apprehension in my voice. "Just to verify." Oh yeah, problem solved. Chalk one up for the new chauffeur.

"The . . . the . . . to verify . . . yeah, that's smart, let's see here," Marv said, and I heard papers shuffling across his desk. "Who do you have again? What's his name?"

Shit. Shit. Shit. Shit. Backfire. I couldn't tell Marv that I had the man I now refer to as "buddy" in my car. I somehow had to fool Marv into thinking that I knew who this guy in my backseat was while continuing to fool the guy in the backseat that I knew where I was taking him. There was only one way to fix getting caught in a lie, and that was to lie just a little more to get out of it. I pretended to flip through papers on my clipboard while mumbling isolated facts and sounds of hesitation into the phone, hoping Marv would chime in with the answers.

"Let's see here . . . American . . . Airlines . . . 11:30 . . . in the . . . morning—traffic coming up here, Marv, don't want to take my eyes off the road here—Okay . . . looking back at . . . clipboard . . . American . . . Airlines . . ."

"Ed Warding, right?" Marv exclaimed.

"Yes! Yes, that would be the one!" I replied a little too ecstatically. "Mr. Warding is who is here with me."

"And he's going to . . . to . . . he's going to NBC," Marv said after some more papers were shuffled around on his end. "He's doing some news interview. Is that what you have? You have NBC, right? "

"Yes, NBC would be the same destination as I have written here. And this is the NBC on . . . on . . . on . . . traffic coming up here, Marv, can't look at my notes . . . keeping eyes on the road . . . the one on . . . on . . ."

"On 3rd street, in Santa Monica." Marv sounded concerned now, "That's what you have, right? Am I wrong here? Did he tell you something different? Is he telling you some place different? They have to pay for that! You tell him! You tell him!"

"No, no, we're all on the same page here, Marv. Everything's fine. I'll have Mr. Warren there in about 10 minutes."

"Warding," I heard from the backseat. "It's Warding."

I cupped the phone and gave Mr. Warding a glance of my sunglasses in the rearview, "Yes, Mr. Warding, that's affirmative. We're on our way."

"And it's definitely not *buddy*," he added before going back to his newspaper.

"What?! What is he saying?!" Marv screamed into the phone. "He doesn't want to pay? Is that what he's saying?"

"No, nothing like that. Oh, here comes the tunnel—" I said just before hanging up.

From that moment on, the remainder of my first gig

as a chauffeur was a breeze. I dropped Mr. Warding off at the studio, read the *USA Today* while he did the interview, then took him to his hotel in Beverly Hills. Even scored a $5 tip at the end of it. And I made it home in time to watch *Jeopardy*, the virginity of my first fare finally taken.

My next assignment would prove to be a little more involved than my previous one. It began not with the question of whether I was ready to handle driving a long limousine, and not even whether I was ready to drive that long limousine to another state—but my third assignment began with the odd question of: "Do you listen to the rap music?"

"No, not really," I replied to Marv.

"That's fine," he said. "I ask because the next pickup is a rap band. The Wing-Wang Boys or something. Hold on, I got the name here . . ." Papers shuffled across his desk again. "The Woo-Ting Clan, that's their name."

"Okay, I've heard of them."

"Are they any good?"

"They're popular. I don't know if they're any good, though."

"Well, you'll be taking them to Las Vegas for some fashion award show for that music TV," he said. "I guess they're pretty big shit. Staying at Caesar's Palace afterward. It's a two-day job. Drive up there today, do the award show tonight, you all have rooms at Caesar's, then you drive them back tomorrow afternoon. This is a big job, kid. The pay is tasty. You good?"

Vegas? Oh yeah, I was good. Real good.

I picked up that extremely long limo from a parking garage in Beverly Hills and cautiously drove it up and down every concrete floor a number of times before feeling confident enough to take it on the open road. Once at the hotel, it wasn't difficult to spot The Woo-Ting Clan—I grew concerned about that on the drive over; the only things I had really known about them were A) they were black, B) they wore lots of camouflage clothing, and C) they would be in a posse. And that's kind of what emerged from the hotel lobby, in a surrealist sort of way. Four gangsta-looking guys in fluorescent orange and pink camouflage outfits pulled their suitcases to the valet entrance, each wearing a neck full of jewelry and a big yellow pair of goggles over their eyes. They looked like cartoon hunters off for a big-game weekend in Oz. Or an underwater welding team in the Ocean of Day-Glo.

They rolled their suitcases to the limo and let me toss them in the trunk while they watched, then they stood by the closed back door until I opened it for them. Then they all shared a good long laugh at the concept of a white man having to open the door for black men.

"It's like *Driving Miss Daisy* and shit!" one of them remarked.

Another, already sitting inside, shouted out, "More like *Driving Miss Cracka*!"

I really wanted to lean into the back of that limousine and explain that it was Miss Daisy who was being driven— that *they* were the Miss Daisy, or the Miss Cracka, in this equation—but I did not. I let them have their fun; their people had waited a few hundred years for it, so I gave it to them. But the fourth and last Woo-Ting Clan member, the one they called Ol' Dirty Prick, paused before getting into the limo, and he turned back and looked at me holding open the door for him. He cocked his head to the side and examined my face with his bulbous yellow eyes.

"You look like . . . who is that?" he tapped his lip and

asked me. "That motherfuckin' actor . . . you look like . . . like . . ."

With my hair slicked back, like it was then, I sometimes resembled a malnourished Nicolas Cage, according to a few ladyfriends. We shared the same widow's peak and nose, I think it was. I wasn't sure but I had heard it more than a few times in the past. So that's what I presumed Ol' Dirty Prick was getting at, that I looked like Nic Cage.

I was just about to end his guessing charade when he beat me to the punch, but his answer was quite different from the one I was expecting. "Oh man, this motherfucker look like Judge Reinhold! That motherfucker from *Beverly Hills Cop* and shit. The dork from um . . . *Fast Times at Ridgemont High*, man! Just like him!"

He finally took his seat in the back and I closed the door. Judge Reinhold? Was he serious? Not to discredit Judge Reinhold as an actor in any way, but he was not the coolest nor the most attractive man working in Hollywood. And he really was, like Ol' Dirty Prick pointed out, a dork. Goofy even comes to mind. Was he right, or did all us Germanic white guys look alike to a man of color? Or was he just trying to insult me, like me telling him that he resembled a Gary Coleman of regular height? I wasn't sure which way to take the Judge Reinhold comment but, regardless, that Ol' Dirty Prick really knew his '80s movies.

They were a rowdy bunch as we pulled onto the freeway for our five-hour drive ahead, and they proceeded to blast songs from their new album in the back after raising the bass as high as it would go. They all lit cigarettes at the same time, so I surreptitiously lit my own and kept it down by my thigh and out of sight. The limo soon filled with a putrid, chemical-smelling smoke, which was exacerbated by the fact that none of them lowered any windows. The acrid smelling cloud wasn't pot—I was very familiar with the way pot smelled and could even distinguish California strains from Canada's through scent alone. It wasn't anything in the cocaine family—*that* smell you never forgot. It definitely wasn't an opiate. Were they smoking methamphetamines, maybe? Foreign cigarettes? Were the leather seats burning? Whatever it was, it was making me as high as a kite and quite nauseous. Before I could poke my head through the partition to inquire what the smell was, somebody else back there beat me to it.

"It's fucking formaldehyde, man!" the one they called Ghost Boy shouted. "You dip a cigarette into that shit, let it dry, and it'll fuck you up, dog. Fucking formaldehyde . . ."

"That shit is what they put in corpses, man!" angrily replied the member whose name I think was R.I.P. "What the fuck? You're gonna kill us!"

"I know, bro . . ." Ghost Boy slurred with a long toothy smile. "But you're high, though. Shit's heavy, man. I got a whole jug of this shit at my place."

Fuck that noise. I pushed a little button on the dashboard and the black partition rose between the driver's compartment and the cabin, and I quickly lowered the windows up front so I could breathe. There were no complaints from the Clan about the divider now up between us, so I found a station that played BBC news and sipped from my thermos of coffee and smoked cigarettes all the way to Sin City in my own isolated cockpit.

Once at the Las Vegas Convention Center, I followed the line of limos through the semifilled parking lot to the front doors, where a handful of photographers and cameramen stood beside a dozen big security guards in headsets.

Again, I jumped out, ran around to the other side of the limo and opened the back door—like a good Miss Cracka—and received a faceful of blinding camera flashes once the Clan stepped onto the curb. Before they could disappear into the throng of photographers, fans, and journalists, I grabbed the last one—Ol' Dirty Prick, I think it was—by the arm and asked, "So, what time should I pick you up?"

"I don't know, man!" he yanked his arm away and shouted. "Wait your Judge Reinhold ass over there with all the other limos!" He pointed to a long stretch of desert road just beyond the enormous parking lot, where forty or so other limos sat parked in a perfect line.

"Do you want to just call me when you're finished?" I asked. "I have a phone with me."

"I'm performing on stage, motherfucker!" he shouted back. "I don't do shit like call the limo man! Just look for us!"

"What about someone from your posse? Could they call me when you guys are done?" I attempted, but he had already started answering questions from some TV entertainment show host.

Another limo pulled up behind me and honked, and I looked over to find three more limos waiting behind that one. So I jumped back inside and drove across the parking lot to the barren lane of limos and took my spot at the very end, exactly forty-three limousine lengths from the middle of nowhere. I stepped outside and tried to assess how far I was from where I had just dropped them off, but it was too far to make out anything but the occasional camera flash. There was no way I would be able to see them coming out. Ol' Dirty Prick had it wrong. I debated the dilemma and came to the conclusion that I should just follow the herd.

Once the show ended, all the celebrities would probably pour out together, and then all of the limos would leave in one long mass exodus to pick each one up. Just a nice game of follow-the-leader. It sounded logical enough for the time being.

One topic they never went over in the Limo Driver's Field Manual was what to do if you had to go to the bathroom. It was at least a mile walk back to the convention center, which was out of the question wearing a black suit in that desert heat. There were no fast-food restaurants in sight; no hotels, no casinos anywhere. I even lowered my urination standards, but trying to take an outdoor leak in Las Vegas proved nearly impossible: There were no trees in a desert, no secluded alleyways, and no trash bins anywhere—just sand and limousines as far as the eye could see. I considered the old "open the trunk and pretend to look for something but really be pissing near the bumper" trick, but three limos had parked behind me and three pairs of mirrored sunglasses were now watching me from behind three windshields. I felt like Morpheus about to get thumped by a handful of rogue Agent Smiths.

I couldn't wait any longer. My stomach and groin were aching from an enlarged bladder, and I could feel the early trickles of pee dampening the front of my underwear. I only had one option left: pee in the limo. Not knowing proper limo driver protocol, I lowered the partition and crawled through to the cabin and looked around for any large cups or beer bottles lying around, but the Clan apparently weren't big drinkers. The only thing remotely close were the three lowball glasses anchored into a minibar by a bottle of scotch. That would not suffice; I would have to improvise. I got onto my knees and cracked open the back door about three inches, then, after making certain that every window surrounding me was tinted, I unzipped, aimed, and tinkled through the narrow opening. Aside from a desert breeze shutting the door midstream, the operation was a success. I used Ghost Boy's pink camouflage sweater to dry off the door then tossed it onto the floor by some candy wrappers. Judge Reinhold *that*, fucker!

I had never before been in the back of a limousine and, whether it was the sudden peaceful feeling of a deflated bladder or the residue in the air of the formaldehyde cigarettes, I melted into the soft leather sofa-like seat and felt a sense of tranquility that I hadn't felt in years. I glanced through the tinted windows at all of the shuffling chauffeurs in black suits making small talk with one another outside, or cleaning their windows free from bugs and sand, or sipping coffee and talking on cell phones from their bumpers. Then I looked around inside the cabin of my limo. I had seclusion, I had privacy, I had a minibar, I had a leather sofa-like seat, and I had a television imbedded into the wall. *This* was living, I concluded. To hell with your small talk, limo drivers. Sing your chin music to one another and share your stories of celebrities and freeway traffic, because this particular chauffeur was going to relax, watch some TV, and have a well-earned drink.

I caught the last half of *Jaws* only to find *Jaws II* next on the roster of whatever station this little antennae TV picked up, so I poured another scotch in honor of Chief Brody returning to the waters of Amity. At just about the same time the first teenager was pulled underwater, a handful of limos left our herd to return to the convention center. So I poured the rest of my scotch out the back door, crawled back into the driver's seat, and followed them in. The crowd of bystanders and cameramen had doubled in size at the front doors of the convention center, and I slowly and very carefully drove through the horde trying to catch a glimpse of orange and pink camouflage. But they were nowhere to be found, so I drove back through the enormous parking lot and returned to my original spot among the line of parked limos on the lonely street of servitude. I crawled back into the cabin, poured another small scotch, and resumed my spot on the sofa-like seat with *Jaws II*. Chief Brody eventually killed the big shark for the second time, signaling that it had been about three hours and change since the fashion show had started. Another succession of limos then pulled out of the line and returned to the convention center. I checked my watch to find that 40 minutes had passed since my first attempt, so I crawled back into the front and followed the last limo back to the crowd at the entrance. But, just like the first attempt, no Woo-Ting Clan waiting for me. So I sped off back to Limo Boulevard and took a vacated spot about twenty feet from the front. I stayed behind the steering wheel this time because limousines were beginning to break from formation every minute or two, and I knew the show would soon be ending.

By the time I finished another cigarette, two-thirds of my black-suited people had fled our road—a mere twelve or thirteen limos were all that was left of us. Cars were also beginning to exit the parking lot in boulevard-long lines, and pedestrians soon filled the streets around us—the fashion show had surely ended by that point. Three more limos turned on their headlights and drove to the convention center, so I started up my stretch and followed them back to the entrance. Most of the photographers and camera crews had already left because the majority of celebrities had gone, so I had a perfect view of the entryway as I pulled up. And yet again, no Woo-Ting Clan anywhere in sight. I idled there for a few minutes hoping they would emerge, but two drunks walked by and threw some type of food at my limo, so I sped off back to Limo Road to find it completely empty of all limousines. But I parked there anyway.

It was 1:00 in the morning when I smoked my last cigarette of the pack. I drove around until finding a liquor store, bought two packs of Camels, beef jerky, and some candy bars for dinner, and returned to the parking lot minutes later. Most of the cars had left. Almost all of the overhead lights had been turned off, and the only signs of life were a few straggling audience members and a lone security guard waving a flashlight toward the last available exit.

I was convinced that I had missed the Clan; that they had somehow not seen me when they left and took a taxi to the hotel. If that was the case, though, I figured Marv would have called to chew my ass off by now. So I waited again, but this time parked right at the front doors of the convention center. If they were still in there, they would have to run right into me. There was no way I could miss them now. I checked my watch to find it nearly 2:00 a.m., almost 10 hours since I'd had anything but 35 cigarettes and a candy bar in my stomach. Just as my eyes fluttered closed for a little malnourished nap, the back door sprang open and the cabin suddenly filled with a dozen loud, laughing people. I was startled awake and couldn't make out who was back there—some drunks, the wrong band, a gang—but then I heard someone shout, "Hotel, motherfucker!" and I knew my boys were back safely inside.

I dropped them off at the lobby of Caesar's Palace, parked the limo, and checked in to my room. I love hotel rooms. I love the freshness of them; I love the crisp, laundered sheets;

I love the free HBO and Showtime; I love the pens and polite tablets with hotel logos, and I love taking them. I love the little individual bottles of shampoo and conditioner and the strong jets in the shower. I love the deep silence of a hotel room; I love putting the DO NOT DISTURB sign on the front door and resting assured that I would not be disturbed. I love everything a hotel room has to offer, and the only way I could love it any more was if someone else was paying for it, like this one.

It wasn't more than 10 minutes after brushing my teeth and settling into bed with my HBO when I heard a knock at the door. I sat upright in bed but didn't move beyond that. Who would dare knock on the door of a hotel resident with a DO NOT DISTURB sign clearly posted? It was well after 3:00 in the morning and, even for Las Vegas, that was pretty damn late. Perhaps it was a mistake? Maybe some drunk mistook my door for where the party was? Well, give it a second . . . quiet again . . . might be safe now to recline back into bed and fall—knock, knock, knock, knock. BAM, BAM, BAM.

I jumped out of bed and opened the door to find two of the Woo-Ting members swaying alongside two promiscuous-looking women wearing silver dresses that hugged every ripple and curve of their unflattering bodies like sausage lining.

"What's the deal?" I said after partially closing the door to conceal the briefs that I thought were boxers.

"Hey, Reinhold, can we . . . ?" Ol' Dirty Prick raised a thick brown joint at me.

"There's forty motherfuckers in our room right now," R.I.P. added. "And we just wanted to smoke a little with these fine ladies somewhere chill for five minutes."

"You mean here? It's not that shit from the limo, is it?" I asked.

"No, no, this shit's chronic, man." Ol' Dirty Prick ran the joint under his nose and smiled. "We'll just chill here for a sec, man. It'll be cool."

He had already angled himself past the door by the time he finished what he was saying, so I opened it all the way and went into the bathroom to put on pants and a shirt. When I came back out, all four were lying on my bed and watching the Bruce Willis movie that I had put on, so I sat down in the chair by the window. I watched the joint pass between them several times before Ol' Dirty Prick finally noticed me sitting just a few feet across from them. I hoped he was finally going to pass it my way, but the scowl should have been a good indicator that he wouldn't be.

"What the fuck?" he shouted. "Why are you still here? You said we could have your room!"

"I said you could smoke that joint in my room," I corrected him.

"Naw, naw, naw, naw! We're paying for this shit!" he shouted again. "This here is *my* room now!"

"No, it's actually not." I corrected him again. "Music TV is paying for this room—for *my* room—as well as for my limo service. You really didn't pay for a damn thing here."

"You even act like Reinhold . . . all whiny and shit!" Ol' Dirty Prick said before leaning back against the headrest of my bed, showing no signs of leaving any time soon.

"Hey, let's all just be cool, alright?" R.I.P. said after running his hand up the back of the bare leg of the lady lying beside him. "We're just having some fun here."

They proceeded to spend the next 20 minutes smoking

that joint without once passing it to me. I puffed away at a cigarette and pretended to be engrossed by this latest *Die Hard* sequel on the TV while they lounged on my comfortable bed and did the same. Then Ol' Dirty Prick finally snubbed out the end of the joint on the wooden bedside drawer, and Bruce Willis finally got the bad guy. But the two lovely couples wrapping themselves in my blankets made no attempt at leaving either my room or my bed. Fuckers even had their heads on my pillows.

It was officially 4:00 in the morning, and I refused to take any more of this. I was off the clock, and these momentary celebrities were now just robbing an honest hardworking man of a good night of sleep. The women were beginning to doze off and the guys looked as if that was their plan, so I stood up and clapped my hands twice, which was something that always worked on me when I was a kid.

"Alright, time for you guys to go now," I exclaimed.

All four ignored me so I shook Ol' Dirty Prick's shoulder and said it again. He violently pushed my hand away and shouted, "Don't you ever fucking touch me again!"

I was exhausted and angry and hungry and I wanted nothing more than to punch him square in the face, but I knew that that would probably be the only punch I landed, and the remaining punches would all be showered upon me. So I leaned down closer to the bed, just a few inches from his face, and calmly said, "Get out of my bed. And then get out of my room. I want to go to sleep."

We did that thing that animals do, where you stare at each other until either a fight erupts or someone acquiesces. But in this case, one of the ladies threw up into her hand and ran it to the bathroom. So R.I.P. grabbed the other lady's hand

and walked her to the door while Ol' Dirty Prick shook his head at me, retrieved his sick gal from around the shitter, and finally left.

I tried to settle back into bed but my veins were pumping with adrenaline and my pillows smelled like perm chemicals and grape smoke. But they had left, and the room was again mine; to the victor go the spoils. Although they had kept me up past 4:00 in the morning, I could still get a solid eight hours of sleep in and some time at the craps tables before we had to return back to Los Angeles. The Vegas trip wasn't completely lost. I flipped through the channels until finding a decent horror film on TNT, and when I went to return the remote control to the bedside table I found the stubbed-out roach from their joint. It was like my severance pay. Thanks, Ol' Dirty Prick. I lit it up and, for a nubby little roach, it offered me many, many good hits. I puffed away at it until it warmed my thumb and index finger then I stubbed it out in the same spot my predecessor did. When I tuned back to the movie, I was as stoned as a caveman fight in a gulley of hand-sized rocks. The gentle tug of honest fatigue finally began to overtake me, and I felt my eyes softly fight to stay open before succumbing to the warm, welcoming pool of intoxicated hotel slumber.

BAM, BAM, BAM, BAM rattled the door. My eyes flew open and my heart pounded in my chest—the kind of palpitation that only happens when being startled awake in the middle of a short nap. The sun was just barely beginning to rise through the window—it was still dark in the room aside from the TV's glow. BAM, BAM, BAM, BAM at the door again. No, no, no, not this time, Ol' Dirty Prick. You can go fuck your drunk lady in your own room. I wouldn't be falling for that shit again. I smothered my head under the pillow and drifted back to sleep. I vaguely recall hearing some more muted knocks at the door, but it wasn't until someone wiggled my bare foot that I awoke. I tore the pillow from my face and shot upright to find the hotel manager and all four of the Woo-Ting Clan standing at the foot of my bed. The reality of the situation didn't register right away, and I glanced at each and every face surrounding me trying to find an answer to a question that I couldn't put into words. "Is it?" was all that I could ask.

"Sir, Mr. Reinhold, I apologize for entering your room like this," the suited manager said apologetically, "but they said you were their chauffeur, and they couldn't get a hold of you."

"We're leaving!" R.I.P shouted at me from behind the manager. "Grab your shit and let's go!"

"Music TV might have paid for this shit, Reinhold," Ol' Dirty Prick then said, "but I say when we leave! So go bring the limo around and meet us downstairs in 10 minutes. You're driving us home now, Miss Daisy."

"Yeah, it's too hard to sleep in this hotel!" one of them added with a sneer.

They left in a herd of laughter accented by an apologetic smile from the hotel manager. Touché, Ol' Dirty Prick, touché—didn't see that one coming. I brewed a minipot of coffee, splashed my face, and packed up my belongings in 7 minutes, then retrieved the limo and pulled it around to the front of the hotel in just under 12 minutes. The Clan came out 20 minutes later and, after I loaded their luggage into the trunk and held the back door open for them, I leaned into the cabin and informed them, "You all might want to wear your seatbelts for *this* ride."

I got in front and raised the partition between us and

didn't lower it again until it was time to say, "We're home." As all four slowly wriggled awake on the long leather seats in the cabin, I pulled their luggage from the trunk and sat it onto the curb by the back bumper. I then opened their back-door and returned to my driver's seat and smoked a cigarette until the last member vacated the limo. All four stood beside their luggage on the curb, and I think they were waiting for me to carry their suitcases into the hotel lobby for them. But that wasn't going to work for me. I tapped on the gas pedal just enough to jolt the car forward, which slammed the back door shut. Then I drove off and left them standing there with raised arms and colorful insults.

Marv called minutes later, just after I had parked the limo back inside its garage, and asked if I had the energy to do another job that afternoon. I explained an abridged version of my night with the Woo-Ting Clan to him, and he explained to me that this next gig would pay $145 and it didn't involve leaving Hollywood. So I agreed. I switched into my Lincoln Town Car and drove back to my apartment, tried to take a nap but couldn't, and instead took two showers, ate a TV dinner, and brewed a half-pot of Starbuck's French Roast. When I returned to the parking garage later that afternoon to retrieve the limo, the Vegas weekend finally began to take its toll on me. I could feel my motor skills hampered by fatigue; I began yawning uncontrollably and my eyes wouldn't stop tearing up. Not normally two points that I would mention as vital to a story, but it does lend itself to the reason I didn't see the large concrete pillar at the passenger side of the limo. It was a horrifying sound as large ribbons of navy blue steel tore off from the back door and coiled in jagged wave-like peels near the wheel well. And even more horrifying than the sound of that steel shredding was the sound of Marv taking the news. He began yelling into the cell phone as soon as I said it and didn't stop for 10 minutes.

Marv said he had rented out all of his other limos for the night, and this next fare—the up-and-coming Caucasian hip-hop star Johnnie G—was supposed to have been a big favor for a big client at Capitol Records. So I lied a little and told Marv the damage on the limo wasn't all that bad and wouldn't be very noticeable at night. And he believed me enough to let me finish the job. I was able to conceal the damaged back door from Johnnie G and his publicist and manager when I picked them up from a home in Encino, but arriving at the Grammys was an entirely different affair.

There was only one way up to that giant red carpet, and that was straight through the flashing, cheering madness of a very well-lit welcoming committee of television crews, international press agents, reporters, cameramen, fans, and security personnel. Before I could yell into the back to tell Johnnie G that the back door facing all those flashing bulbs and adoring fans wasn't going to open no matter how hard he tried, he continued trying nonetheless. So I opened my own door and hustled the few feet to the driver's side backdoor—the door facing *away* from the crowd—and opened it for them. Johnnie G crawled out with a confused expression followed by his equally confused manager and publicist. The cameras began flashing madly as they circled behind the limo to get to the red carpet, where a barrage of laughter and finger pointing greeted them. It was at that point that Johnnie G noticed the obliterated back door with its trestles of ripped blue steel forming what looked to be a giant three-fingered fist. Then Marv noticed the same thing as he watched it all on live TV coverage from his home, and he called me minutes later to fire me.

That next day, I drove my Lincoln Town Car back up to Marv's house in the hills, and I parked it back in the driveway just where I had found it. I ran my palm over that glossy black steering wheel one last time before walking down to Sunset Blvd. and hopping on the bus in my black suit and mirrored sunglasses.

When I got home a little later, my dusty Celica was still parked in the same spot as when the horn had bellowed out so violently two weeks before. I guess I hadn't even touched it since becoming a chauffeur. I suppose it's like returning to an old, fat wife after carrying on a lurid affair with a beautiful woman half her age—it just wasn't the same, and could never ever be the same again. But she was still my wife, so I sat down behind her wheel and started her up. It wasn't that I hated my Celica now, but I blamed her for all that had happened, and all I could now see were her faults: both bumpers were missing, the vinyl seats were ripped to hell, the windshield was cracked, the dashboard was blue and plastic and tattered from the sun, that stupid The Club was still on its steering wheel, and it reeked of gasoline at every rev.

After the Celica had a few minutes to warm up, she must have noticed the sad expression I now carried. In a soft, forgiving tone she said, "You are one of us, lover. We're not the flashy type. We are the same, you and me."

"Never," I whispered back.

"Did you have a good time? How was she? Did you like how she handled?" she began to ridicule me.

"You haven't earned the right to call her 'she,'" I roared at the Celica.

"Well, I'm glad you're back, regardless," she added very sweetly. "We'll always have the horn night."

I turned off the ignition and whispered, "Yeah, we'll *always* have that, honey." Then I removed The Club from her steering wheel, unlocked all the doors, and went up to my apartment. My days as a swinging chauffeur had officially ended.

THE BLESSED DO-OVER

JOB #74

Oh, Jesus. Thirty-seven years old. Thirty-seven years old and unemployed. Again. Not the 37 part but the *unemployed* part. Between jobs, we say. We don't say we're unemployed or out of work, and we definitely don't say that we got fired. If we got laid off, we'll sometimes say that. But, for the most part, we say we're *between* positions, between jobs, between *things*. We, the people in our apartments during the daytime, that is. We, the neighbors that stream Netflix movies on our laptops at all hours of the night. We, the people who not only look forward to wine stores that offer free wine tastings but require it to occasionally leave the apartment to socialize. We are the citizens in the windows; the ghosts of the waking hours. We are the ones who have the time to watch the crows bathe in puddles of roof water, to watch the garbageman perform his entire task, to watch the old shopkeeper sweep cigarette butts from the sidewalk in front of his store every afternoon. We are the people who have the time.

But to say we're "between" things implied there were things at both sides—both behind and ahead, past and future. It was optimistic on the part of the speaker to assume that there would be some form of a job for them at some point in their future. Behind, most definitely, but ahead, that was pure speculation. Odds were, there *would* be something coming up. It might not be the coolest job in the annals of employment, but it would keep a roof overhead and the belly from grumbling. But still, it was an assumption to think that a job would most definitely be in the future. It was wishful thinking. Pure speculation.

This would be my 74th wishful thought. Seventy-three prior bouts of wishful thinking had kept me afloat and entertained for the better part of the past 18 years. But this upcoming 74th job—this *thing* at the far end of my "between things"—would be different from the others. It would be my first job as a resident of Seattle. Although it took me 36.9 years to do it, I had finally figured out how to unfasten the glimmering shackles of the Golden State. And I moved 1,100 miles north before it noticed that I was gone.

"From where?" always seemed to follow that disclosure.

"Los Angeles," my reply.

And then, without hesitation or prejudice to the person speaking, followed the age-old question: "Ummm . . . why?"

My first few weeks here in Seattle prompted my explanation of "wanting a do-over." I would describe in great detail how I had grown to abhor my hometown of Los Angeles; that I had to get out before it was too late. So I proudly explained to my new neighbors and inquisitive people in bars and bookstores that in a two-week period I had made the decision to move, quit my job, sold my pre-owned luxury car back to CarMax for a lot less than I bought it for, sold all my furniture at a garage sale, found an apartment in Seattle online, mailed a deposit check, and then split. I packed the remainder of my clothes, my fishing poles, a rug, my TV, my Ruger 357 Magnum, and my laptop into a rental car, strapped my new mattress and box spring to the roof, drove the 20 hours up to the Emerald City, and arrived the day before my 37th birthday. The do-over. Life reinvented in 14 days. Adulthood refurbished.

Then, at about the one-month mark of this same question, I realized that their "why?" didn't really pertain to why I wanted a life do-over, but why I chose *Seattle* to do it over in—Seattle instead of *anywhere* else in the continental United States. The rain, they say. It's always raining here. Why would you choose to leave a place that's always sunny for a place that's always gray and raining? I never had a good answer for that. I had my reasons—my many reasons why I chose Seattle—but these new people in my life hadn't earned the right to know me that well. Maybe if we're still friends after a few more months, then maybe I'll tell them that Los Angeles had been ripping my heart out for years; that Los Angeles had slowly been shaving off pieces of my soul and replacing the bare patches with celebrity endorsements and pre-owned Lexuses and more internal conversations than external ones. Maybe at that few-month mark of friendship I'll also tell them that I needed to scare the shit out of myself; that I had grown too complacent with my existence and needed to shake things up by moving to a state where I didn't know a single person and had no job lined up—and with just under $3,800 in my savings account. I wanted to test myself, see if I could do it; see if I could just pack up and start over someplace new. I wanted to redecorate my existence. If I had revealed that much to these friends who had made it to the few-month mark then I would also tell them that I chose to quit a $75,000-a-year job in a terrible recession just to make the Seattle move possible. I would, of course, omit the fact about the Human Resources department discovering my bachelor's degree in communications was just four nicely typed words on a resume. And I would also probably leave out the part about that company urging me to quit on my own accord before they fired and most likely brought me up on criminal charges for false representation. That bit of knowledge would be reserved for the one-year friends. The corporate world is a sham anyways. No one wants to tuck in their shirts.

But the rain. The rain. The question left unanswered. I moved to the rainiest city in the States simply because I came from a city that never saw rain. That's why. There was nothing symbolic behind it. I wanted to be an umbrella type of guy. I wanted to wear scarves with my coats. I wanted all four seasons. So I traded in my sunglasses and T-shirts for fingerless gloves, thermal underwear, and a sinus infection. But I was glad to make the leap. Life is short and, in Los Angeles, summer is long.

The seasons, all four of them—a concept I had never known outside of film and television settings. Back in L.A., the winters were a lot like the springs and falls and autumns: sunny and mostly temperate. On the other hand, the winters of Seattle were like the winters of some Nordic Thor-laden fable, especially to a grown man whose only experience with snow was the fluffy white flocking we put on our artificial Christmas trees as kids (which we also learned some years later caused cancer). That first winter in Seattle was a real eye-opener to the reality of cold. The air outside would turn to ice by 2:00 in the afternoon, and the 90-year-old radiator in my studio apartment gave off as much heat as the stack of books next to it. But where the radiator failed the lack of bed bugs made up for—I'd rather stay cold and unbitten than warm and harvested any day.

For the most part, I guess you could say that I got lucky by moving into the Consultay Apartments in Capitol Hill. Finding that place online was just pure blind luck, too—which, in Christopher-talk, meant it was the second-to-cheapest apartment in the weird part of town. The building was three stories and constructed in the 1920s. It rented mostly to students from one of the nearby colleges. The average age of tenant was 22. Aside from the bearded divorced guy on the first floor and the milfy alcoholic woman who lived in the basement apartment, I was the oldest tenant roaming the halls of that forty-unit complex. The types of guys I knew back in Los Angeles would probably have paid an extra $250 in rent just to live next door to a bunch of cute college girls nearly half their age. But I wasn't one of them. These girls only made me feel older. And lonelier. The young ladies of this peculiar Millennial Generation were just like the throngs of aspiring Hollywood celebrities that I thought I had left behind—with their loud, loud, cackling conversations inside small cafés, graciously allowing everyone in the room the pleasure of hearing an audible version of their Facebook status updates. I came from the older generation of Gen X—the early model of what they're based on now. Sure, we may have slacked and whined a bit during the '80s and '90s, but we got our shit done when it needed to be done. We knew we had to fight to survive, and we did. We were the last real generation to remember a childhood without cell phones and computers, and it showed. We were cut from different casts, our two worlds. The Millennials and the Gen Xers had nothing in common, and neither of us wanted anything to do with one another. We were like werewolves and vampires or the Sharks and the Jets.

But it was a simple glass of Pinot Noir in the apartment courtyard that turned the whole situation around for me. While wallowing at the plastic patio table surrounded by nothing but brick and window, I struck up a conversation about zombie escape plans with a neighbor named Bryan. Bryan then turned me on to our adorable neighbor Mary Beth, who was a student and dead-ringer for Shirley from *Laverne & Shirley*. The three of us started to meet at the patio table for wine, cigarettes, and conversation a few times a week around twilight. Then Mindy, our eccentric neighbor with a flair for camouflaging her weight and insecurities behind gaudy outfits and peacock feathers, started hanging around the courtyard with us. Seth, the apartment manager, started showing up with a six-pack. Steven was a once-in-awhile. And, finally, 20-year-old linguistics major Regan, whom we called "the moocher" for his perfectly timed arrivals at the rolling of the joint, rounded out our cast.

Within a month, the courtyard patio became the communal meeting ground for our every-other-day "jazz, grass, and wine evenings," where age ceased to matter once Stan Getz was on the iPod. We cast out our age prejudices and created a brand new generation at the Consultay Apartments. We created our own temporary generation—an indeterminate layover period where we all chose to dwell in the bedrooms of our lives. It felt like we had all decided to pause time, pause our potential, pause our futures—together. It was a period of life that could have been scribed by Armistead Maupin, where it was just as easy to *get* high with a neighbor as it was to *say* hi. It was the college experience that I had never experienced. The apartment became my dormitory, and the city my new campus. Instead of condemning that younger generation I detested so much, I simply adapted to them like a wolf with housedogs. I was growing backwards, shaving off maturity one month at a time. Those pre-owned cars and 401(k) concerns were drifting further and further away, month after month. I was no longer nearing 40 . . . I was nearing *fuck yeah.*

But even the path to Fuck Yeah had its problems. My savings account had become a part of my tenancy that I referred to as, "That was *so* October." I had to find some work; put a little meat on the rent check. I was barely three months into my new life in Seattle, and my $3,800 surplus had become $2,200 in credit card debt. It seemed the past 90-some days of lounge, libation, and security deposits had taken a heavy toll on my finances. But with a plethora of exotic job experience under my belt, I felt confident I could find some kind of decent employment in my new city—once I really applied myself to looking. Luckily, Craigslist had a Seattle page on their website, so I perused the job postings and sent out four #6 Resumes, four #3 Resumes, a couple of #1s, and topped off the day's search with a wildcard: the new hybrid resume that I had been working on, which briefly highlighted almost all of my various seventy-some jobs.

A full week of Internet job-hunting passed without any returned calls or emails, so I drafted a few more resumes—tailor-made for the Pacific Northwest—and sent them out. I had always assumed by being a very small fish in a big pond called Los Angeles I would automatically become a relatively medium-sized fish in this midsized pond of Seattle. But this was not the case. Living in a miniature metropolis with two large colleges meant having to compete with wave after wave of recently graduated 23-year-olds. My elaborated marketing and advertising experience was no match for a punk kid who was eager to learn and "excited about the possibility of growing with a company." I got a few callbacks the next week and landed a couple of interviews, but those resulted in not having enough html-coding experience—a qualification I could not justifiably lie about because I knew the hard way that I would be expected to perform that duty. Times were beginning to get tight by that first week of November. It wasn't as bad as those dire days of 2002 or 2005, but it was starting to get close. I still had about a thousand dollars of wiggle room left on the Visa; that was at least a solid month's rent and survival right there. But I was quickly bottoming out, and I had made a solemn vow not to return to Los Angeles with my tail between my legs—for at least a year.

The malls were just beginning their ambush of holiday music, which prompted two thoughts as I shopped for a decent shirt to wear on interviews: A) I'd have to worry about buying Christmas gifts at some point, and B) The Christmas season meant plenty of retail jobs.

I was already downtown so I walked west toward the water and stepped into Macy's department store. And low and behold, along with their *own* ambush of holiday harmonies, they were just then starting to hire their seasonal-employee sales force. Almost always, any job involving a cash register and customers was one that I would avoid at all costs. But I knew a little something about department stores and their holiday hiring tactics, as well as a simple way to make a solid week's paycheck without having to do any work. It was a little backdoor trick I developed in my 20s, and it almost always worked at the higher-end department stores, especially about this time of year. But you could use it only once per store nowadays, what with all the computer records and such. But it was simple: Get hired for a temporary Christmas sales position, which is usually pretty easy to do when you hit them right at November; boast of your prior sales experience in men's clothing or home furnishings, so you're assured a solid position on the sales floor; attend the paid week of training, which almost always took place in a large casual room with a giant dry-erase board and a dozen other aspiring salespeople; and then you quit at the end of the paid training week—I prefer doing this part over the phone. No suit and tie, no cash registers, no customers, no confrontations—but $340 of cold, hard cash on its way to you in the mail. Next month's rent would be halfway there just for sitting in a classroom mildly stoned for four and a half days, watching multiple "safety in the workplace" and "proper customer experience" videos on a TV, and pretending to learn all the discount key codes on the cash register. It was just like summer school, only air-conditioned and better dressed.

But that was that. I got my $340. The December rent fund was looking better, and Macy's was forever out of the loop. But I still needed to find work. I could probably pull the same scam at Nordstrom, but I couldn't bullshit the attire. You needed some fancy threads to first get the job at Nordstrom, and all I had were a couple of vintage blazers, a V-neck sweater, and some slacks to a suit that never made it out of Los Angeles. It would cost me more to dress for the part than what I would take home in a week. So I went back to sending out resumes from the "home office" for the next couple of days.

The gods of employment soon took pity upon me in the

form of another seasonal job, but this time for a boutique flower store on the wealthy side of town. It seemed that new hybrid resume I had sent out to a couple of vague "hiring Christmas workers" ads showcased my past floral experience (totally genuine and unadulterated, for the record). I was hired along with twelve other semiqualified ex-flower-store employees to set up floral Christmas decorations inside ritzy hotel lobbies. The pay was decent, the work was occasional, and the job involved working alongside a bunch of older married women who needed some extra money around the holidays—the easiest variety of coworker to keep pace with.

Thanksgiving at the Consultay Apartments was a drunken blur of neighbors, food, and wine, and just what I imagined Thanksgiving to be like for Ezra Pound, Hemingway, and Fitzgerald during their first expatriated year in Paris. But that was about the last I saw of my neighbors until December rolled around; it seemed every hotel in Seattle wanted their lobbies ready for Christmas during that one week between holiday storms. My new coworkers and I mostly worked late at night, when the hotel guests were up in their rooms or out on the town. It was a nice feeling to be working again, but it was an even nicer feeling to be working in a position that required no critical thinking whatsoever. This decorating gig fell into perfect harmony with my new growing-backwards philosophy. All I had to do was wrap garland over stairwell banisters, hang designer decorations from Christmas tree branches, and find that one broken bulb in every string of lights that prevented the entire thing from lighting up. There were no deadlines, no angry customers or clients, no cash registers, and no early morning commutes. It was just me and the midnight ladies hanging glittery shit from trees.

December started to get even more interesting after Alex moved into the apartment. Alex—short for Alexandria, but don't ever call her that—was a tall sexy mess of spiky black hair, Parliament cigarettes, and punk rock. She moved into the unit that overlooked our little patio courtyard, and she climbed down from her window one night and joined us for drinks and introductions. We moved the party up to Bryan's apartment for the after-dark portion of celebrating Wednesday, and he fired up Rock Band on the Xbox, and proceeded to wrap his customary bandana around his forehead before setting up the drum kit. I had never had an issue before that night being a 37-year-old dude strumming a pretend guitar in front of a room full of younger people I barely knew, but now with Alex there watching it just seemed so much more pathetic.

"This is kind of gay, man," I confessed to Bryan as we smoked a joint by the whirling wall fan in the kitchen. "Chicks don't dig a grown man who plays a plastic musical instrument."

"You're not that old," he replied. "And you look much younger than you are."

"I was talking about you. You're 31 and you've got a bandana on your head, and you're about to sit down at a pretend drum set. She's going to see us make complete assholes out of ourselves, tonight, right here in your apartment. Maybe Wii bowling or tennis would be a little more . . . appropriate for her first visit here."

"But . . ." Bryan pulled a series of quick puffs from the dissipating joint. "But Rock Band is where I shine. She's fine with it; she's into it."

We burned through a few songs and a few more bottles of wine, both of which flowed easier as the night progressed.

Then I laid down my trusty three-quarters-size guitar and sloppily excused myself to run upstairs to my apartment and grab some more pot; it had been my turn to roll one since Green Day turned into Led Zeppelin and my plastic bass turned into a plastic guitar. As I unlocked my front door, I suddenly noticed Alex standing right beside me. She must have been just inches behind me the entire way up. And she was taller now than back at Bryan's. She was actually gargantuan, standing almost eye-to-eye with me and I'm six-and-a-half feet tall. She was definitely the tallest and probably the cutest woman I had ever invited into that apartment—actually, she was the *only* woman I had ever invited into that apartment.

"It looks like an office in here," she said after taking a seat on my mattress. There was nowhere else to sit.

"Big fan of minimalism. I like to go light."

"The word 'Spartan' comes to mind," she replied to that. "Works for me, though. You should see my place. At least you have a rug."

Over the course of the next 15 minutes, I learned that she had just moved down from Alaska, would be attending school the following semester, and would be turning 23 years old in a couple of months. I'm not entirely sure who instigated the first kiss, but a first kiss on a bed almost always leads to something more. Over the course of the next 15 minutes, I learned that her breasts were extremely large and angelically beautiful; I learned that no kiss, past on up to the time of this writing, would ever compare to the passion and fervor of her lips and tongue; and, finally, I learned that no other bare, pink pussy, again both past or present, could ever taste so much like candy.

"Dude, she's 18," said Seth, the apartment manager, the

next day when inquiring about seeing us swaggering down the hall together the night before. "She's just starting school. She's not even a freshman yet."

"I think you're mistaken," I replied, not even recalling seeing him in the hall the night before. "She said she's going *back* to school. Look at her! There's no way she's a teenager."

Seth then took me to his first-floor apartment, where he brought out her tenant application and thereby proved without a doubt that Alex had just turned 18 years old. "Man, you didn't fuck her did you?"

She was half my age. She could have been my daughter. I was dropping out of college when she was being born. Had I lived in Alaska, I might have gone to high school with her parents. As all these thoughts ran through my head, I couldn't help but smile a little. It wasn't necessarily a proud smile, but more of a grin of recognition. Because my theory was working. I was growing backwards faster than I had anticipated.

THAT MOTHERFUCKER CARLOS

JOB #57

I was finally coming out of a string of bad luck jobs, or so I had thought. My well of easy temp work had ended weeks before that, after management saw the tattoos on my knuckles and promptly removed me from the roster of available office work assignments—which entailed doing mindless filing and data entry for vacationing employees—and instead started giving me all of the manual labor assignments. I had gone from sipping coffee in cubicles and typing dates into spreadsheets to *dismantling* cubicles and *stacking* boxes of spreadsheets into storage rooms. It was equally as mindless and paid about the same, but it was manual labor and not something I was wired for.

It wasn't until the third box-moving assignment, after I had accumulated enough money to cover the following month's rent, when I reminded the temporary employment company of my vast experience *inside* the office. I made it clear that my talents weren't being utilized due to some "silly and miniscule" tattoos on my fingers that weren't even noticeable in most office lighting. The woman at the temp company was chewing her lunch as she reviewed my resume on her computer screen, and I could hear the phone rustle against her cheek with every bite. It was calming somehow, almost woodsy—like brush under stepping feet.

"Yes, you do have quite a bit of office management experience." She sounded a little shocked. "I wonder why . . . Oh. Hmmm. What happened at Priority Medical Labs?"

"Things just didn't work out."

"It says here that you damaged one of their printers. And that you were hostile toward them."

"I was not hostile toward them. They sprung a test on me." I tried explaining. "I wasn't prepared for a test. It was well over a hundred questions . . . and all math. Not my strongest trait."

"But it was for an accounting position. Passing their math exam is mandatory with Priority Medical. All new recruits have to pass it. How did the printer get damaged?"

"They wanted me to print the results after I finished. I was in this little room all by myself, with a monitor and printer. I told them I wasn't prepared. I just wanted to explain things."

"And what about the printer?" she asked as the typing keys paused.

"Well, I didn't know what to do after I finished the test. I knew I butchered it pretty badly. It was early and I couldn't think clearly. I didn't want to give them the printout but I couldn't say that to them, so I tried to delete my test from the computer and that didn't work. Then this little clock icon came up on the screen and said if I didn't push 'print' that it was going to do it for me. I had only seconds to react and I freaked out a little. I dismantled the printer before it could print the results. But I did *not* break it. I just wiggled some things loose."

"It says here they were still able to retrieve your test results from a different printer. It says you failed the test. Then they said you stormed out of the office after they showed you the results."

"I did. But it wasn't out of hostility."

"They don't see it that way."

"Come on, Dottie, there's got to be something you have that doesn't involve moving boxes. I can put makeup on my tattoos. I'm an office kind of guy—a real people person. I have a bad back and no health insurance; there's only so much manual labor I can do before I hurt myself. Come on, there's got to be something."

I heard her type a few words on her keyboard before telling me about a full-time gig that just opened up in Sherman Oaks. She said it was pretty easy and didn't involve moving anything. Then she asked if I'd ever seen *Fast Times at Ridgemont High*, to which I answered, "of course."

"Good. You'll be working at the galleria where most of that movie was shot. So that's neat."

The first thought to pop into my head was Jennifer Jason Leigh's breasts from the baseball dugout scene, when she loses her virginity. It made the job sound sort of enticing before realizing that galleries were also full of stores and cash registers and customers.

"As you can probably see from my resume, my retail sales experience isn't all that . . . sparkling," I reminded her.

"Oh, it's not sales. Not sure what this is. But it's definitely not retail sales."

I agreed to the job, thanked her, and showed up at the

Sherman Oaks Galleria the next morning at 8:00 a.m. to meet with the manager Samantha. Samantha walked me around the outdoor pavilion of the slumbering galleria, where carts selling sunglasses, novelty hats, and cell-phone plans were just beginning to set up for the day. It was about a 100-foot stretch of concrete and grass that ran from the enormous parking garage to the main entrance of the huge indoor mall, with little café tables and flowerbeds peppering the way. She showed me a small table set up near the front doors, and she straightened three stacks of coupons, flyers, and store catalogs on top of it.

"Well, here it is," she said.

"Do you want me to move this?"

"No, this is where you'll be standing. You'll be greeting customers before they come into the mall, handing out coupons and stuff. A lot of our customers here are older, and they don't really know their way around. Most are here for Macy's, which is over on the far side, or Nordstrom, which is on the second floor on the opposite side." She two-finger pointed to opposite ends of the large mall like a flight stewardess.

"And I just tell people that?"

"If they ask," she answered. "And if they don't, just say 'Welcome to the Sherman Oaks Galleria' and ask if they need help with anything."

"Sounds fine. Thank you."

"You sure? Have any questions?"

"No, I'm good. Macy's over there and Nordstrom on the second floor. And someone will relieve me for lunch?"

"Mmm . . . no, not really. Just go grab a bite when you get hungry. I'll come back around this afternoon. You're on your own."

"Cool. I'm good."

I had worn a tie with my button-up and slacks, but as soon as Samantha walked away I pulled it from around my neck and rolled it up into my pocket. Although I wasn't a big fan of social interaction, this was definitely a nice mindless job that didn't require one bit of either manual labor or mathematics. I knew that I was on my last legs with the temp company, and this gig was about the best that I was going to get until I proved myself again. The accounting job was a mistake. I should have never agreed to the interview in the first place. I should have never fabricated the experience on my resume, or the bachelor's degree in the field—there were just certain fake careers better left untouched.

My shift started out wonderfully. A handful of senior citizens had hobbled in with canes and bad hips, and my only duty was to say "Good morning" and maybe flash a smile. The sun finally crept up over the great mall and shined down onto my courtyard, galvanizing the grass, the concrete, and my coupon table in the glow of a comfortable backyard. It was a perfect Southern California day and there I stood getting paid $9 an hour to soak in it. It was the life. It was the perfect job. There were long stretches of time where not a soul came around, and I was able to ponder all the things I hadn't had time to ponder—while getting paid for it. There was such a rush of thoughts and ideas that I used one of the customer-survey pens and the blank backs of whatever I was giving away to write them down before they were lost forever. Brilliance ran from the ballpoint pen that day, and I captured each fleeting notion on a tether made of ink and coupons:

1. Tell a skinny person that they have "those Labor Camp good looks."
2. Perpetual motion is possible by using two magnets opposite one another.
3. Call Grandma and wish her a "Happy Birthday."
4. I am the Jack Bauer of the temporary employment world.
5. The human mind functions like a courtroom, with one litigator representing the *Creative Brandon* and another for the *Analytical Brandon*, plus a sole judge who's the core thinker and who makes the final decisions after hearing both cases.
6. If evolution was genuine, why do monkeys still exist? Or fish? Why do hairy chests still exist? What possible benefit does the hair around my asshole present?
7. Follow a stranger around for an entire week, take pictures of them at various locations, document and time-stamp these locations, then put all these photos and reports into a manila folder and present it to this person. Then wink and walk away.
8. Obese women compensate by having really pretty hair. And smelling good.

My philosophizing and note taking were going great up until about 1:00, when Carlos and his girlfriend emerged from the parking garage. He had been a coworker from my last real job, and he sauntered up to my table in shorts, flip-flops, and a bewildered expression. In my initial agreement of taking this job offer, I had forgotten that I even knew anyone who lived on this side of town.

"Wow, really, man? *This?*" Carlos asked snidely as he

lowered his sunglasses to the bridge of his nose and examined my coupon table. "You work at the Galleria now?"

"It's temporary. Not much out there right now."

"Really? I found another job just fine. This is seriously the best you could do? Handing out coupons and shit at the galleria?"

"I was a professional mover last month. This gig's new, just started today."

"I'd say congratulations, but I wouldn't feel right about it. Really? From writing to *this*? Boy, you really fell far from the tree. You remember Rebecca, right?"

"Of course, nice to see you again," I answered, and his girlfriend and I shook hands. I could see in her eyes that she felt sorry for me and my immediate career choice, as well as for her boyfriend rubbing it in. But I knew Carlos well enough to realize that he was just having a little fun at my expense. We had worked together a few years back writing half-assed TV scripts for a little film company that eventually went belly-up. He seemed to have done alright with himself after the company-wide layoffs, while I was broke and still pissed that my Elvis documentary never saw a set of eyes outside of the Czech Republic.

"Well, it's getting hot out here," Carlos ended the weird five-second stretch of silence. "We need to get a printer for my new Mac. Good to see you, bro. And good luck with this shit."

"Yeah. You too."

The whole dynamic of my galleria job promptly changed once Carlos and Rebecca walked away. As I watched them push open the doors of the mall and shake their heads with a "thank God that's not me" glance to one another, I realized how pathetic I must have looked standing there at the coupon table—not even sitting, like a gentleman, but fucking standing, like a prop.

They never came back out, at least not through the doors nearest me and their car. They must have exited through the front and walked all the way around the mall then circled back to the garage just to avoid seeing me again. I began to feel like I had asked them for spare change or the last half of their cigarette. My shirt felt dirtier and my white socks screamed from my ankles. I couldn't help but inspect every approaching face the rest of the afternoon for someone I might have known or worked with in some better-paying capacity, and my "Welcome to the Sherman Oaks Galleria" greetings became riddled with guilt and conspiracy.

For the rest of the day I did nothing but fill up my back pocket with a dozen more scribbled-on coupons and debase my current livelihood. I stuck it out for a few more days until Dottie called back and asked how I liked the job. She said they missed me at the old company, and relayed that no one could stack boxes both alphabetically and by date like me. She then said my old manual-labor position was still mine if I wanted it.

The legal defense for Creative Brandon blamed Carlos for my decision to leave the galleria job, while Analytical Brandon's attorney tried to prove it was simply time to move on to something a little less in the public eye. The judge sided with Creative Brandon's litigation team on this one, and now history will forever remember the exiting of Job #57 was as a result of that motherfucker Carlos.

MOST OF A DAY AT WHISPERING MEADOWS

JOB #36

"The world is too focused on sex. Everything you see or hear or read—it's all about sex. They're making it out to be the panacea of everything."

"Interesting. I don't think I've ever heard you say that out loud before."

"I've never been this certain of it before. It's everywhere now! It seems like the most common answer to every problem is to have sex. The troubles of this world cannot be healed by vagina meeting penis. Poverty, unemployment, overpopulation, genocide, global warming; these things don't give a good goddamn whether or not you're boning Jody after she puts her kids to sleep. As a matter of fact, most of these problems are *caused* by having too much sex."

"Do we know a Jody?"

"No, we don't know a Jody! Can we focus on the matter at hand, please?"

"Which is that sex doesn't solve the world's problems? We're still on this one? Or that sex causes the world's problems?"

"Not just the world . . . I'm talking about local things,

too. Things closer to home. Like us, for instance. How much time per day do we think about sex? How much money do we spend on stupid dates that end with a kiss and a 'real nice to meet you'? How much porn do we watch on the Internet? If we had the best sex ever tonight, would it magically put a few thousand into my checking account? No. Would it even lend me a ten-spot to treat myself to a Denver omelet at IHOP? No. Sex is a bad investment. Sex is a time-share condo. You put $10,000 in and you get a couple of cloudy weekends a year. Sure, it'll take your mind off of things for an evening, but so will a decent video rental. And speaking of movies, why is the focal point of every film ever made centered around love? Seriously. In the most inappropriate of films—war movies, hitman movies, bank heist movies, zombie movies, horror movies—there's always this thick plot thread about the power of love and how it can shield a teenager from the guy with the machete or forgive all the contract murders a handsome agent committed."

"You've moved from sex to love in your diatribe."

"It's all the same. It's all bullshit. It's a Band-Aid for reality."

"Someone's a Bitter Billy today. I think this is just another good example of you trying to force your beliefs onto society and then scorning them when they don't see things your way."

"You're way off. You're just arguing for argument's sake now."

"A good psychologist might even say that you feel this way because of . . . your little problem."

"*Our* little problem. You're no angel in this matter. And I'll agree with you there to a certain extent. It originally might have been the seed of my stance on this matter, but now it's opened my eyes. Now it's a flower in full bloom. I can see the truth now. In the land of the blind, the one-eyed man is king."

"*I think we just need to get laid, pal. What's your stance on that?*"

"Seriously? After all I've just said, you're going to offer that little turd of advice up?"

"*How long has it been? The last time . . . was with that gal at that bar in Los Feliz. She had the gay guy friend who tried to handjob you at the table.*"

"No, it was the first grade teacher we met on the Internet. The gal from the bar told us she had Hepatitis as we were undressing, and it ruined the mood, remember? Our 'little problem' came in real handy that night. The first grade teacher was the last one."

"*That's right. It was her birthday or something. Man, we were callous with that one. Real Grade-A assholes. I bet she'll think twice about going home with someone on a first date after that night.*"

"The dark side of the little problem. The blame game. But we're drifting too far from shore now. I wasn't finished with my diatribe, as you put it. Sex is going to kill this country. Look what it did to the Roman Empire; it destroyed it."

"*That wasn't because of sex, and you know it. It was perversion, it was greed, indulgence, power; it was a stronger enemy, it was devaluating its own currency, it was the stretching of its armies across half the globe that caused the fall of Rome.*"

"Well, those perverted Caesars near the end didn't help matters."

"*Seven months. It's been seven months.*"

"Since the first grade teacher? Seven months? Well, sex is your thing now. I'm done with it. I wash my hands of it. I could go seven years, if I had to. You're shit-out-of-luck, pal. I'm calling the shots now. I'm Mad Max and this is the Thunderdome. I run the show."

"Not when we're drinking. That's my time to shine."

"You're a selfish son of a bitch, you know that?"

"Back at you. Dick."

The door to the garage-turned-office opened and a middle-aged woman in salmon-colored shorts and shirt walked in with a clipboard. She wore the same phone headset as I did, but the thin microphone on hers rested beside her mouth; mine was pushed up around my eyebrow.

"Hi, you must be our new operator. I'm Denise. Any calls yet?" she asked with an anxious grin.

"Not yet, no." I replied.

She shook her head and glanced at her clipboard. "And you've been here since eight this morning? That's too bad; I really thought we'd get at least a few calls by now. Sorry for making you sit here by yourself for four hours with nothing to do."

"Oh, I've kept myself busy," I lifted Sylvia Plath's *The Bell Jar* from the table. "I'm actually having a really nice time sorting out some thoughts."

"Well, I'm glad you're having a nice time, but I was really hoping we'd have gotten a few calls. We paid a lot of money for that commercial last night. Did you happen to see it?"

"No, no, I didn't," I replied. "But I came up with a pretty good theory as to why I think no one's called by now . . . if you care to hear it."

"Okay," she replied sharply, "let's hear it. I'd like to know why you think our $106,000 commercial failed to garner any interest in our treatment center."

"The timing. You're targeting alcoholics and addicts

to seek your help, so you have to get them at their most vulnerable time: right after the bars close. The counselor before you, this morning, she said you aired the commercial last night at 10, 11, and 12. Most alcoholics I know are still in the bars at that time—they'll usually close the place. You should have aired your commercial at 2:30, 3:00, and 3:30 in the morning. That's when they're depressed and hating themselves—that's when the booze is wearing off, and they're trying to get to sleep to face another grueling day— that's when you can really send your message home."

"Do you know very many alcoholics?"

"More drunks than alcoholics. But it's the same principle, isn't it?"

"No, Brandon, it is *not* the same principle," she snapped back. "An alcoholic has to want to be helped before we can help them. We're not selling a magic pill here; we're offering an inpatient recovery program in a friendly home setting. We offer substance abuse *treatment*, not a substance abuse cure. If someone should happen to call, I hope you can remember that. And someone has told you the procedure for when someone does call, right?"

"Politely get their name and number then transfer them to extension four," I answered. "And don't try to help."

"Exactly. And it's very important you get that phone number. A lot of the times they're curious or scared, and they'll try to hang up before you can transfer them."

"Got it."

"How are you doing on lunch? You need a break?"

"I brought a sandwich and I have my book. I may need to pee pretty soon, though, and I didn't notice any other doors than the one I came in through."

"Oh," her head tilted up a little, "okay, yeah. The

bathroom. I guess we never thought about that; you're going to need to pee. You're our first call receiver . . . I didn't even think about that. I guess you'll have to use the bathroom in the house. But we just got some new . . . *guests* staying with us, so please be aware of what they're going through, and please don't communicate with anyone. One of our counselors will have to escort you in there, for legal reasons. And, I know I shouldn't have to say this, but you can't bring any drugs or intoxicants into that house for any reason. Even cough syrup. There's always someone who tries to sneak in a bottle of pills or a little baggie of something—friends, parents, boyfriends, daughters; that's why we don't allow anybody not in treatment inside that house. We take it very seriously."

"That would explain the counselor patting me down this morning."

"Just tap on the kitchen window when you need to go, and someone will come out," she said before leaving.

Denise had been a welcome intrusion from my four-hour episode of Plath and internal conversation. I took the headset off and walked around the room, when suddenly, and maybe for the first time in my life, I craved interaction with another person. Whether it was the full pot of coffee all to myself, the pristine walls at all four sides of me, or the lone phone sitting on a long barren Formica table, I felt the deep yearning to share a conversation with another living, breathing human being—even Denise again. But she didn't come back, so I ate my sandwich and poured another cup of coffee, and then I returned the headset back onto my head. It was kind of nice getting paid $9 an hour to sit and read a book in a quiet room, but 102 straight pages of *The Bell Jar* was enough to make anybody want to walk into a crowd and stay there. Everything was so still and peaceful around me; the silence in the room was as thick as the tan paint across the drywall walls. No car alarms, no yelling, no trash trucks, no televisions—there wasn't a single sound around me. It almost felt like time had stopped outside of this room—that the rest of the world had paused and didn't bother to invite me. Or, even worse, as if I had died but my conscious mind had refused to accept it, and this tan room was my eternal ghostly afterlife until I admitted that I was no longer among the living. I could have drunk too much coffee, had a heart attack, and didn't even know it. I could have slipped into a coma, and all of this was my active imagination recycling the last few precious hours of its life over and over again: this tan room.

"I think it's called Cotard Syndrome."

"When you believe you're dead, yes, I think that's right."

"Sounds kind of mean. Cotard sounds like retard."

"Nice. Nice mature thought. And you think you're going to meet some beautiful lady and get her to have sex with you with that kind of witty banter? You've got another think coming."

"Candor is all the rage with my kind of gals."

"What's the other one called? That other mental malady? It's a cool one . . . What is that?"

"Capgras Syndrome is, I believe, what you're looking for."

"Capgras Syndrome! Yes, that's a great one! When you believe everyone around you, all your family and friends, are imposters. Man, that's messed up. I bet a few of the *guests* in the house have it."

"We could really fuck with them."

"We need this job too much, pal. This gig is gravy—getting paid to sit here and read a book? This is the graviest job we've had in months."

"I don't think 'graviest' works well as an adjective."

"Agreed. Alright, I really have to pee now. I think it's time we went in and met the houseguests."

The tapping on the kitchen window, as Denise recommended, merely incited a wave from a gangly woman in a bathrobe sitting at the dining room table inside. She didn't look like a counselor, at least not a counselor *against* the use of drugs and alcohol. But she continued waving at me like a scene continuously replaying on a blemished DVD. I attempted to pantomime a clipboard and pen through the glass but the translation got lost somewhere in the curtains. She shot me a bewildered expression before opening the back door and leaning her upper half out.

"Hey, what's up?" she asked with the drawl of a content pothead, but her pimpled face said methamphetamines.

"Hey. I just started working here. Is Denise in there? Or any of the counselors?"

"Nope," she replied. "I'm just watching TV. You got a smoke?"

I pulled out my pack and slid a Basic her way. "I thought we weren't supposed to smoke near the house?"

"I just said the counselors were gone," she said and motioned for a light by bending a thumb.

I lit both of our cigarettes just three seconds before realizing that I was now breaking two very important rules on my first day: the aforementioned "smoking near the house" decree as well as speaking with a patient. The young woman in the bathrobe didn't seem like she had much to share in the way of conversation, so I stood there and smoked quickly, keeping an eye out for anybody with a clipboard. But things then took a turn for the worse.

"Oh God, I so needed that." She tilted her head back

and exhaled through a loud sigh. "This place is like a prison, man. Six days stuck in this dump with all these fucking drunks and speed freaks. Fucking rich losers who can't handle their own shit, man!"

"What's your story?"

"Me?" she asked as decoration on her ready reply; one which she'd probably already shared a dozen times since arriving at the house. "My parents threw me in here! I'm not here by my own decision. Dad gave me the ultimatum: Come here or move out. So I came here. I had no choice."

"What was your vice? Pills? Grass? The White Lady?"

"Me?" she asked again, but this time genuinely. "You think I'm a coke addict? Like these crazy fucks in here? God, no! I'm here because of these . . ." And she raised her half-smoked cigarette to eye level. "My folks found out that I started smoking over the summer, and it didn't mesh well with their ritzy weekend set, so they chucked my ass in here until I quit. Thanks, guys. Thanks, Blue Cross."

"You're in here because of cigarettes?" I couldn't grasp the concept. "But you're a kid! You're not even addicted to them yet?"

"I'm not a kid!" she exclaimed. "I'll be 18 in a few months. And I am seriously addicted to these. You don't know me! You don't know how rough I have it!"

It was then when I wanted to take back the cigarette I had given her and call her a faker; a little spoiled teenage girl reaching for anything that would make her more special. I wanted to tell her that the reason our entire health-care system was so fucked up was because of shallow, self-interested people like her and her parents, who would force their insurance carrier to pay $6,000 a week to cure a girl of her four-month-old experimentation with tobacco—and she didn't even inhale! When my mother found out I smoked cigarettes at 15, she forced me to strike every match in a 2,500-plus box of strike-anywhere matches before being allowed back in the house. It didn't quell my lust for cigarettes, and it may have actually awakened the slumbering pyromaniac inside me, but it was a hell of a more fitting punishment than putting your kid in a treatment facility with upper-crust drunks, lace-curtain junkies, and wealthy wife-beaters.

But before I could tell her all of this, I realized—at least realized how it would look to my employers—that I had supplied a "tobacco addict" in a treatment facility with tobacco, thereby not only breaking two major rules on my first day, but this third one as well.

"I didn't know you were in here for that . . . So, you never saw me, alright? I never gave you that cigarette, alright?"

She smiled, snubbed out the cigarette in the dirt, then threw the filter onto the roof. "Tell you what," then her smile grew even wider, "you give me that pack of Basics and your lighter, and then I never saw you."

Always the optimist, I congratulated myself on buying generic cigarettes that morning. Even as broke as I was, it wouldn't be so difficult to part with a near-full pack of the cheap shit. But there were still over four hours left until quitting time, and with the way this job was crawling along I was definitely going to need a few cigarettes for my afternoon. And even though I didn't like the fact that she was trying to blackmail me, I knew she'd rat me out faster than one of her crackhead roommates would cook up a pale Fruity Pebble on a piece of tinfoil. So I needed to negotiate the terms of this ransom.

"Tell you what. I'll give you half of this pack and a full book of matches," was my counteroffer. "It's a solid deal. Matches are easier to conceal, and you know the counselors are going to find your cigarette stash by tomorrow, so there's no good reason to deprive both of us of these cigarettes."

"Tempting offer," she frowned her top lip to camouflage a mean smile, "but no. I want your full pack and your lighter. Or I just might have to tell Denise that you offered me the very same shit that my parents are paying a lot of money to make me quit."

Damn, she was playing hardball with me. I wish I had something like economic sanctions to threaten her with, but those never worked anyway. I could try to subsidize the deal to my advantage; offer her my new cigarette investment package.

"How about this," I countered again. "You get the half-pack and matches right now, but I also throw in an additional 3 cigarettes per day for the rest of the week. That's 12 additional cigarettes spread safely out over the next four days. That's cigarette security right there. We have a deal?"

"No dice," she snapped back. "That's a sucker's bet. You're not even going to be here tomorrow."

"Yeah, I am! I work here. I'm the new call operator for that commercial they aired. I'll be right back there in the garage. It's really an office. Ask Denise."

"Seriously," she folded her arms, "you won't be here tomorrow. I heard Denise on the phone about an hour ago, and she was yelling at whatever temp job company you work for. She had to pay like $500 dollars to break whatever contract they had. That's where she's at right now."

"Seriously? I was supposed to be here for four weeks."

"Hence the $500 fee to break the contract. I guess that

commercial they did was a total joke. So, are we going to do this deal or what? What other counteroffers you have for me?"

"None now," I answered.

"I get the whole pack and your lighter then?"

"You get shit. You have nothing to bargain with now."

"I'll still tell Denise," she acted frantically knowing her cigarette deal was nearly off the table, "and she could still tell your temp company what you did. That would really fuck you up, man."

I lit another cigarette from the cherried butt of my first, mostly for the dramatic effect of not offering her another one. Then I tucked the pack back into my blazer pocket. "Being 17 and not having tasted the pungent fruit of responsibility yet, you probably don't quite understand that working for a temp company is what you do when you're unemployable. It caters to people like me. I could take a shit on the floor in there and get fired from here today, then start working someplace new tomorrow. I am invincible."

She nibbled on her thumb before asking, "Can you leave me one or two then? You know, a couple of smokes for the road."

I had never before used laughter as a response to a question, but it was effective and worked quite well. I walked into the secluded backyard to pee behind the garage and could still hear her shouting obscenities at me from the kitchen door. She was a terrible negotiator and an even worse insulter; everything had either a "fuck" or a "punk-ass" in it. I returned to my garage as soon as I heard the door slam and poured myself a fresh cup of coffee. The phone still didn't blink or ring, so I opened *The Bell Jar* and resumed where I left off.

"That was weird."

"Very. And I think it also reinforces my theory about sex."

"I don't think it does. No, I'm positive it doesn't. There was nothing to do with sex whatsoever in that situation."

"It was mostly implied sex. Didn't like her one bit. Big faker. Looks like we're getting fired again, though. That's something. An honorable firing."

"That's something alright. Hey, she lost her virginity. I was wondering if that was going to happen. And to Irwin. Seems like a nice enough guy."

"That Plath. She can sure weave a tale, man."

The end couldn't have been better timed; just as I turned over the last page of the book Denise walked into the garage with her bad news. She explained that this would indeed be my last day, as no fault of my own—which is rare to hear in those types of circumstances—but, as a consolation to my newfound unemployment, I could leave right then and get paid for the rest of the day. So that was exactly what I did. And I pocketed *The Bell Jar* as severance.

THE PORN IS MIGHTIER THAN THE SWORD

JOB #69

"Dude, it's fine," Corey said. "We're in fucking Jamaica. This is our last week of filming."

The long tour bus lumbered down the dilapidated dirt road like a frog jumping from electrified toadstool to electrified toadstool. Every pothole and trash heap and who-knew-what-else in our path caused our eight-wheeled mammoth to sink and lunge every few seconds, sending the thirty passengers several inches above our seats before dropping us back into them.

I was sitting in the second to last row, with two very comfortable seats all to myself. In the twenty rows ahead of me sat an exotic and colorful assortment of people, half of whom were treating the bus ride like a singles' beach party, while the other half slept with heads shoved under pillows and jackets. Big bearded guys in bandanas, shorts, and sunglasses, who looked like they should have been touring with the Allman Brothers Band were happily sipping beers in their seats and making conversation with a handful of very attractive blondes in bathing suits. Half a dozen guys in cargo shorts and sleeveless tees were rooting through duffel bags, coiling loose wires, and finessing pieces of camera equipment under dim overhead lights. A brunette lowered the business section of her *New York Times* and flashed two of the bikers her breasts. Then a couple of well-dressed older white men glanced around at their travelmates from behind thin, expensive reading glasses before shrugging them off and returning to their briefcases and Blackberries.

We were a strange, diversified crew in that bus, vaguely resembling a modern-day Shakespearian troupe traveling to our next destination. And paired with the camera equipment stacked everywhere and lights and microphones poking dangerously up from between rows of seats, we could have easily passed for a contemporary, soon-to-be-televised performance of *Hamlet* coming to a town near you—had the Bard dabbled in pornographic themes, that is.

Corey was a gregarious 24-year-old production manager that I had been traveling with for the past couple of months. He had commandeered the entire row behind me, and he passed ahead a wrinkled joint from between the headrests dividing us—its orange lit end illuminating his nose and brow in the darkness. The perplexed expression on my face must have spoken volumes once its pumpkin glow got close enough to me.

"But the producers, they're right there. They'll smell it, man," I explained as the joint crept closer to my lips. Corey and I had already gotten stoned together in a dozen different hotel rooms across the United States, but this was the first time we were doing it in the company of the entire film crew, on a crowded bus, in a country that wasn't our own. Plus, this was my first big writing job and I didn't want to toss away a "Head Writer" title in the closing credits of an

actual television show by getting busted smoking a doobie in the back of a bus like some 1970s movie with Matt
Dillon in it.

"They're already blazing one up there!" He pointed
down the aisle to the midsection of the bus, where a joint
was being circulated between the rows. "Just chill, dude.
This is the last week of the job. It's time to party."

So I took Corey's advice and drew in my 1, 2 . . . 3 puffs
and passed the joint across the aisle to Steven, the other,
older, less-likable production manager. When I turned back
to say thanks, Corey wiggled another lit joint at me through
the headrests.

"Send this one forward when you're finished," he
advised, both hands diligently rolling a third joint in his lap.
"They'll meet halfway."

"Like lovers at midnight," I added, and I was glad when
he pretended not to hear it. I plucked the joint from his fingers just as the first three puffs slowly crept up on me. That
was the problem with really good weed: It took a couple of
minutes before it completely hit you, and then it was usually too late—too late to realize that you were going to be
fucked for the next hour or two.

But I did as Corey suggested—took my 1, 2 . . . 3 puffs—
and passed the thick, smoldering stick through the headrests
to the willing fingers and turned face of the guy in the row
ahead of me. I watched it slowly handed from seat to seat, lips
to lips, row to row, until those two joints did meet near the
halfway mark. And then Corey's third joint wiggled between
the headrests at me, so I took my puffs and passed it to the row
across the aisle from me. How in the hell Corey got that much
pot in the two hours between landing in Kingston, Jamaica,
and driving here to bum-fuck Jamaica, I had no idea.

It took about eight minutes of staring out the window to realize it, but I was as stoned as an Iranian adulterer. I now possessed a perfect clarity, where I could finally absorb the lyrics of the songs on the Bob Marley album that had been blasting throughout the bus since this journey began 40 miles ago. It became so clear to me then. I am *not* going to worry about a thing, and every little thing really *is* going to be alright. The rattling bus began to feel like the Millennium Falcon going through that meteor storm right after its warp speed got fucked up, and the sights zipping by my window were at times both haunting and mystifying—splashes of third-world images briefly hitting the glass then disappearing forever; fleeting moments like windblown pages of a *National Geographic* magazine passing before the eyes. In the black of that Jamaican midnight, a shoeless farmer shepherded three sheep along a dirt path using only a twig to pat them with; a small, very vertical home made from nothing but front doors; a desolate town with darkened store fronts and wind theatrically whipping papers and trash across the ground. And the final memorable sight of that bleak three-hour bus ride before reaching humanity was an open-faced shack, maybe six feet high and wide, made from spare pieces of aluminum siding. It sat barren in the weeds and high grass about 30 feet from the road, and was surprisingly well lit against the backdrop of the surrounding blackness. As we sped by, I could see three barstools and a makeshift counter inside, a couple of liquor bottles behind the vacant bartender. And on top of the aluminum shack was a large plank of wood, most likely a found front door, set up like a billboard to the street. And crudely spray-painted in red letters atop this large plank of wood was its enticing name: MEAT N TINGS.

We finally reached the walled and well-guarded compound that was also known as Whispers, the world-famous, all-inclusive, clothing-optional, hedonism-friendly resort. Once past the 10-foot concrete barriers and inside the lively vacation spot, Jamaica was completely different—it was exactly what one pictured Jamaica to look like. Young white women were walking around in skimpy bathing suits and talking on cell phones, palm trees swayed above warm breezes, and middle-aged couples drunkenly laughed and sipped cocktails from the ledges of pools. I could see the white sand of a beach not more than a stone's throw from the lobby, with small sailboats swaying in its mild current and patches of tropical jungle at either side. It was a paradise.

It took about 30 minutes before we unloaded the last piece of equipment and luggage from the bus, and after the production assistants checked in and handed everyone their hotel keycards, we all scattered off to find our rooms. The "talent" was going to be arriving the following morning, and our first day of filming would begin shortly thereafter—but up until that moment, it was just me, a hotel room, and Jamaica.

I passed two Olympic-size swimming pools, a Jacuzzi, and two outdoor cabana bars before reaching the building where my room was. This resort was so large that they had eight two-story complexes filled with hotel rooms of varying sizes and costs. I was pleased to discover that my room had a nice large queen-size bed, dining table, TV, and even mirrors on the ceiling. I was going to be calling this place my home for the next nine days, so I unpacked my bags and set up my laptop and printer—the traveling office—on the table.

I made it to the outdoor bar I had passed earlier and took a seat at one of the frilly stools next to a heavyset woman in her 60s. She sensed me next to her and turned to face me, her large, sagging, tanned breasts resting merrily at both sides of her belly.

"Good evening," I said.

"It sure could be," she replied.

"I'm going to have a drink now."

She raised her margarita to me, took a sip, and turned back in the other direction. That was a very smooth transaction, I commented to myself—a clean, friendly rejection of her not-so-subtle advances. I was quite proud of myself because, put a few drinks in me, and there stood a very good chance I would be apologizing for my rudeness and playing hide-the-finger with grandma in one of the nearby Jacuzzis. Because that's how I roll when I have drinks.

A smiling bartender appeared from the other side of the counter. He was wearing a fancy yellow short-sleeve and short-bottomed suit, kind of like an antique stage monkey minus the little music box.

"What can I get for you, sahr?" he asked in the type of thick Jamaican accent you only hear in movies. "We have margaritas, daiquiris, wine, and beer, sahr."

"How about a daiquiri. Yeah, let's do a daiquiri."

"Very good, sahr," he said, already pouring my drink from a premade batch in the blender. My natural reaction was to pull out my wallet, but he waved away my effort and reminded me, "This is an all-inclusive resort, sahr. You need no money for nothing."

I gulped most of the daiquiri down. "Oh, that's wonderful. I'll take a recharge since you've still got the pitcher in your hand." He filled my plastic cup again. It took yet one more daiquiri before I got up the nerve to ask this complete stranger if he knew where I could buy some pot.

"Ah, the ganja, mon! Of course, mon!" His face lit up and he fumbled under the bar for something. He pulled up a wrinkled brown lunch bag and slid his hand inside. "How much you want, mon?"

"I guess this doesn't fall under the 'all-inclusive' part?"

"No, mon. This is my own private harvest."

I opened my wallet and pulled out a ten and a five. I let him see it then cupped the money in my hand and slid it across the bar to him as slyly as possible. Being a city toker like I was, you learned to make these sorts of transactions as covertly as possible, especially when doing it across a counter with the bartender. But apparently things were much different in Jamaica; the bartender made no effort whatsoever to conceal the two huge green buds he pulled out from the bag. He raised them to the overhead floodlight and pointed out the purple strands and microscopic crystals as he rotated them from front to back for me. They were two meaty stalks of the Indica variety, each nearly as long and thick as a Cuban cigar, and probably worth about $150 back in the States. I tucked them into my shorts pocket and patted them through the fabric every couple of minutes to make sure they hadn't fallen out while reaching for a cigarette.

When the drinks are free, it's difficult to pull me away. It's not really a matter of alcoholism in so much as it's about getting something for free, and getting my fair share of that free something. My dad always said I had died penniless in a previous life. But, in my defense, the daiquiris were quite small, not a sip over 8 ounces. That's how I justified having six of them in those first 30 minutes.

I was readying myself to go back to my room when a flash of platinum blonde hair appeared beside me, then two large T-shirted breasts leaned over the bar. I recognized those fake tits, then the Puerto Rican-via-New York accent attached to them when she asked the bartender where rooms 400 to 600 were. As he drew out the location on the back of a napkin, she glanced over and recognized me, too. It was international porn star—and the host of the show that brought us all to Jamaica—Carmina Violatta; already a veteran porn actress at the tender age of 25, with more than fifty DVD titles to her credit.

"Oh, hey. You're the writer, right?" she asked.

"I'm your writer," I replied, still getting a proud chill every time someone referred to me by that moniker. Although I had traveled with her and been on set with her a dozen times over the past two months, this was the first time we had ever really spoken to one another. "You're Carmina. I've wanted to say 'Hi,' it's just been so crazy on the sets."

"I know . . . all those people. Just crazy. You ready for tomorrow? Big day. Our first scenes with the finalists. Did you come up with any cool skits for them to do? I liked the sexy spy idea that the cameraman came up with."

By "first scenes" she meant that 8 of the 16 finalists arriving the following day would be filming their first actual porn scenes as directed by a professional adult-film director and crew. That was the concept of the show basically. Our film crew had traveled to New York, Los Angeles, Miami, Tampa, and Las Vegas and collected the 16 best aspiring film actors and actresses after a grueling series of auditions from hundreds of the ugliest people in the nation. And when referring to "auditions" for our new "Search for the Next Best Porn Star" reality TV competition, you don't have to imagine too hard what that tryout process entailed. But out of those hundreds, the eight men and eight women who were able to masturbate with panache in front of the camera crew, the producers, the lighting crew, and the writer, had all won themselves a spot in the show. They would all be coming to this private Jamaican resort for the next nine days to perform various on-camera sex scenes with one another until the best two rose to the top like cream, and were given $250,000 each and a two-movie deal with the porn company producing the show.

As for the "spy idea that the cameraman came up with," I had no idea what Carmina was talking about. But I'd had enough daiquiris in me to smile and agree that it was one hell of a clever idea and deserved some fleshing out. I noticed her suitcases sitting beside her bare tanned legs.

"We got in like two hours ago . . . you still haven't found your room yet?"

"We all just got out of the meeting," she answered. "For tomorrow. Weren't you there? I thought . . . Everyone was there. You're the writer . . . shouldn't you have been there?"

I didn't know anything about a meeting, but yes, as the only writer on the show, I probably should have been there. And that would explain the skit for the spy idea she was talking about. I explained the situation to her and asked her to paraphrase what was talked about, then I sprinted off to my hotel room and fired up the laptop. An hour and forty minutes later, I was surprised to find how easily I had come up with four short scripts for the next day. I printed up four copies of each three-page script and collated them onto the bedspread before me, showcasing their title pages for the mirror on the ceiling: The not too cleverly named *The Spy Who Butt-Fucked Me*; the psychedelic '60s-themed *Austin Cock-Powers*; the oppressive thinking piece *A Raisin Cock in the Sun*; and finally, the *Jaws*-inspired "That's not a scar" boat scene script with women playing the Captain Quint and Hooper characters, which I titled *Great White Tits*.

I stacked the scripts on the little dining table and turned on the TV to put the night to bed. I had totally forgotten about the two stalks in my pocket and pulled them out and studied them under the bedside lamp light. They were so fresh that they were still damp from their last watering. I really wanted to smoke but I didn't put any forethought into a smoking device. No rolling papers, no aluminum can, no tinfoil anywhere in sight. The gift store was closed and I didn't have the energy to hunt down a cola machine. I searched my bag and then searched the room for anything to use; it became a mission after a few minutes. I considered using toilet paper to roll a joint before considering a page from the hotel tablet by the phone. But necessity breeds invention, especially with drugs, and I managed to channel my inner MacGyver and make a pipe from a hotel pen and the little screen from inside the bathroom sink faucet. Although I inhaled more melting plastic than pot, I was again good and stoned and fell asleep to an episode of *Law & Order.*

* * *

I woke up to find that my bathroom's shower had one full wall that was nothing but transparent glass, and it faced the already-full pool right below. I showered knowing that I was being watched by a few dozen middle-aged people drinking daiquiris at 8:00 a.m., and the only thing I did differently from home was spend less time washing my ass and more time washing my groin section—I wanted to at least give the people outside a decent show.

I took the handful of scripts and hustled to the main lobby to join Carmina, the two producers, and most of the production staff in welcoming the 16 contestants set to arrive any minute on the same bus we did the night before. As I gulped down my third coffee of the morning, Sam, the big producer with plenty of actual, non-porn TV shows to his credit, asked why I hadn't been at the all-hands meeting the night before. Instead of explaining that I either didn't hear about it or was just completely too stoned to comprehend it, I showed him the stack of scripts I had written and said, "I had a bunch of ideas I needed to get down on paper." He examined the titles of each, smirked, then nodded.

The large bus then pulled into the lobby, sparing me any more of Sam's inquisition. Its door hissed open and a vibrant and tanned string of 20-somethings poured out into the reception area. First off was the Pink Couple, whom we called the Pink Couple because the handsome pair both had bright pink hair. We would find out several hours later that they both had bright pink pubic hair, too. The colorful pair had been together for several years before deciding they wanted more action in their sex lives, so they auditioned at our Las Vegas tryouts and made it to the finals.

Next off were the twin brothers, whom we picked up in Miami. Looking like a couple of farm boys on a field trip to the big city, the near-identical siblings had auditioned together while drunk, just looking to get laid. But after one of the producers realized how valuable an asset two male twins in the porn world would be, he patted them on the back and gave them two free tickets to Jamaica.

The first of three buxom blondes then vacated the bus, followed by the second, then by the last. Each had hair more platinum than the one prior, and each set of fake tits grew bigger as they progressed. The only black guy then stepped off, followed by a smarmy, long-haired guy in a Fedora and open shirt, who looked like Brad Pitt had he been a heroin dealer in 1974. From our New York audition was the big, barrel-chested marine and his tiny fiancée Brittany or Brianna or something, who were both ecstatic about fucking as many people as possible before they got married in the summer—although he seemed a lot more excited about it than she did. The audition in Miami gave us our token little Filipina fox, who had the typical tight body and adorability factor that most pedophiles drooled over. An attractive brunette woman then stepped off the bus followed by a guy in his mid-30s, both of whom I couldn't place to save my life. When you've watched 500 men and women wank off in front of you, their faces just began to melt into anonymity.

Sam shook everyone's hand as the two assistants checked names off clipboards and handed out room keys. But there were two keys left, so the producer scanned the clipboard for the two names left unchecked. He grabbed Corey and frantically shook his shoulder.

"Where's Donkey Dick?" Sam shouted.

"Donkey Dick?" Corey asked. He took the clipboard from the assistant and reviewed the contestant list. "Oh, the couple from the mail-in audition? The VHS tape guy?"

"Yeah, the guy with the huge dick! Where is he?"

Corey got onto his walkie-talkie to find out what happened while I recalled Donkey Dick's very impressive 12-incher from his home-recorded audition. We had all sat around the office speechless as we watched the tape of this mild-mannered guy in his early 40s, who looked like someone who would do your taxes and do them well, drop his pants and diddle his petite wife with what looked like a child's arm and clenched fist.

"They missed the flight," Corey shook his head and

informed Sam. "They're catching the next plane in tomorrow morning. They think."

"Damn it!" the producer shouted. "They know we've got a tight schedule here! We start filming in a few hours."

"And I think it's just him coming," Corey said under his breath.

"Excuse me?"

"From what it sounds like," Corey clarified, "she got cold feet and backed out."

"But Donkey Dick is still coming, right? We didn't lose the dick, did we? Fuck her . . . we got plenty of alternates with nice tits here. But that dick of his . . . we need that, Corey! You make sure you get the bus to pick him up tomorrow . . . you be on the bus, too. We need that dick here. That thing is gold!"

I could tell Corey didn't want to sit on that bus and drive three hours through barren wasteland to pick up the dick then turn right around and drive another three hours back to the resort, especially because he would be missing out on seeing all these big-breasted women getting screwed and losing any chance he had of sneaking in a sloppy-seconds attempt after the day wrapped up. But this was his first production assistant gig and he took his orders like a man who would make it far in the business.

We all ate a hearty breakfast of jerk chicken Eggs Benedict and jerk chicken omelets after the cast members found their rooms and unpacked. It seemed that every meal at Whispers' all-inclusive buffet featured some variation of jerk chicken. There was something oddly unappealing about it and I couldn't quite put my finger on why until my ganja-providing bartender let me know that it wasn't really chicken at all, but goat. Seems Jamaica had quite an abundance of goats but not very many chickens roaming the coast, and because everything tasted like chicken anyways it only made sense to use goat as a cheaper substitute. Needless to say, I started picking the jerk chicken out of each of my meals.

*   *   *

When one watches a porno on their TV or computer, it seems to have that fly-on-the-wall feeling where you, the viewer, are not really there, and you're not interrupting the sexual act in any way. It's as if you were a masked voyeur glaring through the window at two beautiful people having sex in plain sight, and neither of them knew or cared that you were watching. And the couple seemed very generous in their sexual positioning so that you could always get a great view of the pecker pounding away at that shaved, glistening, pinkish-sore vagina. When it was time for some oral, the male was considerate enough to press her knees against her ribs so you, the viewer, could get a great side view of the tongue action. And when it was the woman's turn to perform oral on the man, he was always selfless enough to hold her hair back so the camera could get a detailed view of his balls slapping against her chin.

This always felt so organic on-screen, but my outlook of porn abruptly changed once seeing it filmed live in a hotel room with a camera crew of six men, a light crew of three men, two grips, one production assistant, two aged producers, and a 40-something female director shouting, "Lift your fucking leg! Lift your fucking leg! We can't see your cock, genius!" It was horribly unsexual. The same scene was shot repeatedly, moans and screams were faked until hoarse, lights were being readjusted during the titty-fuck scene, pussy farts were pooting out during position changes, excrement was wiped off the sheets after a sweaty anal-sex incident, and an unlucky cameraman got a forehead full of a twin's jism when he went in for a poorly timed close-up.

The grizzly sights were just the steak on this macabre dinner plate; I still had a couple more side dishes of my other senses to contend with. The air was thick and unbreathable and smelled of warm, filthy ass; the moistness would glaze across your face and mix with your own sweat, which dripped down onto your lips and tongue. You began to taste her sore asshole, his body odor, and the unmistakable caramel of sloppy sex. Then after close to two hours in that humid hotel room, our first scene would finally end. The twin and the Filipina girl wobbled out of the door and collapsed onto chaise lounges beside the pool. It was the next couple's turn now—same warm room, same wet bed, same soiled sheets waiting for them inside. I gave the producer and director each a script for the upcoming scene then found the next couple—1974 Brad Pitt and one of the platinum blondes—making out at a nearby Jacuzzi, and I gave them their scripts to study. They were already three daiquiris deep apiece, and his Viagra had kicked in about an hour prior, giving him a perfectly horizontal and unyielding erection as he jumped out of the water and happily followed his scene partner to the hotel room. I only stayed for the first 30 minutes of their oral scene before I snuck back outside to the pool area for a cigarette. But from what I saw, that Pitt kid was good. Whether it was raw, natural talent or just the moustache and '70s sunglasses, he appeared to have all the right cinematic moves as he lapped at the blonde's crotch like a hungry handless man with a bowl of warm soup.

From outside, I heard the director shout at 1974 Brad

Pitt to jump to his feet and "spray her in the face" just seconds before a loud cheer from the crew erupted. A minute after that, Brad Pitt came out smiling with the producer patting him on his bare, wet shoulder. Then the platinum blond came out of the hotel room using a damp rag to wipe her face clean, and she jumped into the pool and stayed underwater for a couple of seconds.

The sole black contender in our show, whose stage name was Matrix because of his "underlying complexities as a stage thespian," he explained, was next in front of the camera. He would be teamed up with the second platinum blonde—Brittany or Bethany or something—and I gave them both their *Austin Cock-Powers* scripts and ran through the dialogue with them poolside. I had requested the set location be a silver-walled underground lair on page one, but we were going to make do with the sweaty hotel room for the third time. Matrix was cocky and sure of himself, and he proceeded to playfully slap the blonde's silicone breasts and tell her to get ready for his "chocolate fuck attack." She was nervous, I could see it all over her—partly from knowing she would have to have sex on-camera with a dozen people watching, but I think it was mostly because she would have to fuck Matrix. I remember her audition back in Las Vegas, slowly and proudly masturbating for the camera as if she were lovingly churning butter in slow motion, even with the entire crew and the 100 other audition hopefuls in line watching her. She wasn't nervous at all that day, but here she was now smiling frantically and lighting a cigarette from the butt of another. She was a handful of years older than the other contenders, probably not much younger than me, but she seemed born for this job—born to entertain with her body. She was sweet and kind of maternal, and it was just a shame Matrix was her partner; she deserved one of the twins at the very least.

But the complex thespian Matrix brought with him our first casualty of production: No matter how hard he tried, and no matter how many Viagras he took, the Black Stallion could not get an erection nor anything even near it. The director must have shot for three hours in hopes of penetration, two hours of which were the blonde giving him a blowjob. Then finally the director shouted, "Oh, fuck this!" and the light crew turned off their bright overheads. Bree or Brenda came out of the room with both hands caressing her jaw, and Matrix stormed out moments later loudly blaming *her* for his lack of a boner. On and on, he blathered; how she was too old, how she gave the worst blowjob ever, how her tits were too fake, and how she had probably deprived him of his chances of becoming America's next big porn star.

But our first day of scene filming had officially ended. A full nine hours had passed in that little hotel room, with four of the couples having completed their first on-camera vignettes. The other four would be filming the following day—in that same room, but hopefully with cleaned sheets.

The last actual bit of filming for our first day would be Carmina's wrap-up interview, where she and a couple of "celebrity judges," who were actually two retired porn stars and a radio DJ from Miami, interviewed each of the eight tired actors and asked them how they thought they did, what they could have done differently, and who they wanted to fuck in their next scenes. The camera crew had set up the scene beside the pool with a gorgeous view of the beach and sunset in the background, and tiki torches were put out for the total package shot. There was an awful lot of honesty shared in their interviews, especially when two of the women compared their first scene with getting molested by their fathers when they were children—but that could be edited out in postproduction. Then Matrix ended the Dr. Phil moment when he whined about how crummy his scene partner was again, now immortalized on digital video, and that her blowjob felt as if he had rested his "huge cock" in a bowl of tepid water.

After that, it was official: Our first day of filming the finale in Jamaica was over. Everyone went back to their rooms for a shower or quick nap then we all returned to the enormous outdoor courtyard buffet for another jerk chicken and margarita meal. Between the cast and crew, there were about fifty-five of us there. And after gorging ourselves on goat and libation, we all scattered off in different directions to investigate the mysteries of the resort with our wide-open night ahead. Every bit of that place was clothing optional—even the gift store—and although public sexual acts weren't condoned, they also weren't hard to find. The resort had six or seven lagoon-like pools, a few dozen palm-shielded Jacuzzis, and open bars every 60 feet, so receiving an underwater handjob, joining a poolside orgy, or getting blind-ass drunk was an option pretty much anywhere you went, whatever direction you chose. But over the course of the past two months, being so submerged in the seedy, behind-the-scenes underbelly of pornography, my desire for sex or any kind of intimacy had diminished to almost nothing. The romance had been taken out of the process for me; the sweetness, the mystery, the taboo—it had all been violently removed from the sexual act because of this job. It's a bizarre moment for a man to see a pair of breasts and a vagina right in front of him, there for the caressing, yet all he can think about is getting as far away from them as possible.

So instead of joining Corey, Steven, and some male crew-members watch four of our female contenders daisy-chain each other at the Jacuzzi, I snuck off to the empty beach, smoked a joint, and deliberated how long it would take for the novelty to wear off of being in zero gravity. Seriously, watching a pen float at eye-level would definitely have a short entertainment shelf life.

I was already beginning to loathe these people whom I was writing dialogue for. Not so much for who they were personally, but for who they were trying to become. Sex was simply an overrated act that too many people thought solved everything when all it really did was deprive you of the time for doing other, more-productive things. And these people wanted to bathe in that ignorance, and spread it thickly from TV screen to TV screen. I suppose I was that way in my mid-20s, or at least attempted to be because everyone I knew was doing it, but now 10 years later I knew better. I knew that sex either got you killed, got you sick, got you broke, or got you a family you didn't want.

I went back to my hotel room, smoked a little more, and retired in front of something Pierce Brosnan on cable. The next day I woke up to do it all over again with the remaining eight contestants in that same hotel room. The only thing that remotely interested me the entire day of filming was the Pink Couple having their turn on the mattress of dreams. They were cool and collected, and they didn't try to impress anyone with raised legs or fake screams. They simply had sex the way they normally did at home, and it turned out to be quite the romantic scene, according to the judges.

The Pink Couple's climactic finish signaled the end of our second day of filming as well as the end of the First Round of the competition. After another jerk chicken dinner, Carmina, the producers, and celebrity judges drank daiquiris and sorted out their score cards from the past two days, deciding which eight contenders would be staying in the competition, and which eight would be going home (but not really "going home," just no longer in the competition; the losers were allowed to stay at the resort for the remainder of the week). None of the cast or crew were allowed anywhere near them while they debated the merits of a large penis versus a cute face or a bad blowjob versus an attractive, young-looking vagina. But I ran into one of the celebrity judges a few hours later at the poolside bar. He was the editor-in-chief of a major porn magazine and he could really put away the free daiquiris. He told me that the Pink Couple, the Filipina girl, 1974 Brad Pitt, Hershey Soft, Platinum Blonde #3, just one of the twins, and only Brianna or Bailey or something with a B (without her barrel-chested fiancé) would be moving on to Round Two of the show. Aside from Matrix making the cut, I agreed and let him know by ordering the next free round.

Just like *American Idol* or that semicelebrity dancing reality TV show, we also dedicated an entire episode to the elimination process. It was a big, filmed to-do over who was staying and who was leaving, shot on the white sandy beach with all 16 contenders in attendance. Carmina threw out teary hugs and industry advice to the departing eight, and encouraged them to keep on trying—but to keep on trying with a *different* adult entertainment company. The eight who were staying were then told that their scene partners would be shuffled around to make things fair and exciting, and everybody would have a chance to fuck *everybody* before the show was finished. After the cameras shut down for the afternoon, the producers informed the eight contenders that their next-day scenes would be shot out-doors, filmed at a local, privately owned island. It must have sounded like a dream come true to them at the time. Then the next day happened.

* * *

The island was indeed privately owned, just not by a legal, reliable, aware-of-our-arriving source. Seconds after beaching our two small boats onto the isle's shore, three masked men fired rifle shots into the air from behind palm trees. The cast and crew jumped back onboard and we puttered around to the far side of the island and shot our hurried scenes there. The director fell in love with this isolated palm tree growing horizontally out of the sand, and she shot most of the scenes with it as the sole prop. The couples were told to get inventive with it, so they did. The lone twin bent Platinum Blonde #3 across the tropical bark and pounded her from behind, shredding up her stomach in the process. Hershey Soft finally achieved his erection and went all *Cirque du Soleil* on the little Filipina chick he was partnered with: five toes in the sand and one whole leg lifted up and over the palm tree, giving both cameras a clear view of his shaved black balls slapping against her little childlike ass. The Pink Couple was to be divided up for their second scenes, and Mr. Pink was going to give it to little Brianna or Brittney while Ms. Pink was supposed to have fucked 1974 Brad Pitt. But little Brianna or Brittney had a change of heart and didn't want to sleep with anyone that wasn't her fiancé, so she quit the competition right there on the beach. Now having an odd number of actors left in which to shoot two partnered scenes, the director improvised and proposed a threesome. I wasn't too sure how it panned out because I took one of the early shuttle boats back to the resort and went straight for the daiquiri bar.

But all four scenes were shot that day, and it was again time for another elimination round. So later that night after a dinner of jerk chicken soft tacos, the remaining eight cast members collected on the evening beach before a half circle of fiery tiki torches and cameramen. Carmina stood in her bikini and wireless microphone at the center of the group and explained to the camera audience the rules of the competition.

"We've had so much fun watching you guys perform, and I wish you could all stay here with us on the show. But only two of you get the $250,000 and movie deal, so . . . looks like half of you won't be moving on to Round Three, our final round of the competition."

A cameraman slowly walked his lens down the line of shirtless and bikini-clad contestants, getting a nice close-up shot of each of their faces. Carmina bowed her head as if in mourning then brought the microphone dramatically back up to her mouth. She gave each of them a sincere glance.

"Craig, Bella, Jeremy, and Cynthia, please take one step forward."

1974 Brad Pitt, the Filipina Chick, Lone Twin, and Ms. Pink all stepped forward. They were nervous—they weren't sure which way it was going to go; was taking a step forward good or bad? Were they still in the running or were they going pretend-home? They would seconds later find out.

"You four . . . what can I say about you? What I can say about you is congratulations! You're moving on to the final round! And the four of you in the back row . . . you're not. You're going home."

The front row jumped and cheered while the back row

all shook their heads; two of them looked relieved and the other two were genuinely pissed. But hugs and tears were again shared between all, and Matrix again complained in his postinterview about his scene partner's unprofessionalism. From what I could tell, nobody felt too badly about him not moving on to the final round.

* * *

That next morning, just minutes before the final two scenes were to be shot, Ms. Pink explained to the producer and director that she never thought she'd make it as far as she had—it had been the boyfriend's idea to do this all along, and they both thought *he* would have succeeded and not her. And now that he was out of the competition she didn't want to continue without him. The producer snidely reminded her that he had posed this very likely possibility to her many times before agreeing to fly her to Jamaica, and this isn't how Show Biz works, honey. She apologized and apologized and Platinum Blonde #3 was back in the show.

It was all on the line for these last two couples—what they did in these final scenes would decide the competition. We shot at a rented millionaire's villa about an hour away, and Pitt pounded the shit out of the Filipina while the Lone Twin got it on with the blonde twice his size. My presence wasn't really needed at the villa—in fact, I hadn't been needed for the past three days; I had just been sitting around and watching people screwing—but the producer wanted to get his money's worth out of me, so there I was, smoking cigarettes and eating at the buffet table from setup to wrap-up. I had no impact on the entire day of filming, and the only thing my laptop did was beat me at chess.

It was a torturously long drive back to the resort because I got in the crew bus that Corey wasn't on, so I had to sit with a dozen guys who I didn't know and who didn't smoke pot during long drives like this one. But the finale was now finished for the most part—at least all the scenes involving sex. Once back at Whispers, I spirited off to my hotel room with two daiquiris and a bunch of candy, and decided I never wanted to date again.

The next day, the crew set up their cameras and tiki torches beside a tropical pool for our grand finale, where we would find out which two would leave Jamaica with the two-movie deal and the $250,000. The entire cast was reunited as if they hadn't seen one another for months, when in actuality they had all just shared a breakfast of jerk chicken sausage and waffles an hour before. The cameras followed Carmina as she walked her microphone to each of the 12 expired contestants and gave a little recap of their journey through the competition—no doubt it would be peppered with video highlights of their auditions and Round One sex scenes in postproduction. Then she approached the final four and retold their rise through both rounds to make it where they were now. Then, with tears in her eyes and a Puerto Rican accent on her tongue, sweet platinum Carmina announced the winners to be 1974 Brad Pitt and the little Filipina chick. It all sort of felt like one of those situations where you knew there was a surprise party waiting for you behind the door, but you still acted surprised and probably overdid the shocked expression a bit once the door opened. But it was official. The show was finally officially over. In a day and change, we could all—cast and crew alike—check out of this sodomite resort and return to whatever city we called home, and probably never see one another again . . . not counting on a TV screen or magazine.

But realizing this pending conclusion just made it feel weirder. This show that was at one time just a simple, crazy job offer, then pages and Post-it notes taped to a rented office wall in West Hollywood . . . it had actually grown flesh and cameras and a budget and tits and cocks. This two-month fuck-fest had taken me to Miami's ritzy South Beach and put me in a waterfront, $450-a-night hotel room. It had shown me my first taste of New York City and Jamaica. It had introduced me to per diems and limousines and bleached assholes. It had also illustrated for me just how far people were willing to go for a taste of fame. Had it not been for this job, I never would have imagined that hundreds of men and women would wait in lines for hours just to undress and masturbate in front of a camera crew in hopes of a little stardom. People you would never imagine, too. At the early auditions, only 10 percent of the tryouts actually looked like someone you would see performing in a porno movie; the other 90 percent looked like homely regular people you see every day: your balding 45-year-old neighbor with all the plants, the alcoholic lady with big red glasses who works at the grocery store, the old smiley black guy who drives the bus, the Renaissance Faire gal who acts out role-playing fantasy games on weekends and dates from Craigslist. And we had to watch each one of these dregs undress and pleasure themselves to too-near completion, from the West Coast all the way to the East Coast. And it was all finally finished. I could return home to Los Angeles with about $8,000 more in the bank than I had when I left, my name in an actual TV show's titles as "Head Writer," a few new contacts for future porn-writing gigs, plus my newfound disgust for anything to do with pornography, including writing it.

The following night I left my laptop in my room and decided to tour the resort and maybe even socialize a little, seeing as it was our last night in Jamaica. But I couldn't find anybody I knew. I sauntered down the beachy paths wondering if they were all avoiding me and having some grand party in a secret location. It gave me time to reflect on the past week, and I came to the conclusion that I had A) acted like a royal asshole to every porn star and aspiring porn star in the show, and B) I was pretty much whoring myself out just like they were. This show had been my own taste of fame, just like the contestants, only I had used my words to jack off for the camera. I wasn't really all that distraught once realizing it—it was an entertaining, well-paying, and eye-opening ride the whole time, and my literary sodomy was a hell of a lot easier to take than some of the contestants' *actual* sodomy. But it did bother me that I had been treating "the talent" so asshole-ishly, looking down upon them from such great heights where Head Writer titles bloomed. I had always prided myself on being empathetic and open to people from all walks of life, especially the underdogs and the misfits. I *was* a misfit, after all. I should have embraced these people, and wrote for them scripts that might have revolutionized their porn scenes, and brought tears to the eyes of romantics and boners to the laps of the masturbators. But I hadn't—I had given them a rewritten scene from *Jaws* that had two ladies comparing their breasts. I had been a dick to them; I knew it, I saw it, and I even began to relish in it, to be honest. And then to discover that we were the same! We were the same, my bare-backing brothers and semen-spilt sisters. We were both whoring ourselves out for that sweet taste of fame and fortune.

I heard laughter and splashing nearby and walked a little closer to a lit but empty pool. On the far side was a big bubbling Jacuzzi set into the stone floor with Carmina and a few of the crewmembers getting in. I walked closer wanting to at least say "hi" as some sort of amends for being kind of a prick to them over the week. Then Corey appeared from a side path with a handful of margaritas.

"Dude, where you been? I've been knocking on your door." He handed me a drink, got into the Jacuzzi, and handed out two other drinks. "We're having a little wrap party for the crew here. Get in."

"Yeah, get in the Jacuzzi!" Carmina added with that colorful accent and her tanned boobs bouncing in the water. "You work too hard. The show's over; it's time to have some fun now!"

I kicked off my flip-flops and eased in between Steven and a brunette "celebrity judge" porn actress. The two cute production assistants we picked up in Miami were also in there plus a few of the cameramen and their very liberal wives. We each took turns running to the cabana bar to retrieve new rounds of margaritas every 15 minutes until someone finally got wise and brought a pitcher over. Then a few joints were passed around, and then we all got a little naked once truth or dare started. As I took a puff and passed the doobie to the topless porn star on my left, I realized two things: A) what an amazing bar story playing truth or dare in a Jamaican Jacuzzi with pot-smoking porn stars would be and, B) there weren't many "truths" to be had when you're playing truth or dare with drunken porn stars and porn filmmakers. There weren't many secrets to keep in a crowd like that. Within the first 30 minutes of the game, almost everyone there had admitted to having had some form of a same-sex sexual experience in their life, cheating in a relationship, past STDs, trying heroin, even tasting their own semen. So our truth or dare turned into more of a game of dare-or-really-dare. I made out with one of the cameramen's wives right in front of him before getting dared to do naked push-ups over an equally naked Carmina without getting an erection. Corey was dared to do a titty-fuck with the brunette porn star then the 20-something production assistant, and compare the two. Fingers were poked in orifices left and right, and margaritas were poured down tits and penises and between ass cheeks into eager open mouths. It was a Jacuzzi party worthy of its own TV show, but it was only as amazing as it was because there were no cameras around to capture its glory. We could all let our guard down and just let tits be tits and peckers be peckers again—no camera angles or lifted legs or job titles. We were just nine people in a Jacuzzi getting drunk and doing weird shit to one another.

"Hey, whatever happened to Donkey Dick?" a cameraman drunkenly asked with his face slouched between his wife's armpit and breast. "I wanted to see that thing live, man."

"I think he went to the wrong resort," one of the assistants replied, the top half of her bathing suit floating beside her.

"That prick of his was *huuuge*, bro," Corey slurred. "Homeboy was fucking ugly as hell, but that prick was huge!" He went back to sucking on the neck of the other production assistant.

"Fuck it," the cameraman whose wife I made-out with said flatly. "I don't want to think about any of that shit anymore. The show is done, man. This is all *us* now."

That said it for all of us. A few moments of silence followed while we all drunkenly absorbed the two-month cost for our night of freedom, then we returned to the laughter, the margaritas, the joints, and the underwater hand-jobs. My only regret that night is not being able to acquiesce to Carmina's final dare for me to stand at the center of the Jacuzzi and whack-off to her fondling her breasts, then unload on her stomach for all to see. Because I discovered that, like a large portion of the male contestants who never made it past our open-call auditions, I couldn't perform in front of a crowd either. I gave it one hell of a try though.

WAX IS THICKER THAN PRIDE

JOB #27

My elderly Cadillac Brougham muscled its way up the long, winding road to Universal Studios like a fatigued ox pulling up marshland. Clouds of exhaust bloomed from the rear of my V-8 as the transmission skipped and whined and tried its very best to complete the uphill task. After a rattling and somewhat religious quarter-mile, my rusty chariot and I both decided to settle on the first parking structure three-quarters to the top of the hill, where only employees were supposed to park. I let my tired Brougham rest in an empty spot and hoofed it to the top of the hill in my brother's missing blazer and tie.

The big studio's outdoor promenade, the sightseeing extravaganza known as CityWalk, looked fantastic in the weekday brunch hour. The surrounding façade buildings leaned in comically overhead, giving each and every spectator a surreal worm's-eye view of a fictitious life—a true cartoon environment. The dozen or so movie theaters, which all of this was originally built around some years back, still clung to the rear of this tourist trap like an emperor's castle besieged by a hundred years of defeat, deforestation, and magnificent repopulation. But the true heart and lungs of this consumer-adoring beast were the souvenir shops, celebrity-endorsed bars, and fancy restaurants, which stretched on for as far as the eye could see.

About five thousand tourists from every part of the world packed this enormous, winding boulevard—shopping bags in hand, visors on foreheads, and cameras brushing softly against eyelashes. Wheeled food carts sold $4 sodas and $7 hot dogs to the Asians; gift shops peddled Woody Woodpecker dolls and Frankenstein magnets to the Europeans and Southerners; and the Mexicans walked around with trash bags and brooms, themselves being the caretakers of this cathedral of Americana.

Any place that had tourists also had job openings. That was the theory, at least—a theory conceived during a red wine conversation with a neighbor who once dissected his own poop with a plastic knife in a search for internal bleeding. So here I was, wandering around this massive casino of retail employment after taking job-hunting advice from a grown man who I won't ever have dinner with again.

My search began at an upscale coffee shop near CityWalk's entrance. The way I figured it, I knew how to make a mean-ass café latte from a previous three-week stint as a coffee-house waiter, not to mention my many-years patronage of any and every local Starbucks in the Los Angeles vicinity. So I walked in and filled out an application, then asked to speak with the manager.

The Barista Chief stepped out from the back room and plucked the paper from my hand. His eyes drifted down my neatly printed, written-in-all-caps application before saying,

"Okay, looks pretty good. We'll call you if we need someone." I decided not to shake his hand before leaving.

I walked back into the mash of tourists outside and lit a Camel. I should have gotten a coffee, I thought to myself. That would have been so nice. Nothing's better than sipping a coffee, smoking a cigarette, and watching strangers: a voyeur with his friends.

Because I had nothing but time on my side, I reflected on the last time I was up here at CityWalk. It must have been three years before, still in the armor of my early 20s, when I pulled a six-day stint inside the great Universal Studios theme park working as something called a "Character Escort." Because of my height advantage, the position seemed ideal, they said. Basically, as a Character Escort, I spent my days—my six days—protecting a midget inside a 50-pound Woody Woodpecker costume from a swarm of children with knees made for testicles and hands primed to pull on loosely sewn tails. The cast of other wandering characters included a seven-foot Frankenstein, a six-foot Chilly Willy, an average-sized Charlie Chaplin impersonator, but yet I always got the duty of protecting that fucking three-foot prick from children and teenagers twice his size. By day five I had given up and resorted to garishly waving my index finger in lieu of pulling little redneck kids off the back of the little man in the red bird costume. He complained, I got fired, end of reflection.

Once you left Universal Studios, there was no going back. By the late '90s, Universal had a very thorough computer database of information, and they kept a very tight, comprehensive list of past employees and why they were "past." But CityWalk was a different story; it was still part of Universal but it was mostly franchise restaurants and independently owned stores. And the places that were semi-affiliated with the studios didn't have the same computer databases of past employees readily accessible to their judgy fingertips like they had *inside* the studios. Luck was on my side out here. Out here in CityWalk, I was beyond the perimeter of suspicion.

So, I flicked my cigarette butt onto the cobbled ground and decided to check out a nearby toy store—partly to apply for a job but mostly to see some toys. Three attractive teen-age girls in matching ugly green T-shirts paraded through the store, adjusting items on shelves and smiling to customers with prices on the tips of their tongues. They were all about 17 years old, Hispanic at first glance, with straight brown hair and large curving bangs at the eyes. They had each painted a light foundation of makeup across their foreheads, eyebrows, and cheeks, revealing just a hint of the heavy cake that would be applied after quitting time.

"*Como está?*" I said to the cute one with the green, angled eyebrows. The eyebrows then lowered, and not in my favor. "Are you guys hiring?" I tried more humbly.

She gave me an application, and, after borrowing a pen, I walked back out to my bench in the courtyard, lit another cigarette, and filled out the paperwork. This application was easier than most others: a mere one-pager with condensed Job Experience and Education History segments. Being a professional job hunter makes it mandatory to always have a rich plethora of job skills at my beck and call. Even if those job skills were mostly fabricated and loosely reinforced by a list of job contacts consisting of out-of-service phone numbers, "because it was *years* ago," and phone numbers that are coincidentally the same as a friend's. On the application, I had decided to try out the past "hot dog vendor" position (for the money-handling aspect), the "thrift store clerk" position (for the customer aspect), and, just for the hell of it, I tossed in the liquor store job.

Three prior jobs were all you really needed for retail. And as long as you were Caucasian and looked semipresentable, no one would ever try and verify more than one from the list provided, which was almost always the most recent.

I returned to the toy store and was quickly approached by the 40-something store manager, who was also wearing the same green T-shirt worn by the teenagers. Three seconds of watching him saunter over and it was obvious that this guy really loved his job—the confident walk, the moustache, the complete removal of sideburns. He took some kind of pleasure in having a dictatorial role, even if it was just as the manager of a toy store. I was positive he would perform his duties to the best of his abilities.

He took my application and looked it over, which gave me enough time to more closely look *him* over: shined brown loafers, white socks, cream-colored khakis, that fucking green shirt, and a sterile side-part of brown hair. His closer scrutiny of my application revealed both farsightedness and a wedding ring. Poor gal. Probably named Tamy or Vicky; now she never leaves the house. I bet she was cute in her 20s in a Bakersfield sort of way, but she plumped up by 40. They probably have three kids—two girls and a boy—maybe six, eight, and twelve years old by now. The two had been high school lovers, moved here to Hollywood to pursue her career in film and his in screenwri—

"Says here you worked at a hot dog restaurant," he paused and stared at me. "What happened with that?"

I had to nod a few times before getting my bearings

back. "Yes, the hot dog job. I decided to go back to college to finish my degree. The hours there weren't flexible, so I had to find employment elsewhere." To be honest, I got fired because I got caught stealing cheese. But this manager only needed the abridged, made-for-TV edition of my termination story.

"Have you ever worked up here at Universal before?"

"No, but I'm excited about the opportunity to."

"What was your major? What did you study?"

"Journalism," I answered. "I'm a newsman."

"Are you still going to college?"

"Oh, no, no. I'm all good now."

"So you got your degree in journalism then?"

"Oh yeah," I answered, my degree actually being a three-year Frankenstein's monster of journalism, English, cinema, and art semesters.

"I just . . . I can't wrap my head around this, Brandon. You have this degree in journalism yet you're applying for a $7-an-hour job at a toy store? Why is that?"

"I've seen too many ugly things in this life," I answered. "I just wanted . . . to be around something that was good."

"All right. I see," he replied. "Now why are you *really* applying at my toy store?"

"It's a long story."

"Is it?"

"No, no, I suppose it's not. It's the same story. I just really need a job."

"Why don't you get a job on a newspaper?"

"Have you seen that Internet? Just giving the news away for free. It's a new world out there. Dying breed, they're saying. A dying breed of good brick-and-mortar newsmen."

"Is that so?" he said before pausing, sizing me up. "So if

I hire you here and this *dying breed* of journalism picks back up, you'd quit the toy store, right?"

"I'll shoot you straight on this one: I'd be tempted to, yes. But would I? I don't really know. I don't really know. I'm a loyal man . . . I am. From hard-working German blood. Would I leave . . . ? No. No, I would not leave. I would not leave this toy store if you hired me."

"I believe you about 10 percent."

"Hmmm."

"I'm not going to hire you for the store," he said with a suspicious glare, "but I do have something else for you. Why don't you follow me, Brandon. This might be more your speed."

The manager waved to the teenager at the counter and signaled "two minutes" with his fingers. We then exited the store and I followed him into the CityWalk crowd heading east. I wondered where he was taking me; if there was perhaps some amazing position as a reporter for the *CityWalk Gazette* hidden deep at the back of the crowd. We passed the security offices and information desk and through the large circular courtyard where the restaurants dwelled like pillared walls around a Roman coliseum. We passed the waterfall ballet, which erupted from the ground in spontaneous vertical intervals. We finally stopped behind a horde of nearly twenty people, and I then realized that there was no cool office or cubicle'd desk waiting for me there. The manager looked over at me and smiled, and I knew that whatever it was within this assembly of T-shirted tourists would be my new job.

"Well, here it is," he said proudly.

"I'm not going to be shaping balloons or anything, am I?"

"No, nothing like that. Nothing like that at all," he replied.

I felt some relief knowing balloons wouldn't be involved—I had never done *that* before, and didn't relish the idea of it being on any of my resumes. So I followed him deeper into the crowd and heard an astonished German sigh noisily to my left and some form of exclamation in Japanese or Korean to my right. I was intrigued. What was causing such shock and awe within this gathering? What could elicit such alarm as to make a heavy German man sigh noisily and an Asian woman exclaim something I didn't understand?

The manager then clutched my elbow and pulled me to the right of the crowd, circumventing the tightly knit wad of shorts, flip-flops, and baseball hats. And seconds later, we were standing right beside the object of all the commotion: It was the goddamned Wacky Wax Cart.

"Good God," I whispered a little too loudly.

Standing six feet high and five feet wide, the Wacky Wax Cart looked like a wood-paneled brick of shit left on a cobbled road to dry under the sun. It sat before the crowd of onlookers like a pudgy Christian facing Romans. There were no toys or dolls or digital cameras turning pictures of happy couples into emblazoned coffee cups or one-of-a-kind mouse pads. No, the Wacky Wax Cart had its own unique brand of shame to offer, especially for its newest employee: four bubbling 5-gallon tubs of colored wax circling an even bigger tub of bubbling white wax. Above these five tubs were three glass shelves full of hardened wax hands, each in a different position and color. One wax hand was obviously a teenager's, showcasing the middle finger in red, white, and blue stripes. Another was the two-fingered peace sign, and yet another was the all-too-trite thumbs-up. A dozen or so solidified hand gestures conveyed countless finger statements, giving this cart of gaudy limbs the impression of either being a miniature sign-language school for deaf kids who really liked colors or some bizarre torture chamber.

A petite girl on the soft side of 20, who also wore one of the green T-shirts from the toy store, repeatedly dunked her dainty hand into the tub of white liquid wax, giving each coat a second to cool and harden between dunks. She pulled her pale, glistening limb out for the sixth time and finally revealed it to the crowd, eliciting a loud wave of *oohs* and *aahs*. As her hand hardened into its permanent outstretched-fingers position, she asked an English couple beside her, "Okay, what color should we make it?"

"Red!" the Brit screamed.

"Blue!" someone from the crowd then shouted.

"How about red, white, *and* blue?" a patriot in a wheelchair barked.

"Okay," the Wacky Wax technician replied, "red, white, and blue coming up!" She dipped the bottom of her coagulated hand an inch into the vat of red wax twice then she turned her hand over (thumb-side down) and dunked that side into the vat of blue wax twice. And when she lifted her hand to the crowd, a red-white-and-blue-striped appendage saluted them.

The manager nudged me on the shoulder and nodded to the girl with the patriotic hand at the cart. I could have walked away right then. I considered it deeply. I could have feigned a case of the trots and hustled to the public bathroom to plan my escape. I could have laughed, shook my head, and walked back to my car. I could have done any number of things to get out of that particular predicament. But I needed a job badly. So, I nodded my head several times as if to say, "Wow, what a job she's doing! I'd like to be a part of this action," and continued to watch the show.

"That's Becky," the manager leaned in to me and said. "You're going to be working with her. She's a pro at this." And the job just got more appealing.

We both watched Becky as she elegantly pulled off the wax glove by sliding what looked to be an oiled tongue depressor between the wax and her palm. By contorting her fingers and thumb into a cone position, the wax hand gingerly slid off while keeping most of its shape intact. The crowd cheered again, even louder than before. Becky then turned the hand simile upside down and filled it with tiny granules of wax, inserted a wick into the knuckle of the index finger, sealed the vacant wrist with a quick dunk in the white wax, and again showed the crowd her finished hand candle—her finished Wacky Wax hand candle.

"Okay, who's first?" Becky asked the crowd. "Who wants a wax sculpture of their hand?" Half of the crowd then immediately dispersed while the other half looked among themselves for the first to come forward. A large fireworks explosion then crackled overhead and the sunny sky lit up into hues of pink and blue. It was Universal's *Miami Vice* stage show, and the crowd then realized that the studios were officially open for the day. The remaining onlookers shuffled off in one fantastic herd, leaving just Becky, the manager, and me standing there at the cart.

The manager approached the cart and opened the cash register. He flipped through thin stacks of 1s, 5s and 10s and frowned. "Becky, this is Brandon," he informed her. "He's going to be starting tomorrow."

"Great!" she replied.

We shook hands and smiled at one another. She was

cute, rather elfish looking, with a haircut like Mia Farrow or Peter Pan.

"Still sound good, Brandon?" the manager asked.

There were about forty people that I knew who worked at offices inside Universal Studios, some even nearing executive status by now. My own mother worked there, people I went to high school with, ladies I had dated, ex-coworkers I had known had moved on from old jobs to work there—and here I was, at the far end of my 20s, readying to accept this offer. How much self-respect would I squander by taking this job? How much dignity would I lose when someone I knew saw me making candle fists in an amusement park for $7 an hour? And that fucking green T-shirt . . .

It was right then and there, during his offer to take the job, when I really wanted to leave. Fuck being employed; fuck making rent; fuck being a tax-paying citizen—I wanted to laugh as hard as I could and run away into the crowd. I wanted to fire up my Cadillac and drive to Europe and never look back. I had already started deducing the best possible route through the boulevard of tourists when my stomach suddenly shut down, which then sent a collapsing feeling through my abdomen and chest. I was starving, and the four cups of coffee and six cigarettes I had for breakfast quickly mixed with my naked stomach acids to form a stew of pain and fire. I was so hungry that I felt like vomiting—I was so hungry that I felt like I had *just* vomited, swallowed it back down, and needed to vomit again.

Making candle hands for tourists. It could have been worse. Shit, it had been worse. The summer of 1994, that was bad. Most of '96, that was bad, too. End of reflection.

"Well?" he asked again. "How does it sound, Brandon? You kinda faded off there."

I was very hungry, and I didn't want another 1994 on my hands. I needed food, and I needed rent, and I needed this job. I needed to suck it up and grow a pair. "It sounds real good."

"Great, great!" he exclaimed, the burden of finding some asshole to work the Wacky Wax Cart finally off his agenda.

"See you tomorrow then?" Becky asked me.

"It looks that way."

"Come by the toy store tomorrow about 8:00 in the morning and you can fill out the paperwork," the manager said. "I'll give you a shirt also."

"A shirt? *That* shirt?" I asked, pointing at the green thing covering his chest.

"One just like it," he replied proudly, "this one's mine."

I did my best to smile and sauntered through the crowd and back down the hill to my Cadillac. I drove back to my apartment in time to watch *People's Court* and make three grilled cheese sandwiches and curse the day I gave up journalism for art and film and English.

Seven a.m. came swiftly and furiously into my slumbering apartment. I had forgotten what mornings were like. I had forgotten how good coffee tastes in the cool dawn hours. I had forgotten how delicious a hot shower feels, and the invigorating smell of soap at first light, the touch of a car's headrest on wet hair. I had forgotten all the forgettable moments of getting ready for work.

I parked my Cadillac in the same parking garage halfway up the hill—this time legally—and walked up to CityWalk. I stopped by the toy store and the manager gave me my green shirt, a nametag, the semifilled cash register tray and keys, and some words of encouragement. I changed into my new green shirt in the bathroom near the storeroom and left before the manager could say anything more.

The walk through the dormant CityWalk was relatively calm this time. The entire place was empty except for a few uniformed employees milling around the various stores preparing to open. I caught a very thorough glimpse of myself as I walked by a glass storefront. This new green T-shirt that fit over my thin chest like a starched cotton box; the new nametag pinned near the center of my new green cotton box; my perma-pressed slacks; and my lucky leather wingtips with the good arch support. What an asshole, I thought to myself. What a Grade-A asshole.

I arrived at the Wacky Wax Cart, opened the cash register, and deposited most of the money inside, leaving some out for my lunch and basic necessities. Stealing money on the first day was one of the golden points behind starting a new retail job—no boss would ever accuse an employee of being stupid enough to steal on the first day! They would simply chalk it up to error: The new employee was unfamiliar with this particular cash register; the new employee was both nervous and excited and pushed the wrong button.

I quickly crossed the empty courtyard and bought myself a $3 cup of coffee and returned to my Wacky Wax stool. I sat there at my stool and sipped my coffee and smoked my cigarettes as more employees began streaking across the courtyard. I turned on the heaters below the vats of wax, like the little "To Do" list taped to the side of the register had suggested. Even more Universal employees began arriving, each in their various department uniforms and salary color codes. They greeted each other politely, and held the doors for one another, and congregated in little hordes by lobbies and benches. Nobody looked my way. Nobody fucked with the Wacky Wax Cart.

The sun finally broke over the east end of the façade, and the employees quickly dissipated into their appropriate offices like cursed gargoyles returning to their perches at the first break of dawn. I had already finished six cigarettes since stepping out of the shower that morning, and the fact that it was now only 9:40 a.m.—plus the notion that I was most likely going to burn through an entire pack before quitting time—brought on high acclaim for the side of my brain that recommended buying the generic cigarettes today.

It was about 11:30 when the manager walked over and inspected the cart for dust, debris, and customers. He glanced at my green shirt and smiled—but a strange smile. It was a smile that declared: "We both stepped in shit now."

"The shirt looks good," he said.

"I feel very authentic."

"What does that mean?" he asked, nibbling on his moustache with his bottom lip.

"I really feel like I'm part of the program."

"That's good. Listen, the crowd should be coming through in about an hour or two. Have you tested things out yet? Did you make anything?"

"I wanted to make sure the wax was good and ready first."

"It only takes about 30 minutes before it's ready, but you wouldn't know that; it's your first day. Here, let me refresh your memory on the process," the manager said, and he proceeded to dip his hand into the vat of white wax several times, then the red wax, and then the blue wax. Hoisted then in front of my face was a red and blue fist attached to a thick tan arm, but I don't think his colorful waxwork was what he was really attempting to convey.

"Nice one," I replied.

He then smashed his colorful fist against the side of the cart until the still hardening wax broke off his hand and fell to the ground. Didn't even aim for the trash can.

"One more thing," he added. "Sometimes the parents want a wax hand of their baby or their kid, and kids usually don't like having their hand dunked into hot wax, so . . . "

"*So* what do I do?" I asked seconds later, after his "so" trailed off.

"*So* you be careful. Practice first."

Before he walked off, I jumped in with a "One last thing." He paused and begrudgingly turned back around.

"What is it?"

"Am I here alone?"

"Until 2:00, yes."

"Is that wise? I mean, this is my first day and all. What if the crowd demands too much?"

"I'm right over there at the store if you need help," he replied. "Becky will be in at 2:00 and then you can take a lunch and all that."

The manager walked back to the toy store, and I attempted my first wax hand. After too many deliberations on which gesture to choose, I settled on a sort of claw-hand with the fingers pursed like they were going to pluck an eyeball. I dipped my talon into the vat of white wax several times—it was indeed hot but somehow comfortable, like taking a scalding bath on a cold night. I decided on green with black tips, so I dipped my hand all the way into the green vat then partially into the black. I elevated my hand in front of my face and watched as the wax hardened and set before my eyes. Not bad. I could handle this job for awhile, I thought to myself. Might even be interesting. I'd be outdoors, cute tourists . . . and Becky.

I had traveled back into Pretend Land for several minutes thinking about my new coworker before I remembered something about pulling the wax glove off before it hardened. And it was now pretty hard. So I poked the wooden tongue depressor down in between the wax and my thumb only to find out the reason why I was supposed to have removed the wax before it congealed: body hair. The hair on my fingers and wrist had bonded with the thick layer of wax coating them, and no matter how much I pulled and yanked, whined and whimpered, it wouldn't budge. The green wax hand with black fingertips had attached itself to me. I weighed my options: If I slammed it on the register to break it off, I'd have a hundred little wax pieces clinging to my hand. A hundred small pains. A hundred small pains were much worse than one big pain. One big pain. There was only one thing to do: I was going to have to yank it off.

With my remaining good hand, I gripped the wax claw and readied myself. I gave it a small tug to assess the coming agony, and a subtle "ooohhh" seeped from my lips. It was going to be bad. I glanced around first to see if there were any tourists or managers watching, but the coast was clear. I gripped the wax claw a little harder now and centered the force around the knuckles region, then yanked as hard as I could. It was a colossal yank—one worthy of the "FUCK!" I shouted at the storefronts.

I looked down to my left to find a normal, ordinary hand clutching a stretched green and black *thing*. I looked down to the right to find a swelling pink entity with trembling fingers. Attached to that was a wrist—once hairy but now bald and cherry-colored. There was a perfect line of separation between my hairy forearm and my bald wrist, where the wax had ended. It looked like I was wearing a fur sleeve that was too short for my arm. My knuckles, which didn't have much hair to begin with, now had none whatsoever. I lifted my new hand closer to my face and studied the unfamiliarity of it; inspected its crimson glow; examined the dots of blood forming everywhere.

Inside the remains of the green wax hand I found a two-inch collar of short brown strands, like a vivid still shot of a 1970s porn vagina. The four patches of hair from my knuckles were found a few inches deeper inside, like little hair islands. Like Hawaii. I couldn't do much more than stare at it and regret the college thing again. There was no way I was ever going to do that to my hand again, hair or no hair now. Starving or not, this job just became expendable. I would work this gig until the first paycheck came, or until the first time someone pissed me off enough, then I'd be gone. I'd find something else. Something better, and that paid at least $10 an hour. The good times were just ahead.

As the day went on, I turned three tourists away with stories of faulty wax and a manager who had just had a heart attack. And when Becky came in at 2:00, I showed her my hand and relayed the story of how it got that way along with a secret decree from the manager for her to perform all the hand waxing duties while I managed the cash register and healed. And I spent the rest of that day behind that cash register smoking cigarettes and not much else until the manager got wise to the operation and shut us down. I showed him my wounded hand and tried to explain my actions, and he said I should go home, put some Bactine on it, and not come back.

So my new green shirt and I left. And we never saw Becky or CityWalk again. But I walked away with an honest day's pay, along with about $14 that wasn't that honest. And I have never been happier about getting fired than I was that day. Because sometimes it's just easier being terminated for the right reasons than quitting for the wrong ones. And on top of that, fuck the Wacky Wax Cart.

A STARING CONTEST WITH 40

JOB #80

Seattle didn't fix me. I really thought it would have. Hoped it would. I made the move in my late 30s. Left my hometown to start over—start fresh—start again. But my ghosts followed me here too. There's no avoiding the ghosts of the past. There's no new clean white slate, no new Word document to start another story on. The life you led is yours forever. You own it. The events of your past stick with you for the next 10, 20, even 30 years. Who you were at 23 is who you'll be at 33 and 43—just a bit smarter and a tad more cautious. No one tells you that, but it's true—that's life. You are you and you will *always* be you. You will always be the asshole that cheated on someone you cared for, that quietly tore the condom off in the middle of a one-night stand, that didn't help the meth-addicted neighbor when she fell down the stairs right in front of your apartment door on a three-day high that her children couldn't make better—you just stared through the peephole at her until someone else came. You will always be that same person . . . that same asshole. But you learn and you gain new experiences and become a better person each passing day. But even as time goes on, just below that shiny new paint job, you will always be you and it would be a crime to pretend that you weren't.

That's my version of life in a nutshell. That's how this 80-some-year lease on mortality unfolds. You can adjust your future but you can never alter your past—it's with you through the good times and the bad, the strange nights and the bland days, the Saturdays spent in bed and the Mondays spent at work. You are you, and there's no way to rewrite how it all began.

So you move to Seattle. Partly to find someone to love, but mostly to get the hell away from someone you had loved. You move to find your own kind. You move to discover a new land and a new you. You move to reach your hand into the pond and retrieve that scaly lust for life that you once kept in an aquarium near the bed. You move to both get lost as well as be found. And there's something so romantic about going to a bar or restaurant where no one knows you. When you move to a new city where you don't know anyone, you can do those sorts of things. You can reinvent yourself every single day, and enter an establishment like a shadow in the wake of the couple before you. With your newspaper under your arm like a proud badge of dining autonomy, you saunter into the diner and take the small booth near the back. You keep an eye on every person that enters and deliberate how many of them are foreign spies. Two for sure, and then you order the eggs with hash browns and bacon. Coffee. Cream and sugar. Fuck orange juice.

And the waltz of walking home drunk is something I've gotten too acquainted with. Seattle is a drinker's town, and I'm a "problematic drinker," as Alcoholics Anonymous puts it. The rainy days and nights drive people into pubs and bars and restaurant bars and hotel bars, where Happy Hour still reigns supreme. Most writers would relish the thought of a city that encouraged its most creative patrons to spend their evenings knocking back potent, locally produced beer. But I am one of the few wordsmiths that I could think of that couldn't write when I drank. Never been able to. When I write, I'm a cigarette and coffee man. And lucky for me, Seattle is also a coffee drinker's town, with just as many nearby cafés as there were nearby bars. Feed the monkey until it gets good, in one way or another.

I did some of my best work in a coffee shop on Pine Street. The morose interior and free Internet seduced me inside, and the French Roast kept me coming back. I was making a meager living as a freelance writer for a seafood company at the time. The projects were few and far between, but the job allowed me the lifestyle of avoiding any type of work in an office other than my own studio apartment's "home office," which was just freelancer's code for a desk and a computer near a window. I was able to wake up at a reasonable hour before walking to Bauhaus Café, ordering my French Roast, and checking my emails for work—an act I had pictured all real writers performing. Most mornings found my Yahoo inbox basking in that empty pink no-new-mail glow, but once a week or so I'd get a project that involved writing the appetizing descriptions on packages for new seafood products. Some human does indeed write that, and usually in his underwear after getting high.

The most recent example of my literary seafood prowess was for a new product called Lemon Pepper Tilapia, whose upcoming package would boast a glossy image of a broiled and seasoned fillet beside the italicized description: *A moist, flakey tilapia fillet glazed in a tangy red pepper and citrus marinade.*

Boom. I got paid for that. Paid well, too. If I could have knocked out a couple of those every day, I'd be a rich man. But it was far from every day—it was about three projects like that a month, which meant about $850 income per month. With $700 for rent and another $100 in bills and minimum-due credit card payments, I was barely able to feed myself a meal that didn't involve cheese slices and toast. But I was finally a working writer in my newly adopted city, and pornography, tourists, and cash registers were in no way involved. I had proven to myself that I could just pack up and move into a strange new life, and survive.

At the age of 40, most people were already naming their third child, maybe halfway through a 30-year mortgage, or counting down the days until retirement. But at 40, I was just finally starting to figure life out. All those retail jobs, the bouts of unemployment, the soul-crushing office positions and laborious livings—they're just periods every writer must go through to stir up the sediment of new experiences and fresh challenges, kind of like an unprovoked fistfight or falling in love or pneumonia. All those crappy, crappy jobs, I have come to find out, would be the chapters in this fickle writer's book of life.

AFTERWORD

Starting a new job, no matter what profession or position it is, always requires an incubation period before allowing your true character to start shining through. What you do and don't do, say and don't say, in those first two weeks can sometimes mean the difference between a month of employment or a year or more. The butterfly does not simply start a new job; it must be a quiet caterpillar during the first week, gestate unassumingly in a cocoon-like state during the second week, then it is finally free to flap its wings and shine once that third week rolls around.

These ten simple rules are intended to help ease you comfortably through those first two awkward weeks at a new job, and guide you past the pitfalls and snares that will undoubtedly arise. Because coworkers are savages and the 9-to-5 is a goddamned jungle, and every new employee is just a defenseless cub out there all alone.

1.   Read a newspaper on your lunch break, not a book.
Reading a proper newspaper in a communal lunch area immediately conveys to your new coworkers that you possess intelligence, have an interest in world affairs, and are up to date on politics. The newspaper also makes for a perfectly ambivalent prop, neither declaring your sexual preference, level of internal craziness, nor general discriminations. And the *proper* newspaper is essential, of course. *The New York*

Times says you are classy and wise, while the *USA Today* says you scored an Egg McMuffin on your way to work. But still, even the worst newspaper is almost always better than reading a book during your first week. Most people might assume that flipping through a hardcover at a table by the coffee machine looks rather literary and French, which it does, but it also tells everyone watching you (and they are) exactly what you're made of. Henry Miller implies you're a pervert, Dave Eggers says you are an asshole, poetry paints you as a pretentious fruitcake with a degree in art history, and sci-fi and fantasy books clearly suggest that you spend most evenings sorting through downloaded porn pictures and categorizing them into easily accessible files on your computer's desktop. And don't even think about bringing a recognizable bestseller into work; that just screams you're into Oprah.

2. Never say too much.

This rule can be applied to almost any situation in life, but should definitely be practiced during that first week or two at a new job. You may think a frank, detailed response to a question might be warm and friendly, but it is almost always not the case. New coworkers are usually just being considerate when asking how you're doing; they don't really give a shit about your grandmother, the movie you saw, or what you made for dinner the previous night. Keep it short, vague, and right to the point.

A good example of this is

Coworker: "Good morning, new employee. How was your weekend?"

You: "Great, but never long enough."

A bad example of this is

Coworker: "Hey, new employee, how was your night?"

You: "You know, really interesting. I had a woman over last night, and I kept having to get up and go pee because I was drinking beer. I'm usually a wine person, you see. I was getting really self-conscious about it by the fourth trip to the loo since she had only gone once this whole time. But I really had to go again, so when she went up to use the bathroom I sprinted into the kitchen and peed in the sink. And this may sound crazy, but I really enjoyed it. There's no splash involved and no stream direction to maintain. And because the sink is like waist height, you can actually go hands free and rest your junk on the porcelain edge—and, boy, is that refreshing. I actually washed a couple of dishes while I was there.

3.   Always fall back on a smile and a "Hey, man."

Meeting a dozen or more new coworkers in the span of a few days will always lead to forgotten names and titles. Reciting a person's name out loud upon an introduction will help you to remember it a little easier, but even that bit of advice is easily forgotten. So I recommend familiarizing yourself with the "Hey, man" approach to greetings, responses, and replies.

A good example of this is

Coworker: "Good morning, new employee."

You: "Hey, man." (add smile here)

Or when you accidentally run into a new coworker outside of work

Coworker: "Hey! Brandon, right? We work together. I sit like two desks down from you."

You: "Heeeeey, man. Good to see you." (add smile here)

4. Set the tone by leaving the minute your shift ends.

Sure, staying an extra 15 or 20 minutes on your first few days makes a good impression and lets your manager or boss feel he or she made the right decision hiring you. But then you'll begin to feel guilty the following week when you attempt to leave on time, because you already set the tone for being an overtimer. It's like throwing out the "I love you" too early into a relationship—once it's been voiced and come out of your mouth, you'll always be expected to end every single phone call with those three weighty words. A "take it easy" will no longer ever suffice.

Plus, nothing reeks of professionalism more than turning off your computer, whipping on your blazer, and making it out the door before 5:01 has even had the chance to tick.

5. Only use disguised or invented cuss words.

If you are like me, then self-censorship is next to impossible. Profanity has become such a part of my vernacular that "Shit" and "Fuck" and "Goddamn" are spoken as frequently as "I" or "Me" or "Good morning." But there are two acceptable ways to curse in the workplace without sounding like you're a pillaging pirate and a possible threat. Again, *not* cursing at a new job is definitely the best approach, but if you can't then these two alternatives might be of interest to you during those first couple of weeks:

    A) Invent new cuss word sayings. Some good, safe examples of this are
      · Turd blossom!
      · Frank's ass!

- Chocolate whisper!
- Rickets on everything!
- Crippled Asian!

B) Disguise profanity within a soft adjective blanket so it gets lost inside, or tuck it ahead of a playful suffix that is much more colorful than its vulgar predecessor. Some of these soon-to-be old standards are

- Warm shit taco!
- Re-god-damn-diculous! (John Wayne came up with this one)
- Asshole-shiner!
- Pickle shits . . . went!
- Cock-a-dingo!
- Buttercup motherfuckin' raspberries!
- Blue, blue, bitch, and white!

6. Always wear a blazer to an office job.

A good blazer or suit jacket looks professional, exudes authority, and makes a simple T-shirt and jeans really shine. This same blazer can be worn just about every day, but I recommend at least three variations. Plus, the blazer is like the man's version of the purse: any halfway decent one will possess no less than five pockets, so there's plenty of room for keys, cigarettes, wallet, sunglasses, cell phone, and even a pocket-sized book or journal.

7. Do not get stoned at work during those first two weeks.

This may sound like a great way to make a shitty job a little more fun, and it really is, but just don't do it during those first two weeks. Don't get stoned at work even if it's with a fellow coworker. I've done it. Repeatedly. This is why I can wholeheartedly tell you it is a poor idea. Why? First off, the paranoia associated with being stoned in a public place is multiplied tenfold at a new job. All those eyes that you think are watching you, really are watching you.

If you're in the office world, there are always surprise one-on-one meetings with a supervisor you never knew you had. And they ask detailed questions and expect detailed answers in return. Plus, computer passwords and logins are easily forgotten during those first 10 business days, and there will always be a point when you have to ask a complete-stranger coworker how to contact the payroll department about something. None of that is cool when stoned. And if you're in the retail world, God help you, there will always be that *certain* customer that approaches your cash register with some sort of deformed jaw or an axe to grind with the first asshole in his path. Again, not cool stoned. The only exception to this rule is if your boss asks you to go out and smoke a joint with him or her. This is perfectly acceptable.

8. The Irritation Tax. Or, successfully stealing from the workplace.

Stealing is always frowned upon in any retail workplace—let's just start with that. But there are always those customer interactions or supervisor squabbles that warrant stealing from the cash register—because it makes you feel better, plain and simple. It's immediate revenge. It's compensation for dealing with an asshole. It's what I like to call the Irritation Tax. Nothing drastic, mind you. But if a heavyset customer yells at you about their incorrect food order, that's worth $5. If an old woman raises a stink about an out-of-date coupon, I'm afraid that's only $2, but if a manager or supervisor ridicules or humiliates you, that there is a solid $8.

And if you are going to enlist the help of the Irritation Tax, do it during your first five days there. Most employers would never think a new employee would be brazen enough to steal that early into a job, and they'll assume you simply made a mistake because you're still figuring out the cash register or credit card machine. Don't get greedy, don't get caught, and definitely don't steal during the two weeks that follow. They'll be watching you closely by now, and you'll need to show them what a model employee you really are. But by the next month you'll be in the clear, and you can once again reap the rewards of the Irritation Tax.

9.   Wash your hands after using the toilet.

You cannot believe how fast rumors spread among coworkers when a new employee drops a deuce in the bathroom and makes a straight-track back to his desk. It may not get you fired but it will certainly remove any chance you have of making friends.

And keep in mind, when you enter a new place of employment into an existing assemblage of people, you will most likely receive a nickname until coworkers get to know you better—especially if you have followed rules one through eight above. And this nickname is one that you will never, ever hear to your face. It is a moniker that the cool clique usually assigns to you, and will most likely highlight some physical quality or trait about you.

Some true-life examples of this are

A) **"Blowjob Tits"**—A bleach-blonde with big breasts, who looked like she might have been a prostitute at one time.

B) **"The Hatchet"**—Another bleach-blonde co-worker who was quite attractive save for the huge, jagged precipice of a nose.

C) **"Spanky"**—A chubby male coworker who bore a striking resemblance to the *Little Rascals* character.

D) **"The Polack"**—A nice, Regular Joe-type of coworker who made the unfortunate mistake of stepping in dog shit on the sidewalk and tracking it across the carpet in front of all our cubicles.

E) **"The Twirler" then "Shit Bird"**—He was a strange Asperger-like operator working in the customer service department who would twirl a thin necklace over his palm during every phone call, all day long. It seemed to relax him. Then he became "Shit Bird" once I ran into him in the bathroom leaving a stall after a horrendous, eye-watering crap. And he did not wash his hands. He just walked right back to his cubicle and began twirling his necklace again, until it was time for a fellow coworker's birthday celebration, where he proceeded to grab handfuls of pretzels and chocolate cookies with those feces-stained fingers of his. He killed the party.

10. A shitty wage ain't all that bad because . . .

Sometimes it's worse being paid well at a job than it is to be paid poorly. Not all the time, but sometimes. Because with a decent salary usually comes more work, more responsibility, and more pressure. Getting paid a competitive, middle-class wage means having to show up on time every morning, tuck in your shirt, and explain to the Human Resources department why you don't want to contribute 5 percent of your salary to a 401(k) account because of the impending financial apocalypse . . . or because you'll most likely quit within a year's time. A well-paying job means finally having health insurance, which is good, but then that ushers in all sorts of panic attacks about what the doctor may find now that you can afford to get a check-up. So you don't get a check-up. But you do get prescription reading glasses by Prada on your new company's vision plan, and you get your teeth cleaned on their dental plan, and you take out a $13,000 loan on a four-year-old luxury car because the lot offered you a $500 trade-in for the piece of shit you drove there in, knowing there was a pretty good chance it wouldn't get you home if you didn't sign the deed. Then you're suckered into a $350 monthly car bill plus $200 a month on mandatory premium car insurance, and this is for the next three to five years of your life.

It becomes a vicious cycle, this well-paying-job game. You make more money so you spend more money, and you have to keep that same stupid job, or one just like it, simply to pay off all the stuff you bought in order to keep your mind off of the job. And fuck getting up at 6:15 a.m.

ABOUT THE AUTHOR

Photo by Will Miller

Brandon Christopher is an artist, novelist, and journalist. He has published over a dozen short stories and essays in magazines, literary journals, websites, and anthologies. He also published his first book, *Dirty Little Altar Boy*, through Ghost Pants Press. He is also a writer and producer of several documentaries and TV biographies, including *Just for the Record—The Rolling Stones*, the highly acclaimed 16-hour documentary *The Definitive Elvis*, and *The 50 Worst Movies Ever Made*.